THE HOUSE ON HUMMINGBIRD ISLAND

Also by Sam Angus

Soldier Dog

A Horse Called Hero

Captain

SAM ANGUS

THE HOUSE ON HUMMINGBIRD ISLAND

Illustrated by Steph Laberis

MACMILLAN CHILDREN'S BOOKS

First published 2016 by Macmillan Children's Books
an imprint of Pan Macmillan
20 New Wharf Road, London N1 9RR
Associated companies throughout the world
www.panmacmillan.com

ISBN 978-1-4472-6303-6

3 5 7 9 8 6 4

A CIP catalogue record for this book is available from
the British Library.

Printed and bound by CPI Group (UK) Ltd, Croydon CR0 4YY

For Grey

PART I

April 1912

You don't usually see a horse like Baronet – or any horse at all – on the deck of a ship mid-Atlantic, unless, that is, you're travelling with someone like Idie Grace.

Baronet whinnied with joy for the salt spray on his muzzle, the sun on his back, and the ladies in the lounge chairs turned at his whinny, like leaves disturbed by a breeze. They lifted their glasses and murmured.

'Heavens – a horse.'

'Has no one called the captain?'

'That's her – with it – look, it must be the Grace girl . . .'

'Has she no hat?'

'Is there no one in charge of her?'

Idie thought of her governess and said to herself, *No, there is no one in charge of me, because when we reached the Bay of Biscay my governess declared she wouldn't come out of her cabin till the seas stopped shifting so.* Idie's smile surfaced, together with her sense of mischief, and she told Baronet, 'Now there's only Numbers, and he's not used to small girls or horses, so you and I can do as we please. See, I've taken my hat off and shan't wear hats or stockings ever again.'

'*Her mother was a beauty, in spite of everything . . .*'

Idie paused. *Her mother was a beauty.* She held that close and repeated it in her head, *My mother was a beauty.* She'd write it in her book. She whispered to Baronet to stay very still and listen to what else the ladies said because Idie gathered the things she overheard and stored them like rare treasures in a special book.

'*That hair – just look at it. From her father's side of course . . .*'

Idie winced. Her hair was the wrong kind of hair. She knew that because Myles and Benedict and all the Pomeroy Graces had straight, sunshiny hair. Nevertheless she lifted her hatless head and stuck out her chin to show the ladies she didn't care what they whispered behind their fans.

Even if the sea is smooth and flat as a plate, it's tricky to manage a high-spirited horse on the deck of a ship. There were more obstacles, awnings and bulkheads and things, than Idie had counted on and she wondered what Baronet would make of them all, but he simply nuzzled her to tell her of his interest in the salt and the sea.

'You think I'm all right, Baronet, but other people think there's nothing right about me at all.' An arrowy dart shot through her sunny mood. Despite all her questions, and without anything that amounted to an explanation, Lord Grace, known to all as Grancat and the only father Idie'd ever known, had sent her away from Pomeroy, off to a place so far away that there might be no going back. The only good that could come of leaving Pomeroy, Idie had told herself, was that she might find out about her mother.

'Come, Baronet, hurry.'

Baronet's nostrils flared in puzzlement at the lack of grass in evidence on the surface of an ocean. Idie tugged at his head rope. They must reach the prow before the flustered captaincy marched him back down to the stinking belly of the ship. Scandalized whispers ran from chair to chair. People were always watching; that was the problem. Well, now they had something to watch: a fine horse was stepping out to take the air on the deck of the *Majestic*.

'*Call the Captain! Someone call the Captain!*'

'*They sent for her, you know, to fetch her back.*'

'*No place for a young girl, that house, so large and remote.*'

'*I've heard it's haunted.*'

Haunted? Idie started. Haunted was not good. Haunted would in fact be a negative.

'*Well, it would be, after what happened there . . .*'

After what happened there? What *had* happened there? But Idie felt their eyes on her and tossed her head and led Baronet on.

'There's no other relative, of course, only her.'

A tide of consternation and curiosity swept like a bow wave before their progress along the deck. A group of men in panama hats who were smoking and playing bridge raised their brows, a little more admiring, perhaps, than the women, and stared.

'My word, look at that. A horse . . .'

'That's her . . . the Grace girl . . . you know – the one . . .'

'That animal is a beauty.'

Idie wondered if it were a bad thing to be a beauty, but in Baronet's case she didn't suppose it was. Forced to stop by an inconvenient set of stairs that barred their way, she turned Baronet and led him to the deck rail. Baronet nuzzled her as if to say he knew her defiance was the angry, fragile issue of shock and pain.

'Look, Baronet, we're at sea and we don't know where we're going nor why.'

She bit her lip, remembering how Myles and she had huddled behind the plaid curtains of Grancat's study, listening as plans were made for her departure. Idie had become an eavesdropper, listening behind curtains and doors, concentrating with all her being on what was said.

'Only Miss Treble can be induced into accompanying the child, and she only on account of the money,' Grancat had said.

Treble, Idie's governess, was idle and cumbersome; a woman of no discernible age and no apparent purpose in life. Myles had sniggered at the notion of Treble being in charge of Idie, and Grancat had murmured, 'Treble, good God . . . heaven help the child. Webb, of course you must accompany the child and see her installed.'

Algernon Webb, known to the family as Numbers, was an accountant or lawyer or some useful combination of both, and he'd been at Pomeroy so long you could almost forget he was there at all. Idie peered between the curtains. Numbers appeared a little alarmed about accompanying Idie on such a voyage; his eyebrows having escaped so far up his forehead in shock at the idea that she began to worry they might never be able to come down again. On Myles's knee lay the Idie Book, in which Myles wrote the things they learned about her. So far he'd written:

1. *Idie is not the same as us.*
2. *But she has the same name [GRACE].*
3. *Grancat is mine and Benedict's father but not Idie's.*
4. *Someone just gave Idie to Grancat, like a kind of parcel.*
5. *Then [later, when Idie was bigger] a letter came telling Grancat she had to go back to where she came from at the start.*
6. *Grancat says it's because she is a lady of property*

now. We don't know if that's good or not.

7. *Grancat says that Blood is THICKER than Water. We don't know what that means, but the result of it is that Idie has to go to a small and faraway place called Hummingbird Island.*

Myles's brow furrowed as he pencilled a new entry:

8. *It is in the WEST INDIES and they are dangerous and only Treble will go to them them because she is greedy for the money. You have to pay someone a good deal to go to them because they are awash with brigands and bandits.*

9. *Idie won't ever come back because the Indies are so far away.*

Round tears crawled down his grubby, freckled cheeks. Myles made fatter tears than anyone else. Grancat said that was because Myles's heart was so much bigger than other people's. Myles was slow and thoughtful and life came less easily to him that it did to Benedict, who was quick and reckless, but Benedict was mostly too busy and grown-up to want to play with Idie.

10. *We won't be allowed to visit her because the Indies are hellish hot and only pirates live there.*

Idie crept away. She had her own book. Across the

cover she'd written 'My Mother', and this book was the only secret she ever kept from Myles and Benedict. Alone in the attic, Idie opened it and reread the first entries:

> I don't belong at Pomeroy because my hair is the wrong colour.
> Myles said he doesn't think I ever had a mother, but I do because all children have mothers.
> Then he said my mother didn't love me and that's why she sent me away.
> Grancat said she DID love me and that's why she sent me away, because sometimes it is kinder to do that.
> First my father died [a long time ago] and now my mother is dead too.

Idie took up her pencil and added:

> My mother lived in the West Indies so now I have to go to her house.
> I have no other relative except for my Pomeroy cousins.

Then she'd put that book down and taken up another, *The Flora and Fauna of the Indies*, and pored over the coloured plates in it.

2

'*Trescientos escudos.* On-ly *trescientos.*'

A large bird, a white and lemon-yellow parakeet, was held high above the heads of the crowd on the dock.

'I'll have him.'

The young girl with the mane of dark hair slipped between the trousered legs and pastel skirts of the crowd. Numbers followed in her slipstream, dabbing his face with a handkerchief and apologizing at least twice to everyone he passed.

'Miss Grace! Miss Grace!'

'On-ly *trescientos escudos.* Ve-rrry fine . . . ve-rrry good . . . very handsome . . . ve-rrry clever . . . ve-rrry booot-ti-ful.'

'I want him – I'll have him,' Idie told the man, breathless.

The hawker eyed the fine embroidery of Idie's collar.

'*Trescientos escudos.*'

'Yes, yes, I want him.'

'Ve-rrry clever. Name of poet: Homer. H-O-M-E-R. Famous poet. Bird of the ambassador of Brazil.'

There were cockatoos and parakeets and lorikeets and all sorts on the dock in the Azores, but Idie supposed that they hadn't all belonged to ambassadors.

'Miss Grace –' pleaded Numbers – 'do wait, Miss Grace.'

'*Trescientos escudos*,' insisted the hawker.

'I have three hundred escudos,' said Idie, loud and determined.

The parakeet dipped his head and inspected Idie sideways.

'*Trescientos escudos –*'

'Miss Grace, I do not think – where is Miss Treble? Should we not consult Miss Treble on the matter? I am sure—' petitioned Numbers.

'Miss Treble has counted herself out of the equation by choosing to remain in her cabin, where the whisky is to hand. She says whisky is medicinal in a case of seasickness,' responded Idie in a loud voice, adding, 'Besides, she says the Azores are NOT SAFE, that no one she knows has disembarked there and returned alive.'

'Oh dear. Oh dear.' Numbers cast about. 'Well, you see, about the parrot, Miss Grace, you must be moderate, be prudent, Miss Grace. Moderation and prudence . . .' Numbers glanced nervously at the large bird and dabbed his face and said, 'They live a very long time, you know . . .'

Homer moved his head with the spasmodic twitch common to all birds and his crest oscillated like the ornamentation of an oriental emperor. He fastened a resolute eye on Numbers and plumped out his nape, then his breast and finally, when, like a soufflé, he'd quite doubled in size, he said, '*TRESCIENTOS ESCUDOS.*'

Numbers stepped back in alarm, but Idie squealed with delight.

'You SEE, he TALKS.'

'Ve-rrry fine bird, talking bird, *senhorita*, ve-rrry clever bird. Name, Homer. *Trescientos escudos.*'

'Miss Grace, it'll be awkward, do you not think, very awkward, to have a parrot . . . ?'

'*Parakeet.* And he will talk to me. NO ONE ELSE talks to me . . .' Idie spoke loudly. The crowd grew silent; heads turned. Sweat broke out on Numbers's brow. 'YOU never talk to me and Miss Treble is too inconvenienced by the mild swell that occurred THREE days ago in the Bay of Biscay to leave her cabin.' Idie noted with satisfaction that Numbers was foraging in a pocket in a flustered sort of way and she continued triumphantly, her voice rising. 'So, in the absence of any other companionable companion, and because whisky isn't quite so medicinal as Miss Treble thinks, Homer will step into the breach and talk to me.'

'Ve-rrry clever bird.'

Homer dipped his head in receipt of the compliment, then began to edge his way, claw over claw, towards Idie. He placed one large, many-jointed claw on the bare skin of her arm, inclined his head a fraction to her and said, 'YOUR EXCELLENCY.'

A smile burst over Idie's face.

Homer curled the segments of his claws around her small arm. He shuffled and bustled and waggled his rear quarters, then waggled and bustled again till his rump had billowed like a cloud. When he was quite sure he was looking his most magnificent and was installed in the most commodious manner possible, his tail feathers lifted again and settled over Idie's arm, like the gown of a dowager over a throne she has no intention of relinquishing.

With the great bird on her small arm, Idie turned. The crowd parted for them, then closed and clustered after them, watching and whispering and shutting out the hapless Numbers.

With the acquisition of Homer, Idie's spirits rallied and she realized the point of having money of her own. However, Homer proved a disappointing companion on that lonely journey, because he took a dim view of sea voyages, dropping his head beneath his wing and refusing to talk for a long while.

Numbers and Treble kept to their cabins and Idie wondered that she should have been sent to the end of the world in the charge of two such un-seaworthy grown-ups.

One night after dining alone with a despondent sherbet crested parakeet, she wrapped a cardigan around herself and slipped out of her cabin. She paused at Treble's door, wondering whether her governess had grown accustomed to seas that shifted. The door was ajar and Idie heard Numbers talking in a hushed tone.

'I never know what's coming next, what mood or prank will take her. I cannot talk to her. I have no wife nor child, and I fear lack of practice ties my tongue, Miss Treble.' Idie peeked through the gap in the door. Treble was running a plump finger through her ringlets. Numbers, however, was evidently not the sort of man to notice the fetching gestures women might make, thought Idie, because he wrung his hands and ploughed on, 'She's resorted to a parrot, God help her, for her own amusement and to mock me. She's precocious, but she knows nothing of the world, wasn't received by neighbours, rarely went beyond the bounds of the park at Pomeroy. They've told her nothing. She doesn't know where she's going nor why, and like a wounded thing she snarls and holds her head high and I – anything I tell her would only wound her more deeply.'

You WILL tell me, said Idie to herself. *Whatever there is to know, I must know it.*

'Mr Webb, don't worry yourself. That child requires EXPERIENCED MANAGEMENT. Leave everything in my hands. When the sea's calm, I'll be quite myself and I'll *tame* the child.'

Idie snorted. *Tame the child? Well, Treble might find that Miss Idie Grace CANNOT be tamed.*

Numbers answered. 'I am most grateful to you, Miss Treble. I wish you goodnight and a speedy recovery.'

Idie made a dash past the cabin for the stairs.

There was a dance on the quarterdeck. A band was playing waltzes under the awning, couples dancing by lamplight. Idie stood behind a post and watched, her eyes travelling from one woman to another, resting on their dresses, their faces, their hair, wondering what sort of clothes her own mother had worn, and then why it was that her mother had lived in a house that had ghosts in it, and why she had sent her daughter away, and why she, Idie, was told nothing about anything. Idie never so much as glanced at the men. Grancat wasn't Idie's father, but he dwarfed all other men and was all the father she'd ever wanted.

The wind grew fierce and the waves tall. The lamps were put out, the couples crept below deck, but Idie lingered. The hull was gleaming beneath the water as if lit by a lantern. Idie crept along the deck rail and saw how the wake had turned to a ribbon of fire and how the waves broke about the boat in luminous starry showers. Floating lights gleamed on the water and were gone, and the fishes were grown silvery as if lit with a light of their own.

'It's the salt that makes light when the ship meets a rough sea.'

Idie turned, surprised for she'd not noticed anyone else still about on that part of the deck.

A tall, dark-skinned man approached and said, 'It is not safe. Come, miss, I take you back inside.' His voice was slow and sing-song and strange to her, but Idie considered him and concluded he had the kind of uprightness about him that was desirable in an adult. 'You are going home.'

It was part question, part statement. She scowled, cross that he, like everyone else, knew about her, and said through her teeth, 'It's NOT home.'

'Miss Grace, it is a fine place.'

He knew her name too.

'It is good you are going home,' he repeated.

'Pomeroy is my HOME,' said Idie sullenly.

'That house is tall and grey and –' he paused, searching for the right word – 'big and cross and frownin' at the world.'

Idie started. He knew Pomeroy. It was him – the man who'd come with the letter for Grancat, the letter that said she had to leave, the one that had changed everything and meant that nothing would ever be the same again.

'Your home, Miss Grace, Bathsheba –'

'Bathsheba,' breathed Idie.

'It is white and low and the sun always there like she shining only for it, and it lying there, just smiling back at the world.'

Idie considered the notion of smiling houses and frowning houses and conceded that there might be an advantage to a house that smiled, but not if it were troubled by ghosts, so she asked, 'Why do they say it's haunted?'

He shook his head. 'It is a fine place, with creeks and gullies and hummingbirds . . .'

Creeks and gullies and hummingbirds. Idie considered these. Well, of course there would be hummingbirds, and hummingbirds would be a positive, but he hadn't mentioned monkeys, so she asked, 'Are there monkeys?'

He smiled. 'Plenty of monkeys, plenty of mongooses . . . Oh yes, miss, it is a fine, fine place. You needed there, Miss Grace. Is good you goin' home.'

The ship lurched and plummeted into the valley of a wave, flinging Idie against him. He caught her and led her back to the lower-deck stairs and paused there, and she asked, 'Does it have ghosts?'

'Ghosts everywhere, for those that look.' He smiled, yet his tone was serious. 'Don't you go lookin' for them, Miss Grace; don't you go searching.'

She looked at his face, remembering how he'd stopped under the turkey oak to shelter from the rain and stretched a hand over the railing to the horses huddled there. It was perhaps because of that, because he was the kind of man who talked to horses in the rain, that Idie asked, very quietly, 'My mother . . . Did you *know* her?'

He looked then right into her eyes and nodded. Idie's heart turned over,

'Tell me – what was she like?'

'Your mother she planted the trees, she fill all the inside and the outside with flowers –'

'And . . . ?' Idie's voice was barely audible.

'She was strong and kind and capable and all the things a mother needs to be.'

The door to the lower deck opened and Numbers stood before them. He started with shock and said, 'Ah, Miss Grace, there you are, and Nelson, I see –'

Idie saw he was alarmed to find her with the man called Nelson, and the mischief in her bobbed like a cork to the surface and she said, 'Yes, here I am. And I have been having a MOST interesting conversation with Nelson.'

'Good night, Miss Grace, Sir,' said Nelson, and slipped away.

The wind roared, the waves grew tall as trees, the captain cursed, women screamed, plates smashed. Treble wept, prayed and vomited.

'We're going to a fine place,' Idie told Homer

to console him, 'with gullies and monkeys and hummingbirds.' In her book she wrote:

> My mother was a BEAUTY.
> I am going to her house.
> It is white and smiling.
> It is called Bathsheba, which is a very nice name for a
>   house.
> She filled it with flowers.
> She was strong and kind and capable and all the things
>   a mother needs to be.

Those words were, for a long time after, a light to live by, a little fire at which to warm her hands.

3

Hummingbird Island was shimmering and strange as a fairy tale. The emerald-skirted hills stretched their violet crowns into fleecy lilac cloud. Some careless eruption of the seabed had perhaps thrown them up and left them there together in a happy cluster, as if just floating on the silvery sea.

Idie whispered to Treble, 'Myles says they'll drain our blood for ink and dry our skin to parchment.'

'Quite so, quite so.' Treble was busy adjusting her bonnet, but as Idie's words registered she spun round. '*What* did you say child? No, no, that cannot be so.'

The harbour was a kaleidoscope of steamers and schooners, carriages and cranes, masts and palms, awnings and warehouses, casks and crates, a mesmerizing rainbow of brilliant otherness, greener, yellower, pinker, than any greens or yellows or pinks Idie had ever seen.

Baronet was led, snorting, down the ramp. He struck the cobbles and roared with joy as if the island had appeared there in the sea especially for him. Dazed by the swooning heat, Idie waited on the dock. Dark, bare-backed men walked past, sheaves of cane on their heads. A line of turbaned ladies followed, baskets on their heads, and Idie marvelled that everyone carried things on their heads instead of in their hands and wondered if she could soon go about in such a way.

Treble, her feet finally on ground that did not shift, shuddered. 'Mr Webb, this is most unsuitable. Have no arrangements been made for us?' Treble was turning pinker by the minute in the heat, and all her ringlets were unravelling.

Numbers put his hat on, took it off, put it on again. 'Yes, yes, there will be someone – Gladstone will come.' He cast about and beckoned vaguely across the sea of straw hats and parasols.

'Miss Grace, Gladstone Mayley, your foreman, has managed the estate at Bathsheba most loyally and for some forty years.'

'Whoever he is, he's late, Mr Webb, and it is most unsatisfactory,' said Treble. Ruffled by the sun and the unsatisfactory unsuitability of everything, she was wavering like a blancmange, putting Idie in mind of Myles, who'd said, 'It'll be vile and horrid and you'll melt like wax.'

Idie gave a wicked smile to think of Treble subsiding into a pinky-peachy puddle between the casks of rum.

'Ah, there's Gladstone with Nelson.' Numbers raised his hat in the direction of two men bent in close conversation.

Treble looked their way and flinched as if with shock. 'No, no, that cannot be so.'

Gladstone, the older of the two men, made his way towards Idie's group, but Idie's eyes were on Nelson, the man who'd known her mother, the man who'd gone all the way to Pomeroy and been turned away at the door. He'd had no overcoat then, Idie remembered, and in that rain his clothes would have been wringing wet.

'Gladstone Mayley is Nelson's father, Miss Grace. The Mayleys have always been good and loyal. Unfortunately Nelson no longer works at Bathsheba, though two or more of his children do.'

'I see,' said Idie.

Gladstone stood before Idie and bent a little, raising a hand to his hat. 'Miss Grace?'

'There's some mistake surely,' Treble hissed at Numbers.

'I am Gladstone Mayley, mistress, your foreman,' the man said to Idie, lifting his hat.

Treble started and blinked with shock that the people of such a place should speak with so educated and English an intonation.

Gladstone looked at the large bird on the small girl's arm and a broad grin breached his solemn face.

'This is Homer, and this is Baronet,' said Idie proudly, gesturing to them both, and with a quicker sweep of her hand she indicated, 'Mr Webb, my lawyer, whom I believe you know, and Miss Treble, my governess.'

'There's some mistake, Mr Webb,' Treble hissed again. 'I did *not* expect—'

'Miss Treble, what exactly *did* you expect?' asked Numbers, a touch sharp.

'Here comes Sampson with the handcart,' said Gladstone.

Sampson was young and sort of long and his suit stood nervously and separately about him as if on its first outing.

'I may faint,' announced Miss Treble. Idie noticed with mild curiosity that in the heat Treble had indeed grown still more unsteady and sort of liquescent.

'Mistress, I am Sampson Sealy,' Sampson said, smiling broadly. 'Welcome.'

He looked at Baronet and rubbed the soft parts of Baronet's nose, 'This horse is happy to be here.' Sampson took sugar from his pocket and held his palm flat.

'See, I told you, Baronet. I told you there'd be sugar,' Idie whispered, wondering if everyone here went about with sugar in their pockets every day.

'Plenty of sugar.' Sampson's smile was still there, as if it would now stay happily on his face forever. His skin was pitted and gnarled by some childhood disease. His arms hung sort of accidentally about his sides as though they might come loose at any minute and Idie wanted to bind all the bits of smiling Sampson Sealy together with tape in case he came apart.

'I may faint,' Treble repeated in a trembling voice.

Gladstone started forward. 'Quick, help the lady, Sampson.'

'Certainly not,' said Treble, adding forcefully, 'Mr Webb, lend me your arm.'

Sampson had strapped the luggage to a trap. Baronet, harnessed alongside, was expressing by the high carriage of his head his superiority over the trap ponies. Numbers murmured to Treble that he regretted he could not see them safe to Bathsheba, it being such a long way there and the hour growing late.

'It's quite all right,' said Idie promptly. 'Baronet is just as good at looking after me as you are.'

'I'll come by on Monday,' he answered.

'Yes, yes, do, dear Mr Webb. Do come by on Monday,' said Treble, and Idie was mortified by Treble's simpering and by the straining apricot frock that was probably inappropriate on a governess. Numbers and Gladstone conversed quietly, then Gladstone mounted and Numbers waved them off.

They passed a ladies' lyceum, some quaint Regency-style houses, a statue of Lord Nelson and a cricket pitch.

'Oh! It's all just like a little England,' murmured Treble.

A white country track curved through stately

palms with swaying feathery tops and fields of high, whispering leaves.

Gladstone gestured. 'Sugar cane, mistress.'

'There *are* monkeys, aren't there?' asked Idie, disappointed she hadn't yet seen one.

'Plenty of monkeys,' Sampson assured her in his slow, smiling way.

'Are we nearly there?'

'Soon.'

They inched down a steep rough track into a densely wooded cleft and up past a straggling settlement of wooden houses on stilts, all in shades of sherbet and candy-floss and sweet as dolls' houses. Bright-eyed children stared, the girls fingering the looped braids and ribbons of their hair. The road dropped down along a strand of dazzling white and a sky-coloured sea, then climbed again to lush, unfenced hills carpeted in coarse hummocky grass. Dumbed by the heat and humidity, Idie drifted into sleep.

When she woke the sun was low and saffron and resting on the water as if she too were hot and tired and was considering taking a swim. Just then the sun did, in fact, decide to do just that, and with a final blaze of scarlet and amber, sank into the silver sea.

'Mistress.' Gladstone turned and in his face was pooled all the gold of the sinking sun and he smiled a slow smile that made Idie think of surf breaking over a silent beach. 'You are home.'

PART II

May 1912

4

The ponies pulled up before a pair of white stone pillars all tufted with ferns. In the half shadow beyond the iron curlicues of the gate, the sweep of a long drive glowed whitely. The only house Idie had ever known or wanted was Pomeroy and she eyed those white stone pillars a little warily.

No place for a young girl . . . so large and remote . . . haunted . . . well, it would be, after what happened there.

Sampson bellowed, 'Enoch! Come, Enoch. The missus is home.'

Enoch appeared from a stone gatehouse. On his head he wore what was no more than the relic of a hat, straws poking up at all angles from the crown like plumage. He ran towards them in a stiff, rolling kind of way, and Idie thought that he might be very old; as old, quite possibly, as his hat.

'Mistress, Enoch Quarterly,' said Enoch, touching a hand to the derelict hat, and Idie thought it was a mercy he didn't lift it for it might disintegrate.

Homer looked at Enoch with interest and

29

announced in the lilting intonation of the place, 'THE MISSUS IS HOME.'

Enoch's old face crinkled into a smile and, chuckling, he saluted the bird.

A double avenue of palms, tall and straight as the columns of a county cathedral, stood sentinel along the drive. Idie caught her breath and looked up in wonder at their plumes and thought how like feather dusters they were, and how they were high enough to tickle the violet sky. Beyond on either side, low, spreading sorts of trees dotted the ground, giving the impression of English parkland.

Baronet whinnied for joy at the grass, but Idie looked doubtfully at the coarse, spiky tufts that served in these parts instead of lawn and thought of the rich clover of Devon, but she put a brave face on for the sake of Baronet and said, 'See, Baronet, there's grass. We didn't know if there'd be grass, did we?'

The drive wound on and on. At Pomeroy, the drive, while impressive, had not been so long, nor had the trees reached up so far, nor had they had so many sorts of green in them.

The night was racing in – not down from the sky as sensible English nights do but rushing up from the ground.

No place for a young girl.

The whispers she'd heard on the ship batted about in her head, flapping their large wings like crows trapped in there. Disquieted and anxious, she said, 'It's a very long drive.'

All around from every leaf and blade of grass rose a swelling, humming chorus of tiny numberless night things.

'Tree frogs, mistress,' said Sampson, smiling.

'Do the frogs here live in trees?' asked Idie.

'Yes, an' they tiny as my tiniest toe an' they sing *crac-crac-crac*, high in the fustic trees.' Sampson turned, smiling, to her, and Idie wondered if he'd stopped smiling at all ever since Georgetown.

Stars appeared, star after star, second by second, as if to flood the sky. Idie's wonder at the strange, warm night unfurled. She stretched out a hand. She could reach up and touch the stars – they were so low that they might've come close to earth only for her. A tiny red pinprick of light appeared at the tip of her finger and Idie started and recoiled; then they were all around, about her head and in between the trees, and flashing in and out of the very air, a million million lights, sudden and darting and angular.

'Fireflies, mistress.' Sampson's smile grew wider.

Night birds flashed between the trees and it was as though everything had been asleep and Idie's small hand had touched it all to life. She peered about in amazement, breath held.

Still the white drive wound on between the tall palms. The moon appeared and tipped a white radiance over the garden. The tree frogs, as if at a command, fell quiet, and the sudden silence clutched at Idie's throat. There were rustles and fleeting shadows and all the beauty of the place was suddenly grown uncanny, every dark space vibrating with tremulous shadows.

Strange things happened there.

Leaves flashed in the moonlight and there was malice and mockery in their rustling. The ferns grew grotesque and strange; there was a soft, sinister laughter in the rustle of the leaves that curdled Idie's blood.

No place for a young girl.

Her heart pounded. She shook Treble's arm to wake her, but her governess merely grunted and turned her head aside.

The chorus of tiny chirping things started up once more and Idie peered ahead and tried to still the heaving of her heart.

5

A white, two-storey house lay before them. Low handsome trees stood around, waxy blooms strung about their dark leaves like flocks of moons. Pink and orange flowers lay carelessly about the bushes. The air was soft and still as if once a spell was cast over the house that had forever enchanted it and left it there in shimmering dream-like beauty. A veranda ran the length of it, a mass of feathery vines trailing along its roof. Candles flickered on the curved stone steps. The shingles of the roof were silvered by moonlight and the white house seemed, as Nelson had said, to be smiling and to be waiting there specially for Idie.

Male staff, perhaps forty or more, lined the circular stone forecourt. Either side of the steps to the porch stood the house staff in white frilled bonnets and pinnies. *So many of them*, thought Idie. She stroked Homer's nape, grateful for the fact of a magnificent parakeet on her arm so as to keep her end up, being only small and only twelve and the mistress of so large a payroll.

Treble blinked and looked about, her bonnet askew, lank ringlets clinging damply to her cheeks, and Idie felt a little ashamed. She saw the proud carriage of Baronet's head and thought how good it was to have a fine English thoroughbred and a parakeet at your side if you were a lady of property coming to your house for the first time.

This will be my home, these the people I live among and I their mistress, Idie said to herself, and then whispered to Gladstone, 'Do they *all* work here?'

'Yes, missus,' he answered, smiling broadly. 'Some work on the cane, the cacao, the coffee.'

Idie lifted her chin and stood up straight. So they had come because they wanted to see the new mistress. Well, here she was, standing before them; a small, tired girl in a white dress, with a large sulphur-crested parakeet on her arm and a fine horse at her side.

A young boy raised his cap to Idie, then stepped forward to Baronet. 'Reuben Sealy, missus.'

Idie drew a line in her head linking Sampson and Reuben, for their names were the same and their smiles were the same staying sorts of smiles and they were surely brothers.

'Reuben works with Sampson. They do the horses and the blacksmithing,' Gladstone said.

'Do you have hay and a straw bed for Baronet?' asked Idie doubtfully.

'Big kus-kus grass bed,' answered Reuben, beaming.

'My bed is the same, sweet kus-kus grass.'

The thought sailed into Idie's head that she might sleep on a bed of sweet kus-kus grass with Baronet. She felt the watching eyes on her and drew close to Baronet, glancing as she did so back at the circle of faces. She clung to Baronet and whispered, 'The tree frogs will sing to you all night long, and in the morning we'll go swimming.' Her voice wavered, 'We'll have fun, I promise.'

'Go on, mistress,' whispered Gladstone, urging Idie on.

The large parakeet on her arm, her crumpled governess behind, Idie moved around the forecourt.

'Stedman.' The man lifted a hand to his head.

'Bailey.'

Idie walked on, a hesitant smile on her lips, from one to the next. The men dipped their heads briefly, then stared at her, unsmiling and unreadable.

'Skeete.'

These people had been here always. They knew things about Bathsheba she didn't.

'Curtis, mistress.'

'Clement Mayley, miss.'

'Clement is my grandson – he works with me in the office and in the fields,' explained Gladstone, smiling broadly and with pride. Idie drew another line, linking Gladstone and Clement.

When she reached the foot of the stairs she looked

up and saw the long, drooping blooms that hung from the froth of creeper about the veranda. She saw the women, most in pink gingham and white pinnies. At the top, before the door, stood a woman with hair so white and skin so pale that she might have been conjured from trembling moonlight. Idie paused. She breathed a strong, swooning sort of scent that caught and held her there as if captive. She clutched at the stair rail for the scent made her giddy. She saw a bush of ivory flowers at the right of the stairs, their long trumpet throats deeply veined with purple. She turned away from them and caught sight again of the moon woman.

'Who's that?' she whispered.

'Miss Celia, mistress,' said Gladstone, then he urged her on. 'They're waiting.'

Idie took the first step.

'Myrline, miss.'

'Laticia, missus.'

The women bobbed and withdrew a fraction, reticent but staring.

Idie hung back and stood on tiptoes and whispered to Gladstone, 'Do they *want* me here?'

'It is your home, mistress,' he answered simply.

Idie glanced back to the staff lining the forecourt, all their eyes on her, and then to the top of the stairs. She took another step, and another, on upward to the top, the women that stood on either side greeting her.

'Sharissa, missus.'

Idie turned to the other side. A woman stood there, her face hard and riven as a dry, desert land, a towering arrangement of tangerine and violet on her head, the garment that hung over her gaunt frame black and sulphur and tangerine.

'Phibbah Sealy,' said Gladstone. 'Miss Phibbah manages the kitchen.'

Phibbah chewed on an unlit pipe and stared at Idie through eyes that were knowing but strangely young in her wrinkled face. Idie gazed at her, fascinated by her turban and by the glory of all the colours she chose to put about herself. Phibbah Sealy, Idie decided then, was a sort of sphinx, wise and full of secrets.

Gladstone whispered, 'Phibbah cannot speak. She is the grandmother of Reuben and Sampson Sealy. She's been here fifty years or more.' Idie drew more lines in her head.

A girl spoke now and Idie turned.

'I am Mayella Mayley. I been here six months only. I am the kitchen maid and housemaid. And –' Mayella glanced across the stairs at Phibbah, and said in a rush as though she couldn't help herself – 'I'm supposed to help Phibbah with cooking and cleaning, but God be my witness, it's only me as does everything.' The words poured from her, an undulating sing-song murmur. There was more affection than malice in them, and Phibbah took no notice, chewing her pipe and staring into the middle distance.

'Mayella is my granddaughter,' said Gladstone, smiling. Idie drew another line in her head between Gladstone and Mayella, who was perhaps not much older than Idie herself.

Idie stepped up on to the veranda towards the spectral moonlight woman who stood before the door. Idie stared, wondering if there were any blood in her at all, wondering too what sort of age she was, for she was certainly not young, but neither was she old, for her skin was smooth and unmarked as if life had somehow passed her by.

'Carlisle Quarterly, missus, your butler.' A man had spoken but Idie'd seen no man there and she jumped a little with fright. In the shadow by the door stood the man called Carlisle Quarterly. There was something curling, something mocking in the way he spoke that Idie didn't like. If there was no blood in the white woman's veins, then Carlisle had plenty for two. *Quarterly*. Idie drew another, more tentative, line between Enoch and his tufted hat and this man, and now the insides of Idie's head were a spider's web.

Idie turned back. The moon woman's mouth hung open a second or two, as if someone had once told her what to say but she'd now forgotten. Gladstone announced, 'Miss Celia Rhodes.'

'Idie,' the woman said eventually, her English vowels ringing like cut glass, and Idie was surprised that so familiar a greeting should be delivered so coldly. Idie stared some more at her. Celia Rhodes's eyes were strange and yellow and dull with confusion. Those eyes turned now from Idie to Carlisle.

Idie drew close to Gladstone and stood on tiptoe and whispered in his ear, 'Who is she?'

Gladstone looked at Idie, and hesitated.

'Who is she?' repeated Idie and Gladstone answered carefully, 'This is the only place she knows.'

'But what does she *do*?'

'Do? . . . She's just here . . .' said Gladstone.

A few seconds passed and Celia, who was just here because it was the only place she knew, still blocked the door so Idie stood on tiptoe and hissed in Gladstone's ear, 'But *who* is she and *why* is she here?'

Gladstone bent down and murmured, 'Miss Celia is your aunt, Miss Grace. Did they not tell you that?'

'My aunt?' Idie was dumbfounded. She glanced sideways at Celia and mouthed, 'Are you sure?'

'I am sure.' He smiled. 'She is the sister of your mother.'

'The sister of my mother?' repeated Idie, barely audible. *My mother's sister. My mother had a sister and I didn't know.* She turned slowly to face Celia, then, still uncertain, stepped forward, extending her hands.

'Aunt Celia.'

Celia's eyes wavered with fear. Idie looked at her, at the lifeless, mask-like skin, colourless lashes, colourless hair. In none of her dreams or imaginings had her own mother had a sister nor ever such a sister as this.

'Aunt Celia –' she started again, but Celia only stepped back, tremulous and shaking her head as though a ghost stood before her.

My mother's sister will not greet me, Idie said inwardly, wounded. She found that she was shaking, but Gladstone took her arm and led her to the door and said, 'Open the door, Carlisle.'

Carlisle shot a brief, chilly smile towards Gladstone, then turned from him and said to Idie, 'The bird stays outside.'

Idie looked again at Carlisle and paused, taken aback that her butler should speak to her in such a way; doubly taken aback since this came so fast on top of an introduction to an aunt she'd never known she had. She looked at Carlisle and took stock of him. His face was handsome, but had something hard and cruel about the mouth.

Homer plumped his feathers and billowed in a rather magnificent sort of manner and inspected Carlisle with his customary disdain. Idie felt rather proud of him just then and she gathered her strength and held her shoulders back and stood up tall.

'That's for the mistress to say,' said Gladstone gently.

The only butler Idie'd ever known was Silent, and

he'd never seemed to have any view of his own as to what would or wouldn't happen at Pomeroy. Idie considered the lines of waiting staff and watching eyes behind and said to herself, *I will not cross swords with him now in front of his staff because I know that is not right or fair, but the battle lines are drawn. I am drawing them now between myself and Carlisle Quarterly.*

She said aloud and airily so those around could hear, 'That's right, the veranda will suit Homer nicely. You can settle him for me, Quarterly.' She took a step towards Carlisle and held out her arm. Carlisle flinched. Homer fixed his most resolute stare on the man and tilted his head and set his crest rippling. Carlisle stepped back and at that Idie smiled and said breezily, 'It's no matter, Quarterly. I see you are afraid so I will settle him myself.'

She placed Homer on the chair nearest to Carlisle. Homer bustled and plumped himself up and Carlisle took a step towards the front door.

Aha, fifteen–all, Carlisle Quarterly; the scores are even, thought Idie. Then she remembered all the watching eyes and began to wonder what the correct manner of entering your own home for the first time might be.

The door swung open and Idie stood very still before it, her insides flapping as if she were suddenly full of moths.

6

A hall ran the full width of the house. Tall shuttered windows filtered the moonlight, laying it in slats across the polished floors. Palms and ferny things stood about in plaited baskets, a bowl of cut flowers rested on a bamboo side table. Light pooled from oil lanterns on to gleaming wood, and a flight of stairs curled up from either side to a balustraded landing.

My house, she told herself in wonder. *This is my house.*

On either side of the hall closed doors led to other rooms. Idie stepped slowly across the floor towards a carved mahogany chair. She placed her hand on the arm of it, ran it along the smooth wood and fingered the cane back. She turned and placed her hand on a small pedestal table, the warmth of the wood beneath her fingers solid and real. She looked up to the ceiling and to the landing and then down again to the room and turned slowly round and round again. She breathed deeply, smelling the house like a hound. The air was thick and still as if it had been a long time waiting. She cast about the room as if the house itself, the walls of it and floors of it and worn linen cushions, would tell her something, for there were no photographs, no portraits, only the handsome furniture and lamps and ferns in their baskets.

Treble arrived, panting a little from the exertion of the five stairs, and settled like a swamp over the nearest chair. She looked up at the cornices and about at the carved mahogany and cane and said, 'It's all very good, child, very good.'

Perhaps the staff were still assembled outside. It would be up to Idie to dismiss them. She turned to the veranda and saw Celia in the doorway, strange and vague as fog. Not much liking the idea of being in the house with Celia even if she was her aunt, Idie went to Mayella and whispered, 'Where does Celia live?'

'She lives in one house by the stables, Carlisle in the other. Sampson, Clement, Gladstone and I have houses by the sugar works. Miss Phibbah has a room behind the kitchen.'

'I see,' said Idie, because grown-ups often seemed to say that and she thought it made her sound grown-up and knowing.

She heard Carlisle outside, saying, 'Go, Gladstone.'

'He's got no respect,' Mayella whispered to Phibbah. 'Nobody talks to my granfer like that.'

'Why must Gladstone go?' Idie asked.

'Carlisle don't like anyone coming in the house.'

'It happens to be *my* house though and not Carlisle Quarterly's,' said Idie tautly. She spun on her heels, marched to the door and said, 'Quarterly, please tell the staff they may go and you may also go. I will let you know when I have need of you.'

Carlisle looked at her and waited a second, then in a manner so low as to be mocking, bowed and withdrew.

Thirty–fifteen, Carlisle Quarterly, Idie said to herself, and then, extending a hand to Gladstone, said in a loud, clear voice that all might hear, 'Goodnight, Gladstone, and thank you.'

'I will come by, mistress, when you are settled,' he answered, and she said, 'You are welcome at any time.'

Idie went back to the hall, beginning to feel that giving instructions was rather satisfactory and thinking that in fact you didn't need to be grown-up at all to be in charge.

'Come, Miss Phibbah has the dinner ready,' said Mayella, smiling at Phibbah and making it clear that Phibbah had in fact in no way contributed to the readiness of dinner.

'I am a little faint,' said Treble, 'and will retire to my room. Please send dinner up directly.'

'Faint?' enquired Mayella, with concern in her voice but amusement in her eyes as she regarded Treble and the straining chair beneath her. 'A glass of punch is good for that. I bring you up the punch first, then the dinner.'

'Quite so. Punch will be most medicinal,' said Treble. As she made her laborious way up the stairs, Celia followed Mayella to the dining room, Idie turned slowly around the room wondering where to explore first. She breathed the close, stale air and went to the shutters opposite the door and tugged at them, running from one to another and flinging them open. A soft breeze rippled through the still room and Idie breathed deeply. She gazed out into the spangled sky, where the stars were so low it seemed they might at any moment decide to drift sweetly in through the windows. She looked down at the stippled black and silver sea and shivered at its beauty.

She turned back to the room and eyed the two closed doors.

It is your home, Gladstone had said.

She walked slowly towards the one on the right, reached out and turned the porcelain handle. Moonlight lay in silver stripes across a small and pretty room. On a lacquered desk stood a glass oil lantern and a cut-glass vase of purple orchids. Idie picked up the lantern and went to the far wall. There would be a picture on these walls, or somewhere in the house, of her mother. She stood on tiptoe and held the lantern to the cracked, shining surfaces of the paintings. There were still lifes in oil of fruit and flowers and island landscapes and birds, but no portraits. Idie went to the desk, wondering who had sat at it and thinking because of the orchids that it had been a woman's desk. *Her own mother's desk.* She sat at it, where surely her own mother had sat, and tried the drawers. The first was empty, the second empty, the last too.

Idie started at a sound from the hall and rose and ran to the door and saw Celia at the windows, closing and bolting the shutters. Idie stood in the doorway watching, and Celia turned her strange, pale eyes to Idie, a hesitant smile on her lips.

It is my home, Idie told herself. *The shutters will be open if I want them so.*

To Celia she said, 'Aunt Celia, I should like the shutters left open.'

Celia put her hands to her mouth, whimpered and backed away from the window, cowering.

Mayella came running from the dining room, and Idie went to her and asked quietly, 'Why does Aunt Celia not like the shutters open? Why is she afraid?'

'They were always shut.'

'I see,' said Idie, wondering.

Mayella went to soothe Celia, and, sighing at the oddness of things here, Idie went to the door through which Mayella had come. She pushed it open. At the far end of a long table, dinner was laid for two: Derbyshire china patterned with ivy leaves, silver a little tarnished by the climate. Idie paused, her heart in her mouth. The walls were lined with portraits, tall high-up canvases, wrinkled and cracked with age. Idie stepped forward, her legs trembling a little. The curtains lifted gently in the breeze, like ghosts waving faint limbs.

Her fingers clasped the back of each chair as she paused, and the portraits looked down at her as if they'd been long waiting in this shuttered room. Like the Pomeroy portraits, their poses were self-conscious and careful, a hound or two at their feet, a horse perhaps in the distance or an open book in hand. Most had dates and names: John Grace, 1700; Lavinia Grace, 1700; George Grace, 1780; Ivy Grace, 1785; Arnold, 1870. Arnold's large, soft eyes stared through a window to the gate house of Bathsheba and he seemed to be sitting in the very same chair above which his portrait hung. He had no wife beside him, for the last portrait was of Cecil Grace, 1900, and there was no wife beside him either.

Idie stepped closer, trembling. 'Cecil Grace,' she breathed, 'are you my father?' She looked up and saw eyes that were large and soft, like Arnold's, but they were sad and faraway and he sat in shadow, so there was almost nothing you could tell of him, of his skin or the colour of his eyes. *Where is my mother?* Idie asked him silently. *Why is she not at your side?*

The flame of a lantern fell, shivering over the

polished table. Idie whirled around.

Aunt Celia.

Idie'd not heard her footsteps. Perhaps her aunt would always follow her about, drifting behind her like a trail of smoke from room to room.

'Aunt Celia, was Arnold my grandfather?' Idie demanded.

Celia nodded.

'Is Cecil my father?'

Celia nodded, less certainly now.

'Where's my mother's portrait?'

Celia uttered a strange sound, half whimper, half moan.

Idie paused, then asked more gently, 'Why is there no picture of her?'

Celia flinched. Her eyes swam with fear. 'You don't know . . . ?' she whispered.

Idie shook her head.

Just then the door from the kitchen opened and Mayella came in and said, 'Miss Idie, the squash and the guineafowl is ready.'

What is it that I don't know? Why will no one tell me anything? Idie asked herself.

Mayella went to Celia and took her arm and led her through to the kitchen. When she reappeared with a platter, Idie was waiting at the door.

'Mayella, was there no portrait of my mother?'

Mayella stepped back against the door, but Idie

went close to her and asked again, 'Was there no portrait of my mother?'

Mayella put the platter on the sideboard. 'I been here six month only,' she said, and fled into the kitchen.

7

Idie woke with a jolt. She tossed and turned for a while then looked at the bedside clock and saw that it had stopped and that there was no way of knowing what time it was. She touched the tips of her toes on to the rush matting, crept to the window, pulled up the sash, pushed open the shutters and paused there. The dark outside was softer and more scented than the dark inside. The night was just as it had been when she'd gone to bed, the frog chorus coming and going, the white candle flowers in the trees, the darting fireflies, the moon tired and fallen on its back as if faint with the singing of the night, bats flitting in and out of its light stream, jerky and angular, the stars disordered and dancing, not at all in their proper places. Idie wanted to reach out and tidy the stars and nudge the moon back up into her proper place.

A bough creaked and bent under the weight of some night creature. The tree frogs sang and the darkness teemed with flitting, darting, diving things. Idie remembered the upholstered still of Pomeroy, the sloping attic walls, the sprig-printed curtains, the pink-striped wallpaper, and thought how sad it was to be sent around the world like a lost penny to a place where there was a secret and no one told you anything and everything was strange and disquieting.

She thought of her new aunt and that unsettled her some more so she told herself that two sisters were not necessarily alike. *My mother was strong and kind and capable and all the things a mother needs to be. That is all I know, even though I've come all this way to this house that was once hers, and is now mine.* As she stood alone at the window, Idie gathered together all the clues she had about herself. Her arrival in Devon was the stuff of Pomeroy legend: enjoying the pleasurable state of mind induced by six whisky sodas and a bet on a winning outsider at Newmarket, Grancat had been accosted by a stranger on a Paddington platform, a bundle pressed on him.

'Eh, what's that?'

'Grace. She carries the name of Grace, Your Lordship.'

'What?'

'Grace.'

'Good God, man, you've already told me that . . . What sort of Grace? Where's it come from?'

'The Indies, sir.'

'Well, take it back at once.'

'She's no other relative, only yourself, sir.'

The earl harrumphed and then, perhaps due to the sweet state of mind induced by whisky sodas, he peered at it, quite as a matter of form, since he didn't know what to look for in a baby.

'Hmmm, it's the right colour, but it's not a Pomeroy Grace, you know, not one of my sorts of Grace . . .'

'There's only yourself, sir, she could go to.'

'What's its name?'

'Idie, sir. Idie Grace.'

The earl roared with sudden glee. 'Good God, d'you hear that? Idie. Idie – the outsider. My ticket – see, Lady Idie – thirty to one. Five pound to win.' Grancat clapped the open-mouthed stranger on the back, took up the baby and danced a surprisingly agile pas de basque, and then he, who'd never before handled a baby, tucked her under his arm along with the *Racing Post* and chuckled all the way back to his West Country estate.

And there the child lived happily ever after, Idie said to herself, until of course she was sent back again to where she'd started out. And that was when things started to go wrong, because in that place there was a secret and no one would answer any questions there any more than they would at Pomeroy. So the child would have to be secretive too and look in all the corners of the place and listen at doors all over again.

Idie started. The vine leaves scratched against the shutters and the palms made muffled, whispering sounds. She started again, for there'd been other noises too, from inside, footsteps perhaps in the corridor. Idie tensed and listened.

Take charge of yourself, Idie Grace, she whispered to herself. *All old houses whisper and speak at night.*

She crept back into bed, but for a long time she couldn't sleep and grew increasingly certain that someone was in the corridor.

After a long while, her mind turned to the portraits in the dining room. She remembered Celia's whimper when she'd asked about her mother, and felt a sharp prick of fear: *Don't go looking for ghosts*, Nelson had said. There was a secret in the house, and that secret made people afraid and it somehow had to do with her own mother, but Nelson had said that her mother was strong and kind and capable, so why would there be a secret about her? *Strong and kind and capable.* Idie climbed into bed and said these words over and over in her head like a rosary.

8

When she woke, Idie went to the window once more. The garden shimmered with light. Tiny, brilliant birds flitted from tree to tree, piping and fluting. The blue of the sea flashed between the glistening green of the leaves and everything was sparkling and luminous. Idie breathed deeply, feeling the sun on her skin, letting the fears of the night creep back into their shells like snails.

Beneath the window, beside the ivory trumpet flowers, was a low, feathery sort of tree. Tufted pink blossoms lay recklessly about it and amidst the blossoms sat a yellow-breasted finch. Idie watched him and wished Myles were there to tell her what kind of finch it was. Then she thought that it would be afternoon now at Pomeroy, that the horses would be dozing beneath the turkey oak, Grancat in his chair with the *Sporting Life*, Lancelot at his feet by the fire, dreaming rabbity dreams. Benedict would be away at Eton, and Myles, well, without Idie, Myles would be idle, perhaps just drawing on a window pane. He never knew quite what to do with himself if Idie wasn't there. It was she who began all their adventures; she who climbed the trees and explored the roofs and turrets of Pomeroy. She didn't have to be careful; she didn't have the breathing problem that dogged the Pomeroy Graces, didn't have to avoid excitement-inducing activities that triggered the attacks that Myles and Benedict were prone to.

Idie used to think that if she were to have an attack then she would prove she was the same as them, would be one of them, and at lunchtime once, when all were there to see her, she'd thrown herself to the floor and gasped like a stranded fish. Dr White had come and prodded her and listened to her heart and finally pronounced her, 'Fit as a flea. A vigorous hybrid.' 'Vigorous hybrid,' Grancat had echoed, chuckling. 'Quite so, quite so.' Idie didn't know what a vigorous hybrid was, but she had been somehow ashamed because Myles and Benedict weren't *vigorous hybrids*.

She looked again at the yellow finch and thought she'd write now to Myles and tell him that in the house that was her own there were yellow-breasted finches and creeks and gullies and hummingbirds. She took a paper and pen from the escritoire and wrote.

Bathsheba

23rd May 1912

Dear Myles,

> My sun is not the same as your sun.
> Yours is just a faded copy of mine.
> My house has trees with flowers that
> open like moons when everything else
> closes –

She scrubbed that out. Myles wasn't interested in flowers. She wrote instead:

> I have a parakeet but he is a bit uppity
> and doesn't always talk. He sleeps on
> the veranda –

She twisted a strand of hair through her fingers and sucked the pen.

> because there is a strange butler here
> called Quarterly who is scared of
> parakeets. He is not at all as nice or
> obedient as Silent. He has VIEWS OF
> HIS OWN and I don't think Silent has
> any of those, does he?

These are three things I have discovered for the Idie Book:

1. Arnold Grace was my grandfather and Cecil Grace was my father, so you see I AM a Grace. You always said I wasn't but I AM, even if I am not a Pomeroy sort of Grace.
2. I have an aunt called Celia and she is my mother's sister. We didn't know about her, did we?
3. Mayella, she is the housemaid here, has a father called Nelson, and Nelson was the man that came to Pomeroy with the letter. Do you remember that Silent wouldn't let him into the house, but Grancat said he must be all right because the horses seemed to like him.

There's a finch sitting on my windowsill. He is bright yellow. What kind of finch is that?

Love Idie
PS None of the clocks work here, because of the water in the air, so everything is suspended and strange and like being in a story book.

PPS The frogs sing all night. They live in trees.

That was the detail that she knew would most annoy Myles and make him wish he were there. Then she thought how it was only after you got to the end of a letter that you realized what should be in the middle of it and added:

PPPS People play cricket here and Treble says it is just like a little England, so please tell Grancat it is QUITE SAFE to come here.

Then she took her 'My Mother' book from the bedside table and wrote:

I can't find any paintings of my mother but I have to do some more EXPLORING.
There are lots of things that people don't want to tell me.

Then she reread the earlier entries and scowled and crossed out 'I have no living relative' and wrote instead:

I have an aunt. She is my mother's sister. She's here because she's here.

Mayella came in with a tray. She saw the open window and tutted. Idie hid the book in a drawer.

'How-day, Miss Idie? You hungry?'

'Yes.'

Idie was always hungry. Mayella set down the tray of tea and biscuits on the escritoire. Idie took a biscuit and went to the window. The finch flew from the tree to the sill.

'The windows open, then the birds come in, take sugar from the cake, butter from the bread.' Mayella spoke up-and-downly, like the cooing of a dove.

Idie crumbled the biscuit on to the peeling paint of the sill. The finch watched and twitched. Idie waited. It hopped up and pecked.

'You feed the birds, that's why you're hungry. Open the windows and everything comes inside.'

Things coming in through windows and doors put Idie in mind of the night. She frowned a little and turned to Mayella and whispered, 'Does anyone sleep in the house, apart from myself and Miss Treble?'

Mayella's enormous eyes grew bigger if possible than they were before. 'Oh no, nobody sleeps in this house, mistress. Only Phibbah in the—'

'There was –' Idie interrupted – 'I heard something—'

'Oh no, nobody wants to sleep in this house.'

Idie stared at Mayella a little astonished. Mayella's tone had been solemn and deadpan and didn't seem to take into account at all the fact that her new young mistress had just slept in the house, almost alone (because you couldn't really count Treble).

'Only the duppies like this house. They fly in-out, in-out if the windows open.' Mayella's eyes were wide and deep and serious.

'Duppies?' asked Idie, widening her own eyes and trying to make them as big and pretty as Mayella's and at the same time wanting to make clear that things that flew in and out of windows were of no concern to her.

'Keep the windows closed. That stops them coming in and out, in and out all the time.'

Idie grew cross and said, 'I heard a noise in the corridor, footsteps—'

Mayella interrupted, asking with concern, 'Miss Idie, the duppies – did they trouble you last night?'

'No, of course not.'

Then Idie began to wonder if the house was haunted and duppies were in fact just a local variety of ghost, so she asked, casually, 'Are there ghosts here?'

'Ghosts? Oh no, no ghosts, only duppies, plenty of duppies.' Mayella leaned forward and whispered closely, 'They show their faces in flames and hide in cupboards and . . .'

Firstly, thought Idie, duppies were definitely nothing more than a tropical species of Fine Old English Ghost. Secondly, the footsteps she'd heard had not belonged to any species of ghost at all. And thirdly, she thought that Mayella was perhaps very clever. Certainly she knew much more than Treble did about everything, and that made Idie wonder where, in fact, her governess was, so she asked, 'Where's Miss Treble?'

Mayella whispered, 'She slept long because of the punch and then she woke and now she hungry. You dress, Miss Idie. Hurry or the governess will eat all the breakfast.'

Mayella began to hum to herself and to sway gracefully about the room, tidying things. She went to the door and poked her head around it and went back to Idie and whispered, mischief in her eyes, 'Miss Celia is coming.'

'Aunt Celia's coming?' asked Idie in surprise.

Mayella smiled a smile most innocent and beatific, then swiftly slipped from the room. Warily Idie watched the door, and soon enough Celia did come through it, silently, and like a cat on the balls of her feet. But for what reason she'd come, Idie couldn't discern. Without greeting Idie in any way at all, her aunt Celia glided, like moving water, to the centre of the room and looked about.

'Good morning, Aunt Celia,' said Idie.

Celia gave no answer. Her eyes flickered to and fro about the room, till they alighted on Idie's suitcase. She went directly to it and lifted out a dress and held it up.

'Oh, don't worry, Aunt Celia. I can do that –' began Idie, thinking her aunt meant to help with the unpacking. But Celia never looked at Idie. She simply put the dress aside and, as though Idie had not spoken at all, took out another, a grey one trimmed with white lace, and went with it to the armoire. Idie watched, astonished. Catching sight of her own reflection in the mirror of the armoire, Celia paused, then turned a fraction to the right, a fraction to the left. She swayed her hips and watched the folds of her dress oscillate a little to the left, a little to the right. She had a long, graceful figure and the dress moved prettily about her and made her smile at her own reflection. Her hand moved to her collar and toyed with the lace of it and for a second as she gazed at herself she seemed to slide away from the room into a world of dreams, and Idie saw the longing in her and felt sad for Aunt Celia, who was her mother's sister and who was too old surely to be dreaming of sweethearts.

Celia placed Idie's old grey dress right at the back of the armoire as though it were never to be taken out again and next picked out of the suitcase a brown dress with a velvet collar. Idie glanced sideways at Celia's own short-sleeved rose-and-white-print dress and knew suddenly how heavy her own dresses were, and the sunshiny wonder of the morning was tarnished with her aunt doing strange things in her room and with the thick browny-greyness of her English dresses. All dresses, she realized, should be soft and skimming and have no grey or brown in them. Still, she thought, it was rather odd just to walk into someone else's bedroom, even if she was your niece, and go through her clothes just like that without a hello or a may-I.

Celia now picked out a cotton paisley dress with long gathered sleeves. She held it out and said, 'This one.'

Too astonished to do otherwise, Idie took the dress and slipped it on. She'd never had a mother to tell her what to wear, and began to feel that it might be rather nice in fact to be told what to put on each morning, because that way you didn't have to make any choices yourself. She looked at herself in the mirror and felt cross that her dress had long sleeves, but then it occurred to her that it would be easy just to cut them off, so she asked, 'Where are the scissors, Aunt Celia?'

'No, there are no scissors.' Celia's voice was ringing and clear, her face unreadable as a mask, and Idie could make no sense of her at all.

'No scissors?' she asked, a little arch.

'The scissors are in Georgetown.'

'The scissors are in Georgetown?'

'Yes, the scissors are all in Georgetown.'

Idie watched Celia carefully and decided that she was UNFATHOMABLE. Mayella was superstitious but she was shrewd too, while Celia was just strange and there was no getting to the bottom of her. Idie thought sadly of Stables and Stew and Silent, who were as dependable and sensible people as you could ever hope to find, and a wave of loneliness broke over her. No one here was like anyone she'd ever come across before. Fragile after the disturbing night and the oddness of the morning and beginning to feel it might be a relief to see even Treble, Idie went to the door.

9

Idie went slowly down the stairs, her small hand skimming the curved handrail. The light cast dancing patterns through the shutters of the hall and the breeze drifted softly through and Idie thought how sad it was to have a house that was so beautiful but so full of secrets and spirits that no one liked to sleep in it. In the blue-and-white umbrella stand by the entrance stood a fishing net, a black one on a short strong rod, of the kind Benedict used to land salmon, and Idie wondered that she hadn't noticed it the night before. Treble was waiting at the door to the dining room. After all the loneliness and the fear of the night, Idie was flooded with relief at the sight of anyone from home and she ran to her.

'There's no China tea in the house, and the girl has not the faintest idea how to make porridge and—'

Idie interrupted. 'There were footsteps in the corridor – did you hear them? – in the corridor – a man's footsteps?'

An expression of horror dawned on Treble's

face. Her mouth formed a quivering rectangle. 'No, no, you're imagining things. I don't like the cast of your mind, child. You've an improper imagination, most improper; it must be stamped out forthwith.'

'Oh,' said Idie, stepping back, her brief warmth for Treble dissipating. She saw the yellow crumbs of hardboiled egg that were clinging to some of Treble's chins and asked in what she thought of as her new grownup sort of tone, 'How would you, in fact, go about stamping out my imagination?'

'Missus, I'll bring you pawpaw, soursop, pineapple, eggs, fried banana,' interjected Mayella.

'She'll not have the banana,' said Miss Treble, tight-lipped, 'on any account.' Treble had taken an exception to bananas on account of what she called their vulgarity.

'Thank you,' said Idie at exactly the same time. She smiled sweetly at Mayella. 'I'll have all of that, outside, in the company of my improper imagination and of Homer.' *Homer*. She turned to the veranda, saw the fishing net again and stopped, a sudden feeling of dread taking hold of her.

'Homer!'

She tore out. 'Where is he? Where's Homer?'

Mayella came running, Treble too, though less fast because of the tightness of another inappropriate pink confection.

'Where is he? What've you done with him?' Idie asked wildly.

Mayella glanced at Celia, who stood in the centre of the hall, an empty china vase in hand.

Idie turned. 'WHERE is he?'

Celia's mouth opened uncertainly. As Celia hesitated, anger and fear surfaced in Idie as a blinding rush of rage and she went close to her and stamped her foot. Celia recoiled and the vase smashed on the wooden boards. Niece and aunt stood, face to face, the white shards between them on the floor.

'He told me to put the bird in the stables,' Celia whispered.

'WHO? Who told you to?'

'He – he doesn't like the parrot,' Celia whispered hesitantly.

'His name is Homer and he is a PARAKEET and I would like to know EXACTLY who it is that doesn't like him.'

Celia, barely audible, whispered, 'Carlisle.'

'I see. The butler is scared of parakeets, so YOU moved him. And how exactly did you move him? Is this how?' Idie brandished the net.

'He told me to. He gave it to me to use,' Celia breathed, cowering.

'Carlisle is a *butler*, and he is *not* in charge of Homer. I am,' said Idie through her teeth. 'Homer and Baronet are MINE and you will not so much as touch them, for they are all I have.' Her voice had grown in strength and volume as she voiced what before she'd only dimly recognized.

Celia was shaken and wounded for there were tears starting in her eyes. Mayella went to her and took her arm and led her gently from the room, and Idie bit her lip, for after all Celia was her mother's sister.

10

Mayella placed a tray on the veranda table. She saw the large English horse loosely tethered to the hibiscus hedge, and the parakeet perched on the back of Idie's chair, and her eyes narrowed.

'Must I feed the horse and the pigeon too? And where's that pigeon gon' live now?'

'PARAKEET.'

Two of Homer's crest feathers were broken and that made him look a little piratical, but on top of that he was uppity about being trapped by a net, being stabled with a horse and possibly too on account of being called a pigeon. Mayella set out mango and pawpaw and avocado on the table.

'Phibbah is just sitting in the kitchen waiting for the Day of Judgement, and it's only me that cooks and cleans. I must feed the mistress, the horse, the pigeon—'

'PARAKEET.'

Homer withdrew his head from his wing and inspected the food set out for his mistress.

'Homer will live in the house from now on,' said Idie firmly, picking up a fork.

'The pigeon?' Mayella's eyes widened,

'Um-hmmm,' said Idie, spearing a piece of pawpaw with her fork. 'The PARAKEET stays IN THE HOUSE, where I can see him.' She popped the fruit in her mouth.

Mayella hesitated, then her eyes twinkled as some mischief quite visibly sailed into her head.

'Carlisle doesn't like pigeons nor any other bird.'

'EXACTLY,' said Idie.

'Nor the duppies, they don't like pigeons.'

Idie was not quite sure whether Mayella was teasing.

'There are NO SUCH THINGS,' she said firmly, though secretly she conceded that an English ghost wouldn't be that keen either on the presence of large sulphur-crested parakeet in his dominion. Delighted by the new taste of pawpaw, she decided to try the mango and pronged a piece.

'You all big, brave words, mistress, but I see the big dark rings around your eyes and I know the duppies been flying about your head all night.'

Idie rolled the slippery sweet mango around in her mouth, trying to look as though she'd eaten mango every day of her life. 'Oh,' she said, falsely bright and casual, 'and what exactly do duppies do?'

Mayella smiled knowingly as she poured Idie's hot chocolate, but said nothing.

'Gladstone is your grandfather?' asked Idie, changing tack.

'Oh yes. He worked here since he was eight years old. Nelson – he on the boat with you – he is my father. I got seven sisters also and five brothers and all they work here. Only my father, he works in the docks.'

'I see,' said Idie, who had discovered that this was definitely a most useful kind of phrase to have up one's sleeve when one didn't in fact see anything at all. She decided that Mayella was a SAFE person because her father was Nelson, and Nelson knew why fishes glowed at night and that was probably an indicator of integrity, but it was a pity that Nelson no longer worked at Bathsheba, and Idie wondered why he'd left.

'Mayella, please tell Quarterly, when he MAKES AN APPEARANCE, that I would like the shutters to be open from morning until night. From daybreak to day end.'

'Oh Lord, the pigeon inside the house and the shutters open. But Miss Celia like the shutters shut for they was always shut,' Mayella muttered to herself.

'Mayella, why is my aunt here?'

'Why she here?' Mayella paused. 'Miss Celia is here because she is simple as a moon, slippery as glass and the thoughts in her head are like water – any man can give them the colour he wants. That's why she here.'

Idie wondered if Mayella was in fact so very clever that she'd once decided to speak only in riddles and stuck to them ever after. Mayella returned to the kitchen and Idie told Homer, 'Celia is too strange to make any sense and Mayella is too clever to make any sense and no one here is like anyone anywhere else at all.'

'YOUR EXCELLENCY,' said Homer, dipping his head in agreement.

'You must develop your conversation. I need someone sensible to talk to,' Idie told him.

Homer gripped a piece of Idie's pawpaw with his claw so Idie said, 'AND you must not eat any more of my breakfast, because if you do I'll turn you into a feather cushion.'

11

There was no sign of Treble. Mayella appeared to be busy clanking pots and pans against each other in the kitchen and Homer was still in high dudgeon about his missing feathers and also now about all the inferior small and tweeting sorts of birds he'd seen about the garden, so Idie left him to sulk and wandered down the veranda stairs to Baronet. She plucked a red hibiscus from his mouth and lay her head against his cheek, wishing Myles or Benedict were there because it was no fun exploring on your own. She whispered to Baronet that she wouldn't take him swimming today because she wasn't quite sure how to get to somewhere you could swim. 'We'll go tomorrow,' she told him, 'when I've got my bearings.'

She thought sadly how long ago it seemed that she'd stood, suited and booted, in the hall at Pomeroy and asked, 'But when'll I come back?'

The grown-ups had glanced at one another.

'When will you come?' she'd asked, looking at Grancat.

Into the uneasy silence, Myles interjected, 'No one can visit because the South Seas are awash with brigands and bandits and pirates and primates.'

'Am I taking Baronet?'

'Yes, Baronet goes with you.'

'He won't like it because there's no grass and nothing grows there but sugar,' Myles had said, jealous that Idie was to take Baronet with her.

'Baronet goes with Idie,' Grancat growled, murmuring after, 'Poor chap.' Though it was not his son to whom he referred, but Baronet, poor chap, to be cast across a stormy sea and left to reside thereafter in some infernal, grass-less outer firmament.

'It's hellish hot. You'll melt like wax . . .' continued Myles.

'There'll be monkeys and mongooses,' Idie had answered.

'Mongooses are rats.'

She'd turned back to Grancat and asked, 'Why do I have to go?'

And he'd answered, 'You're a lady of property now.'

Idie was silent because she still didn't know what a lady of property was.

'It's because you don't *belong* here,' said Myles.

'Don't I?' she'd asked. 'Don't I belong here?'

Grancat had waited a moment, then said carefully, 'Blood is thicker than water, child.'

What he'd meant by that she'd no idea then and still didn't. She thought about blood and water now, her head still against Baronet's cheek, her hand idly scratching his neck, and tears came to her eyes. She didn't belong at Pomeroy, but did she *belong* here where no one seemed to want her? Only briefly assailed by doubt, her spirit rallied and she told herself, *I DO, I do belong here and mongooses aren't rats and I haven't melted, nor have I seen a single pirate.*

On the veranda, Idie settled herself down in a businesslike sort of way, put Homer on her lap, instructed him to be companionable, picked up her pen and pulled her book from her pocket and wrote:

I haven't discovered anything because everything has been hidden or taken away.

She sucked her pen a little and tried to remember if there was something else to write.

'Hello! . . . Hello there!'

Idie turned, surprised. She closed the book and slipped it between the cushion and the seat of her chair. She squinted, suspicious, at the figure making his way across the lawn. Older than Myles, she thought, assessing his age. He was taller, sort of better joined together than Myles, and had the dark, brown kind of skin that you don't have to hide from the sun. He wore the short shorts of an English prep-school boy, but looked as if he lived always outdoors and had never been in a schoolroom in his life. Idie watched him through narrowed eyes because his mother might've sent him to pry so that she could gossip, except that he had a battered hat and a breezy sort of way of walking, all of which made Idie think that then again he probably didn't have a gossipy sort of mother.

'DING DONG,' said Homer.

Idie scowled and hissed, 'Do *not* embarrass me.'

The boy bounded lightly up the steps and said, in the lilting intonation of the place, 'Are you Idie?'

'DING DONG,' said Homer again.

'Idie Grace,' Idie said tautly.

'Mother sent me, said to say was there anything you needed?'

He *did* have a prying, whispering mother. Idie darkened. She scowled at the floor and drew a line in the dust with her toe.

'Austin, Austin Hayne,' he said, extending his hand.

She scowled more fiercely at the floor and clenched her hands. *Recent encounters*, she told herself, *have, after all, taught me to be wary of people. Not everyone is as good as Benedict and Myles and Grancat.* The boy withdrew his hand. He waited a moment or two, then leaped up on to the balustrade, and Idie was surprised at that for visitors to Pomeroy didn't go about leaping up on things. But it would be fun to do that too and she felt annoyed that her dress wasn't right at all for leaping and that she was anchored to the spot by the large and uppity parakeet on her lap. She tugged at a loose thread of her hem and eyed the boy's red shirt and battered hat. The thread came clean out and left a line of holes about her knees.

'DO NOT EMBARRASS ME,' squawked Homer.

The boy laughed a sudden hooting laugh. Idie stared at the floor because her cheeks were burning on account of Homer's lack of sensitivity to delicate situations. Austin stopped laughing and began to swing his legs to and fro and look around.

Mayella came out. 'How-day, Master Austin. You like some tea maybe?'

'Thank you, no,' said Austin brightly. 'I'll just take some of that honey you've got there.'

He dipped his finger in the honey and licked it, and Idie, who was still cross about being pinned to her chair by a wrong sort of dress and an out-of-sorts parakeet, said, in a high, chin-out kind of way, 'We have bacon and egg and kedgeree at home.'

Austin raised his brows and seemed amused. 'Oh well, this is your home now, isn't it?'

'No, it isn't, and I hate it.'

Austin was silent for a while. Then he took up whistling a rowdy sort of tune and stuck his finger in Idie's honey again and on top of all that he hopped back up on to the balustrade and crouched there. Idie watched him surreptitiously. Mayella moved about the terrace inconsequentially with a broom, a little dab here, a little dab there, and Idie wished she'd go away.

Austin slowly rose to his feet and stood, very still, arms outstretched on the balustrade, like a tightrope walker. Curious, Idie watched him out of the corner of her eye and wondered if boys who stood on balustrades and ate honey from their fingers could in fact also have gossipy sorts of mothers.

Something brilliant as a fragment of fire drew close to Austin, and Idie heard the purring of wings and caught her breath – a hummingbird, its body tiny as a bumblebee and green as moss. It hovered above Austin's hand and then alighted on his little finger and the two of them were face to face, as if talking. The tiny green bird moved from one finger to another, its claws not wide enough even to span the littlest of them. Idie lifted Homer and put him on the back of her chair, thinking it would be nice to stand on a balustrade and let a hummingbird drink honey from her finger. She took some honey and crept towards Austin.

'Keep very still,' Austin whispered, 'and stay close to me. They like red, you see. You have to wear red to be friends with a hummingbird.'

Celia appeared with another vase, set it down on

the table in a fussy, nervous sort of way, then moved down the stairs into the garden. She seemed to do nothing but dream of sweethearts and flowers and slide about the place with vases, thought Idie, annoyed and then doubly annoyed because the hummingbird flew off and was gone.

Austin sighed and licked the remainder of honey from his finger and jumped down, and Idie licked the honey off hers too.

'We live next door,' Austin said.

'Where next door?' asked Idie.

'Well, what goes for next door round here. At Bissett.'

'I see,' said Idie, pretending to know and wondering at the same time where she could find a red dress so she could be friends with a hummingbird.

Austin whistled and looked at Homer, then at the large English horse who chomped freely at the hibiscus, and he stopped whistling and said, grinning, 'I say, isn't there anyone in charge of you?'

Idie was silent because she had just enough worldly wisdom to understand that children were supposed to have someone in charge of them and that her own governess was not really what Grancat would call *fit-for-purpose*. It was bad enough to have been given away by your mother and to be sent around the world like a lost penny without, on top of all that, having to make do with a not-fit-for-purpose governess. In any case,

Idie still couldn't be certain that this boy wouldn't tell tales, and then the people who cared about such things would whisper, so she remained silent.

'There's a pool high up in the gully, almost in the clouds, and it's deep and turquoise and a waterfall runs into it. Shall I take you there?'

Idie *would* very much like to see a pool high up in the clouds, with a waterfall tumbling into it, but she couldn't shed the ashamed, scratchy bits of herself, so what she said was, 'No, I hate it all and everything here.'

Austin's eyes rested awhile on her. 'Oh well,' he said eventually, 'I think it's wonderful. There're rocks and waterfalls and deep swimming places . . . oh well, hey-ho . . .'

Idie thought that was sweet and funny, because Grancat always said *hey-ho* too, at just such moments.

Austin went to the steps.

'YOUR EXCELLENCY,' said Homer, dipping his head. Homer, it appeared, was prone to announcing arrivals and departures.

Austin raised his hat to Homer and said, 'The resident sulphur-crested parakeet is more civil than the new mistress of Bathsheba.'

Idie instantly regretted being so prickly with Austin, because anyone that said *hey-ho* and knew that Homer was a sulphur-crested parakeet, just like that off the top of his head, was probably worth his salt. But there was no going back now so she said, 'No, he's not. He's a very uppity sort of creature.'

Austin leaped over the hibiscus hedge and landed lightly on the grass.

'Hey-ho . . . oh well, I shan't trouble to come back.'

He ran across the lawn, taking leaps from time to time and batting his heels together as if he didn't give a fig what the mistress of Bathsheba did or said. Idie watched him. He knew about pools in gullies and waterfalls and sulphur-crested parakeets and now he'd gone there was no one except Mayella who spoke in riddles and Celia who was sly and strange and Treble who was *not fit-for-purpose*.

After a while Idie took her notebook from beneath the cushion and wrote:

> *Mother's garden is very beautiful. The sun rains through the leaves and makes flapping sorts of light shadows on the ground.*

Then because she had nothing else to write she put it in her pocket and went into the house, determined to find some clues.

12

She paused in the hall.

There was no sign of Celia, but the shutters were all closed so Idie stomped from one to another flinging them open, five in all, two in front, three at the back. The breeze hummed swiftly through the house and, satisfied, Idie paused to consider her next move. Mayella was in the drawing room, dancing, her broom clasped to her bosom like a beau. Treble was in the kitchen, enquiring with loud suspicion as to the laundry provisions in the establishment. Idie peered through the kitchen door in the hope of glimpsing Phibbah, whom she had down in her head as a Mysterious and Magnificent kind of person as well as definitely a sphinx, but Phibbah was nowhere to be seen.

Idie crept upstairs. On the landing she hesitated, then took the corridor to the left. She found a bedroom, the furnishings faded but sweet and comfortable and full of paintings and vases and pretty things. She tiptoed in and opened the doors and drawers. All were empty. She went to the next room and the next and again all were empty. She turned back, crossed the landing, passed her own door, stopped at the next and pushed, and found the room strewn with garments in the spectrum of colours that fill hanging baskets outside public houses, so she knew that room was Treble's. A red ribbon trailed from a drawer and, because that was the colour you needed for hummingbirds, Idie crept across the room and pocketed it and slipped guiltily out.

A cool breeze came from the far end of the corridor and she turned and went that way. The house opened up there to the sea and sky in a sort of open loggia or portico. Stencilled palmate leaves trailed along the cornice and skirting. A small bamboo writing table, a cane chair and a sewing table inlaid with mother of pearl stood together in the centre. Idie sat at the table and placed her hands on the handle of the drawer. The drawer was empty but for a pile of worm dust and a pen, the nib of it tarnished, the clip broken. The other drawer held only a large glass paperweight, a purple orchid preserved inside. She cupped the smooth warm glass in her palm and held it there a while for it had surely been her own mother's.

She sighed, thinking that she'd go and see Baronet because she felt the need just then for the common sense and decency inherent in a good English horse. They'd go swimming, they'd find the turquoise pool high up in the clouds, for she, Idie Grace, didn't need Austin nor anyone else to help her.

She stood and turned and found herself face to face with Celia. *How long had Celia been there?* They stood a second facing each other, staring, and it became like the staring game she used to play with Myles – Myles would always win, but once he'd told Idie that the trick of it was to talk to yourself, so hard and fast that you never thought about blinking at all, so Idie stared and things came into her mind about Celia and she said to herself:

She's here just because she's here
Just because this is the only place she knows
The shutters of my house must be shut
for Aunt Celia
Just because once they were always shut
She's simple as a moon
Slippery as glass
She has pale eyes
And moves like a cat
Her body is wavery
Her insides are watery
She might be a white witch –

It was Celia who broke first, and Idie felt guilty for Celia looked startled and fearful.

'Aunt Celia –' began Idie, turning the paperweight around in her hands – 'did my mother sit here? Was this hers?' She held it out.

Celia stared at it. Lost in a reverie she slowly stretched out her arm. Her hand went not to the paperweight but to Idie, hovering as if in a trance over Idie's hair, then above the skin of Idie's cheek.

Mayella came out on to the loggia just then, took Celia's hand to lead her away and said over her shoulder to Idie, 'Your governess has gone to lie down. The heat is too hot, the sun is too sunny, the trees are too green and the birds too full of song.'

13

The stables stood a little higher than the house, their stone walls enclosing a welcome shade, a breeze singing from front to back.

'Hello!' Idie called.

'Hello!' she called again, going to Baronet's box. She bent and sniffed a handful of the sweet-scented kus-kus grass, pleased that he had such a good deep bed. Idie settled Homer on the water trough where he'd be safe while she was out and went to look for Sampson. She found him in the forge, hammering a set of iron shoes.

'Mistress Grace,' said Sampson.

'I'd like Baronet saddled,' instructed Idie.

As Sampson fetched the saddle, Idie asked, 'Does anyone else sleep in the house, Sampson? Apart from Miss Treble and me, upstairs, and Phibbah in the back kitchen?'

'Oh no, missus, no one goes in the house when it comes dark.' His eyes widened and his happy face set and grew serious. 'Oh no, nobody go in there.

Only the night-walkers, the duppies. The lady ones –'
Sampson stretched his arms out and tiptoed a fairy
circle in his big boots – 'they like the soft beds and
soft drapes of the windows.'

Sampson had seemed perfectly sensible on other
occasions. He was good with horses, and that in
Grancat's view was a sign of good character, but now
it seemed he too believed in spirits that flew in and
out of cupboards and candles. Perhaps everyone here
was superstitious, however commonsensical in other
respects. Grancat said if you lived in certain wet and
sticky places, County Kerry for example, or Cornwall
or an Outer Hebride, you were bound to believe in
fairies and things. In which case every right-headed
person in the Indies might believe in duppies, because
the Indies were sort of sticky too, not wet-sticky but
hot-sticky. Idie was silent while thinking about all this
until it occurred to her that there was another more
important thing she must ask Sampson.

'Did you know my mother?'

'Yes, mistress.'

Idie's heart leaped, for he had not flinched nor
turned away. 'What was she like?' she asked quietly.

'I only knowed her afterward – after . . .' Sampson
hesitated, 'I never knew her when . . .'

'After what? When what?' asked Idie.

'Is not for me to talk of, mistress,' he answered.

'Why? Why will no one tell me anything?'

After a fidgety silence he said, 'Is best sometimes not to know everything.'

'Is it now?' asked Idie, arch. Seeing Sampson begin to back away from her she adopted another line of questioning. 'All right, tell me about Nelson then. Why doesn't he work here any more?'

'He get good work in the shipyard. He won't come back these parts no more.' Sampson waited to see if that might be answer enough.

Idie said, 'Go on.'

'He don't get along too good with Carlisle; that also why he go.'

'I see,' said Idie, who did see why someone would not get along with Carlisle.

As she mounted Baronet, Sampson asked, a little anxious, 'Where you going, mistress?' He'd gathered his arms and legs together in a line and looked long and narrow as a pencil.

'Oh, I thought we might go swimming.'

Sampson's face tightened. 'Don't go to the creek, mistress. Nobody goes to Black Water Creek.'

'Oh,' said Idie, to tease him because he looked so serious, 'I was thinking of doing just that. I very much *do* want, you see, to go to Black Water Creek where nobody goes, because in fact I want to find out why nobody does go there.'

Sampson grew agitated and began to say something, then closed his mouth and then began again, a little desperately, as though he'd just happened upon a warning that would *really* deter a child from going where it was not supposed to. 'The devil walks about there in the night.'

'But it is the day,' said Idie, trying to keep a straight face.

'Is for your own good I say that.'

Sampson looked so deeply hurt that Idie answered gently, 'It's all right, I'm going to the turquoise pool high up in the gully.' She paused before asking, 'What did happen at the creek, Sampson?'

'Nobody knows. The people, they say things, but nobody knows for certain and everybody they scared of that place, but anyway, to the pool is all right. It's that way there.' Sampson indicated with both arms in what looked like all directions at once and Idie wasn't sure which way he'd meant at all.

14

The sun was hot and Idie had no hat, and after a while she let Baronet choose his way along the shady places where the light was fractured and the air cool. Treble's red ribbon was tied around Idie's wrist and for a while she held her arm out in the hope of hummingbirds.

The trees started to grow close and tall, the sun stabbing the leaf canopy in glinting flashes, and Idie drew her hand in, giving up on the hummingbirds on the grounds a red ribbon was not nearly so good as a red shirt. After an hour or so, she grew certain that they were not on Sampson's path at all. From high above, vines dangled like tresses and rooted on the ground. Wizened things, half root, half branch, ran across the path like snakes.

Strange flowers stretched from their rotting beds, and seemed to bloom not according to the month but just as the feeling took them, not at all in the orderly manner of sensible English plants. The air was dense and still. Vines and trailing things hung like cloaks around her. The waterfall couldn't be so far away as this, nor so difficult to reach.

At last there was open sky ahead. The path was less tangled and Idie paused to look about. Somewhere a branch snapped. She waited and listened, then went on. In any case, she told herself, if there was someone there, she could ask how to get back to Bathsheba. The ground grew wetter and softer underfoot. There were now pools of standing water and tall rush, flattened in places, and footprints. She went on, following the flattened, muddied places.

There was a movement in the tall rushes and Idie glanced ahead.

Carlisle Quarterly.

A few feet away, half concealed in the rush, he stood, waiting, as if for her, his thumb hooked into the pocket of his tweed weskit. His nails were long and white and there was a menacing energy in the drumming of his fingers on the plaid cloth. His face was lean and taut, eyes dark as tunnels. The tweed weskit was an odd choice, Idie thought, given the temperature. His stare was intense and discomforting and his voice, when he spoke, curling.

'Good afternoon, Miss Grace.'

There was a sudden gusting sound and Idie looked up. The sky was filled with swooping forms, a thousand thousand tiny birds, heads outstretched, necks outstretched, legs outstretched, were coming in to land. The air vibrated with the rushing of their wings. Idie gasped and stared up in wonder. *Myles*, she thought, *Myles, if only you were here*. Their tail feathers were deeply forked like swallows', their beaks and feet the red of an English postbox.

'Tern!' she breathed, for he'd once shown her an Arctic tern in a book, *The Birds of the Greater Antilles*. He'd dug that book out of the library secretly and he'd pored over it, trying to learn, in his own way, through the birds, about where Idie was going, just as she had taken other books to the attic and pored over them.

Carlisle had picked up a gun. Idie's gorge rose in her throat. With javelin-speed he cocked it, raised it, aimed and fired. The birds screeched in alarm. A tiny body thudded to the ground and another, and it seemed the air was turning to clods, the heavens falling in.

'No, no, no!' she screamed at the skies, but they'd come from the frozen Arctic, they'd flown twenty thousand miles, and were too exhausted to go elsewhere. Carlisle loaded and fired again.

The air screamed with the shrieking *ke-arr, ke-arr, ke-arr* of the birds. The gun cracked and the water spurted as they fell and Idie was torn to pieces with horror. Carlisle swigged from a flask, then reloaded and fired, quick and keen and accurate.

Idie flapped her arms at the sky and screamed, 'Go away. Go somewhere else! Don't land here!'

Carlisle watched the small girl waving at the

heavens and laughed. He raised his gun, and a tiny thing, seconds ago living and weightless and airborne, thudded dully to the ground a foot or two away from Idie.

Nauseous, she fell to her knees and held its warm silvery body and stroked the black cap on its head and held it close.

'Was there a storm at sea?' she whispered through her tears, wiping the dribble of red blood from its white cheek. 'Was that why you had to stop here? Were you so tired you had no choice?'

When the spasmodic jerking of its wings stilled, Idie looked up. She stared at Carlisle and saw how the silverwork of his gun flashed in the sun. It was an English double-barrelled shotgun, like the one Grancat kept under his bed to repel invaders such as Vikings. This one was just the same as Grancat's; even the silver crest was the same. That gun wasn't his.

Consider the lie of the land before you make a move.

This had been one of Grancat's rare pieces of advice. Carlisle Quarterly was her employee, but so far there'd been no indication that he intended taking orders from her or anyone. On top of that he was a grown man and twice her size. It would be a commonsensical precaution to keep a large horse at one's side if one was only small and in a sticky situation, so Idie laid the tern aside in a bed of rush and went to Baronet. Leading him, she walked slowly towards Carlisle.

'Quarterly, I command you to stop. This instant.'

Carlisle bent down to a box and filled his pockets with cartridges. Idie moved closer still, her eyes drawn again to the silverwork of his gun.

'I have told you to stop.'

'And if I don't, Miss Grace, what then? What will you do?' he asked as he loaded the gun.

Deeply shocked, Idie hesitated. Silent had never spoken to Grancat in such a way.

Consider the lie of the land. Consider your options.

Idie looked about and saw the box and kicked at it, kicked and kicked again till all the green and gold cases lay scattered and half buried in the rush, the empty box on its side. Carlisle cursed and knelt to scoop them up. The gun across his knees and cursing still, he searched about for cartridges, then put aside the gun and fumbled for them with both hands, all the while glancing anxiously up at the sky.

Idie grabbed her chance. She snatched up the gun and raised it, struggling a little for it was long and heavy. Only the tip of her forefinger reaching the trigger, she said, 'I hold a loaded shotgun. It is pointing at your head, Carlisle Quarterly. The silver crest tells me that this is a Grace family gun and therefore does not belong to you. So I advise you to do AS I SAY, WHEN I SAY, FROM NOW ON.' It was rather fun using the words adults used on children;

they sounded so much more satisfactory when used this way around.

Still on his knees, Carlisle dropped the cartridges he held and looked up.

'Good,' said Idie. 'Now, you will start by telling me which is the quickest direction home.'

To herself she said, triumphant, *Forty–fifteen, Carlisle.*

15

'I was worried, mistress, thinking you had gone down to the creek, and nobody want to go there to find –' Sampson broke off in alarm when he saw the shotgun lying across the small girl's knees.

Idie thrust Baronet's rope into his hand and said, 'This place is TOPSY-TURVY. MOST TOPSY-TURVY.'

'Where did you go? You go by the lake? Who was there? Somebody there shooting?' Sampson's eyes darkened.

'As it happens, the butler was there. Shooting, on a Tuesday afternoon.' She handed Sampson the gun. 'I don't believe this belongs to him.'

'You see him? You see Carlisle there?'

Idie nodded.

' Carlisle . . . You take good care, mistress, if he's about the place. He thinks he's the master here.'

'Yes, that does seem to be rather the case.'

'Missus! Missus! Sampson, you seen the missus? Where the missus?' Mayella called. She came up running, saw the gun in Sampson's hands and her eyes widened. She turned to Idie. 'Mistress – there you are. I've been looking everywhere for you and now the dinner is cold.'

Idie collected Homer from the water trough and, bearing him on her arm like a shield, followed Mayella towards the house. She sighed noisily to see that the shutters were closed. *All right*, she thought, *the shutters will be a game between myself and Aunt Celia.*

She placed Homer on the back of a chair and he made his way claw over claw along it and peered between the candelabra at the bread basket.

Mayella lowered her voice and whispered, 'Carlisle, he scared of animals. He don't like that pigeon.'

Pick your battles, Idie. Pigeon, parakeet, does it matter? So she plucked a slice of bread from Homer's claw, and replied only, 'Homer doesn't think much of Carlisle Quarterly either.'

Mayella laughed. 'Oh no, none of the animals out of the ark like Carlisle. This pigeon sees Carlisle and he trembles and his crown shakes like all of God's wrath is in him.'

Idie thought about this and came to the conclusion that Mayella had given her a golden key to dealing with the problem of the butler.

'That is precisely why Homer and Baronet will live *in* the house, in here, with me, *always from now on.*'

'The horse? Oh Lord.'

'Mm-hmmm,' responded Idie.

'And must I feed the horse also?' asked Mayella as she placed a soup tureen on the table. 'Oh my word, the new missus, she think she Noah himself, and she going to make this house her ark . . .'

16

For the first time in a while, Idie encountered Treble.

Treble tended to emerge, on what she saw as the high-risk venture from her room to the dining room, at precisely the three times a day that a meal was likely to be forthcoming. Today, however, her hair had been coaxed into ornate loops about her face and there was such a swaying to her walk and such a floating to her dress that she appeared to be *wafting through* the corridor. She'd become at the same time somehow less substantial and more voluminous, and Idie watched her in wonder, thinking that Treble was prone to growing vaporous at tropical temperatures. In any case, it was good that she hadn't said anything about the missing ribbon.

'When dear Algernon comes,' Treble giggled, 'then, have no fear, I will take everything in hand.'

'Dear Algernon? And who is he?' Idie asked, noting now that Treble's lips were a violent shade of pink.

'Mr Webb, my dear, Mr Webb.'

And what on earth could he do?

Idie despaired of them all. Aside from Grancat, all grown-ups were apparently no help at all. She'd go and find some hummingbirds instead.

For a long time she stood waiting upstairs on the loggia, her arm stretched out over the railing, but no hummingbird came. She edged further along the railing, thinking again that a red ribbon around your wrist was not nearly as good as a red shirt.

She sighed and licked the honey from her finger, thinking she would've written to Myles again if only he'd written to her, but things had to be fair; he must write to her before she wrote again to him.

She heard a snort from the hall. At least Baronet was happy. He found the hall here as much to his liking as the hall at Pomeroy, and this had had a most pleasing and satisfactory benefit: Idie's own requests that the shutters be opened had been ignored, but it appeared that the demanding whinnies of an impatient horse who desired a view of the garden and all the goings-on in it were responded to most promptly. Since Baronet had taken up residence in the hall, the shutters were opened every day at dawn.

Baronet snorted again and Idie peered over the railing to discover what the current object of his indignation was.

A dun-coloured mare was tethered to the veranda. Idie appeared to have a visitor. She thought she might pretend to be out, but Baronet whinnied and Idie's curiosity got the better of her caution. She made her way downstairs, meandering a bit and trying to look as though she didn't know anyone had come to visit at all.

Austin, the boy who knew about pools in gullies and had clouds of hummingbirds at his beck and call. He sat on the railing, a piece of Guinea grass in his mouth, looking out into the fustic trees and swinging his legs.

'Since you think more highly of animals than you do of people, and since you're stuck here on your own, I've brought you some company.'

'I don't need company,' said Idie firmly, but she looked about, curious to see what kind of company he might have brought.

'Well, if you don't like her, she'll amuse Homer.'

'Homer has a low regard for everyone except himself.'

'He has something in common with his mistress then . . . Anyway, let's see.' Austin turned and addressed Homer, eye to eye, the pair of them in profile to each other. 'Homer, I'm going to introduce you to Millicent, and if you have any sweetness in you, Millicent is the girl to melt your heart.'

The name of an animal was always a serious consideration, and Idie thought Millicent a silly sort of name because you couldn't go about the place calling out, 'Millicent, Millicent!' and retain any sort of dignity at all.

'Millicent is rather keen on pawpaw, as well as mango and cake and many of the finer things in life.' Austin helped himself to a piece of pawpaw. Mayella had evidently served him tea, and that made Idie cross because she herself would rather like some tea too.

The pocket of Austin's coat suddenly bulged as though it had taken on a life of its own. There was something very trembly and excitable and keen on pawpaw in there. Idie told herself that she wasn't interested at all in the kind of animals that fitted inside people's pockets.

'Millicent takes strong likes and strong dislikes to people. She is a fine judge of character and can keep people she doesn't like away, and that is the great advantage of her. It's useful to have someone who can do that when there are all kinds of people about the place one might not like.'

A tiny, ferrety nose peered over the rim of the pocket and Idie could no longer pretend not to be interested.

'A mongoose . . .' she breathed.

Homer squawked and his neck ruffled like a courtier's collar and his crown began to tremble as though he were experiencing his own special earthquake whose epicentre was a small lady mongoose, and Idie sighed, 'Homer, it's *only* a mongoose.'

Austin spoke to Millicent, 'Come on out, Millie. I think the mistress of Bathsheba is all right, just a bit snooty.' He continued conversing with the mongoose as though Idie were not there at all. 'And you are especially averse to duppies, aren't you, Millie? Well, this house is full of duppies, even though some people think they know better and don't believe in them.'

Millicent sat up on her hind legs and tail in a begging position, with all the soft pink pads of her forepaws outermost, just as Mayella appeared with a large and handsome pineapple tart. Millicent's nose trembled in the direction of the tart and she rubbed her tiny paws together and made a sort of chuckling sound that made Mayella squeal and made Idie giggle.

'Millicent is rather partial to a hard-boiled egg,' Austin said.

'Mayella, Homer would like some banana bread,' said Idie, her nose a bit put out about Millicent being favoured with egg and tart when she and Homer had been ignored.

'And must I be feeding the mongoose also?' complained Mayella, walking away. 'The pigeon, the horse, the mongoose . . .'

'Millicent, you will have to make friends with a large and uppity parakeet if you are to remain here,' said Austin.

'Millicent isn't staying here. Homer doesn't like her.' Idie knew she was being pettish and that really she wanted to write straightaway to Myles how she sat down to tea with a mongoose whose name was Millicent.

Austin ignored her. 'Millie has to be inside, of course. She is quite spoilt and thinks she is quite a cut above an ordinary sort of wild mongoose.'

'That may be the case, but Baronet does not like mongooses and Baronet lives in the hall.'

'Oh yes. Horses should always be in halls.' Austin's face was deadpan, but Idie giggled and Austin smiled and they both smiled at each other and he said, 'Baronet appears to be more used than most though to coming in and out of houses.'

'Of course,' answered Idie. 'You see, Grancat never minded that he came in and out as he wanted and he'd send Silent, who is the butler, to the kitchens for a salver of scones and cream but not for cutlery, because no sensible horse can be doing with such things.'

'Grancat?' Austin queried, amused.

'Father, well, sort-of-Father,' explained Idie.

'He sounds a rather good sort of sort-of-father to have.'

Idie was silent and the tears were starting in her eyes and Austin asked quietly, 'Do you miss him very much?'

She nodded.

'Do you love him very much?'

Idie looked up at him as though he'd asked a rather silly sort of question and said, 'Oh yes, everyone loves Grancat.' Smiling now for the joy of speaking of him, she went on, 'Stew, she's the cook, said Grancat had lots of *foibles*, and that foibles make you do things like wear, from daybreak to day end and all at the same time, two binoculars round your neck and two pairs of reading glasses stacked on your head. Grancat says it saves time if all these things are immediately to hand when needed. He says you must always be practical and pragmatic about everything. And you must always *save time*. That's why he slides down the banisters to breakfast and wears his cuffs loose about his wrists, because if you are saving time you can't be doing with stairs or buttons or cufflinks.'

'I see,' Austin said. 'Grancat, Stew and Silent.'

'And Stables. And Numbers.'

'Yes. What a sensible system.' After a while he asked quietly, 'Will Grancat come and visit?'

'Well, he *says* he'll never come. He says it's just common sense to be suspicious about all the parts of the world that lie beyond the bounds of Pomeroy because you can never be so certain anywhere else of tea at four and dinner at eight as you can at Pomeroy.'

Austin laughed, then after a minute he whispered, 'Where is your governess?'

Idie answered, 'Treble is expanding *by the minute* so she's more than three times the normal size now and should be called Quadruple. Anyway, now she looks like a sunset crossed with a soufflé, and she says she won't rise from her bed until dear Algernon comes because everything here is unsafe and unsuitable.'

Austin grinned, but it suddenly occurred to Idie that he himself was remarkably free, even by the standards of Pomeroy, to do as he pleased without any sort of grown-up about, so she asked, 'What does your governess think about you going about all over the place all day with all kinds of animals in your pockets?'

'Oh, there's no money in my house for governesses and things like that. You see, Father is supposed to be a rector, but he's not a very good one. He practises his sermons on the stuffed animals in his study, but never gets any better at them because a stuffed crocodile can't fidget or shuffle or fall asleep. He's *really* a sort of amateur biologist, because when he's not doing sermons he writes papers about endangered species and sends them off to anyone that'll read them. Specimens arrive in boxes and cages from all over the place and some of them are alive and some of them are dead, but Mother's always trying to send them off again somewhere else before he knows they've arrived at all.'

Idie, always curious about mothers, asked, 'And your mother?'

'Oh, Mother's a poet, so she's sort of forgetful of

everything, and mostly what she forgets, in the best possible way, is that she's got a son at all. Anyway, because of Father being a rector who wants to be a biologist and Mother being a quite unpublishable poetess, I don't have to have a governess.'

Idie decided then, on the grounds of her being an poetess and forgetful, that Austin's mother definitely wouldn't be prying or gossipy.

Mayella reappeared with mashed egg on a gold coffee saucer. Millie's tail grew bushy with excitement about the egg. With catlike delicacy, she poured herself between the teacups towards the gold saucer and demolished the egg. Mayella said, 'She's hungry, Master Austin. Maybe one day she eat the pigeon.'

'Millicent will not eat Homer,' said Austin rather severely.

Mayella whispered, 'A mongoose will be good for round here, will look after the mistress and the pigeon, and keep the duppies away . . .'

Idie rolled her eyes and said, 'THERE IS NO SUCH THING as a duppy.'

As Mayella left, Idie went close to Austin and whispered, 'Except perhaps Carlisle Quarterly. He might be a new variety of duppy . . .'

Austin made his curious sort of hooting laughter and said, 'I know, let's find out if he *is* a duppy.' He stowed Millicent away in his pocket and tiptoed into the dining room, Idie following. They crept between the portraits and the chairs to the kitchen door. It was slightly ajar and they stood behind it, waiting and watching.

Phibbah sat at the table chopping a squash, and there was some venom in her chopping as if on account of Carlisle being in her kitchen. Celia stood close to Carlisle, facing him and wringing her fingers and smoothing her skirt and wringing her fingers again. He whispered to her and she nodded. Then he touched a finger to his mouth and whispered and she touched a finger to her own mouth as if playing a game of Simon Says.

Austin winked at Idie, bent and placed Millie on the floor. Millie paused, nose twitching, then rushed like a ribbon into the kitchen. Carlisle squealed and leaped up on to a chair. Then Homer took fright and squawked and Baronet clattered about the hall. Idie and Austin giggled and Phibbah's eyes sparkled with merriment and even Celia had a faint smile on her lips, and all the while Millie sat at the table on her hind legs, paws to her mouth, chuckling and looking very wicked and very delighted.

17

Celia came to Idie's room the next morning and went to the wardrobe. She made a habit of this, to which Idie had grown accustomed. Besides, Idie didn't care about dresses except that they be comfortable, so she let Celia choose what she should wear, seeing as Celia seemed to want it that way. Each morning Idie would say, 'Good morning, Aunt Celia,' and each morning Celia would turn away. Idie thought, *Celia is like a small bird, timorous and easily alarmed. She is a tiny bit like a June Bug too, a bit annoying but harmless.* But this time, when Idie said good morning, Celia ventured a brief timid smile. *Little by little,* Idie told herself, *she will grow to trust me little by little.*

She took the heavy brown dress Celia handed her, at the same time noticing that the stuff of Celia's dress was soft and fine, with a fresh white-green print. Idie felt the familiar drag on her spirits as she wriggled into her dress, because clothes that were good for Devon were no good for the Indies, and in any case what she wanted was something red. After a while she said,

'Aunt Celia, where can I get some new dresses from? Mine aren't right at all.'

Celia paused then and turned and after a moment she half whispered, 'Like this?' She picked up the hem of her skirt and lifted it out at the sides and swayed as if she were a girl dressing for her first dance, and that made Idie feel a little queasy and sad for her, but she nodded and said, 'Yes, though could it be a red one, please.'

18

Austin didn't come that day, and Idie knew it would have been more fun if he had. At dusk when she returned from a ride, she handed Baronet's reins to Sampson and paused, surprised to hear Numbers's voice coming from the little estate-office building next to the stables. She squared her shoulders and stood up straight. It was about time he came. He owed her an explanation for the *topsy-turviness* of things.

Idie walked to the window, thinking to call to him, but he was talking and his voice had that sort of whispery tone to it that put Idie on alert and made her think she should creep up and listen.

'Her father's generosity caused expectations to be raised in certain quarters, and that's unfortunate for the child, most unfortunate. Problems may well arise from that generosity. Oh dear. And of course when her father died, her mother was faithful to his wishes concerning the arrangements he'd made for Carlisle Quarterly – even going so far as to put them in her will. Am I right in thinking Carlisle Quarterly still lives on the estate and is employed in the house?'

My father wished Carlisle Quarterly to live here? My mother too?

'Is so,' Gladstone answered gravely.

'Oh dear. What a legacy they've left. Oh well, no doubt the girl'll learn to live with the situation. And Celia Rhodes? Is she well looked after, as her sister would have wished?'

My mother wished her sister to be looked after. That is why Aunt Celia must live in my house.

'Yes . . .' Gladstone paused and then said, 'I am glad, sir, that Miss Grace never knew her mother. It is better so. She was never the same again.'

My mother was never the same again. But never the same after what? How could I ever be glad I never met her?

'Yes, we've much to be thankful for. The land is good and profitable too . . . I'm afraid I've had word from Devon and must return. As you know, I'm also trustee to Pomeroy. Poor Pomeroy, unlike this place, she can't stand on her own two feet. There're envelopes his Lordship won't open, things he can't look square in the face, things he can't say. All he tells me over and over is, "I leave the place FEET FIRST, Numbers, FEET FIRST," and it's my lot to keep the banks at bay, to hold them off until His Lordship goes.'

Idie wondered why all of a sudden everyone was speaking in riddles. Even Numbers. *How did a house ever stand on its own two feet? How did one leave a house feet first?*

'There're sons, are there not?' asked Gladstone.

'They're young and will find their way in life. Ah well, everything here is ably managed by yourself, and that's a great comfort. You've always had, and have, my complete trust.'

'Miss Grace should want for nothing, sir.'

'Good, but she must be protected from rumours and gossip. I'm given to understand that anything personal was removed from the house. Is that so?'

'Is so, sir. The women did that on account of a superstition. That happens, sir, frequently when—'

'Yes, yes, quite so, but make sure if you can that she doesn't learn what happened from anyone wishing her harm, from anyone wishing to hurt her by saying what we don't dare.'

What we don't dare? What was it that no one dared tell her?

The men stepped into the doorway and Idie shrank back. They shook hands and Numbers made his way across the lawn.

Idie took out her book and wrote:

After something happened my mother was never the same again.
No one will tell me what that something is, and because of that I have to listen at doors and windows.

Whatever it is that happened causes rumours and gossip.
My mother wished Celia to be looked after.
She was faithful to my father's wishes. That means she
   put it in her will that Carlisle could stay at Bathsheba.

Idie put her pencil down, thinking how sad it was to be sent away to the other side of the world by one's own mother and how Myles had said that if your mother sent you away then she couldn't have loved you and only *not very nice* persons sent their children away to the other side of the world.

Grancat had heard that and he'd boxed Myles about the ears and then he'd said to Idie, 'Remember, Idie, Myles has also lost a mother. He's angry and sad about that too and that's why he says horrid things sometimes.'

Idie thought some more, picked up her pencil and wrote:

My mother wanted her sister to be looked after, and that
   means that she was a nice and kind sort of person.

19

In the early evening Idie found Treble accommodated on the veranda, the froth of her skirt spilling over her chair and quite concealing it, Numbers standing nearby. Treble was twisting a ringlet through her fingers and gazing at *dear Algernon* and Idie giggled that Treble should find in Numbers sufficient reason to rise from her bed and brave all the dangers of the place.

Treble waved girlishly as Idie climbed the stairs. 'There she is, the dear child.'

Numbers stepped back and set the drinks trolley wobbling as Baronet advanced up the stairs.

I expect some answers, Idie told herself, pleased that Baronet was following her on to the veranda, because he was proving a useful means of putting certain adults at a disadvantage.

Numbers glanced at Treble, but Treble appeared not to notice the fact of a large thoroughbred mounting a flight of stone steps up to an elegant veranda. 'Miss Grace . . .' he began, but he couldn't meet Idie's eyes, either on account of the horse or the mongoose about her neck or the parakeet on her shoulder or her shorn, sleeveless dress.

Treble interrupted. 'Dear Algernon, would you care for some punch? It is almost the hour.'

Numbers persisted. 'Miss Grace . . .'

'Yes, Mr Webb?' answered Idie, very prompt.

He paused, looking weary and nervous and old. He removed his glasses, rubbed his eyes, opened his mouth, closed it again.

'Fishes do that. They open their mouths and no words come out,' said Idie.

Baronet picked his way between the wicker chairs into the hall. Numbers rubbed his eyes awhile and then shook his head slowly from side to side, in the way grown-ups had of displaying their disbelief.

'Miss Grace –'

'Child, I will call for lemonade for you, punch for Algernon. Do sit down, dear Algernon. Of course you'll be staying to dine. I will slip upstairs and prepare myself.'

Since Baronet gave every appearance of intending to stay in the hall, Numbers sat gingerly on the edge of a chair. As Treble retreated, he took a deep breath and said, 'You see, Idie, I do feel a little like that, like a fish. I am in deep water . . . I've no experience of talking to young girls . . .'

Idie, at first disarmed by his frankness, then

grew cross. Of what use at all was another grown-up who wasn't capable, commanding and able to find solutions?

'You're *supposed* to be my lawyer and trustee. A fish in deep water is of no help to me when I find myself in topsy-turvy circumstances. Besides, I am a *child* and it is not *normal* to take a child from one place and land it in an entirely different place and leave it there.'

Numbers bowed his head to accept the truth of this, then spread his fingers wide to tell her that there was nothing of course that he could do about it. 'Miss Grace, the circumstances are extraordinary, not at all in the normal run of things. I could've worked for perhaps forty years and never been confronted with such circumstances.'

'You're not confronted with them, I am,' she retorted.

'Quite right.' He looked down and his hands strayed to the arms of his chair. 'Quite right.' He picked up his hat, put it down, picked it up, and so on, while Idie heaved a loud, long sigh.

'Miss Grace, you must . . . You are mistress here, you must –'

'What *must* I do and why?' demanded Idie. 'You tell me, why am I here? *Why?*'

'You have responsibilities to this estate and the people on it, Miss Grace.'

'I want to be at Pomeroy. I want to be with Grancat

and Myles and Benedict and –'

Numbers said with a trace of sadness in his voice, 'This is your home now, Miss Grace.' He sighed, 'I am afraid I must return to England.'

'You can't just go. You can't leave me here,' she burst out.

'I will return when I can. There are minor complications here –'

'Ah, the COMPLICATIONS,' said Idie, in a loud, drawn-out kind of way.

Mayella brought out a tray: fresh lemonade for Idie, punch for Treble and Numbers and banana bread for Homer, who eyed the bowl with his customary suspicion.

'Mr Webb, about the complications, where shall we start? The fact that I don't know why I was sent to Pomeroy nor why I was brought back again, the fact that no one will tell me anything . . . Where would *you* like to start, Mr Webb?'

Numbers blinked and started at the anger in Idie's tone and after a while he said, 'You're not alone. Miss Treble is with you. She will be a guide and support –'

Idie snorted. 'She's unsuitable and *embarrassing*, and in any case she's permanently indisposed because of the punch. First it was the shifting sea, now it's the punch.'

'No, no, she's a most affectionate person, and there's no doubt she cares for your well-being.

She's taken many matters in hand.'

'Don't go . . .' Idie pleaded, changing tack in desperation.

'Miss Grace, all is not well at Pomeroy. In any case, I was asked to bring you here; that was all. Now you're settled . . .' He glanced at the mongoose draped sleepily about her neck, at her bare feet, and said, 'I shall perhaps, however, make a recommendation that an assistant governess be sent out to assist Miss Treble.'

'Grancat doesn't believe in governesses.' Treble might not be fit-for-purpose, but Idie certainly didn't intend to have *another* governess. '*And* the butler doesn't seem to be a butler at all, *and* things move in the night and fly about the candle flames . . .'

Numbers looked at Idie in alarm. 'Miss Grace, you are overwrought. Your imagination has the better of you – it's the change in climate perhaps which has set you off balance . . . In time you'll be happy here; in time you'll understand it's for the best.'

'In *time*? I don't want to be happy *in time*; I want to be happy NOW.' Then Idie felt ashamed of this outburst, which was petulant and perhaps beneath her. She paused, and then reached out an arm to him and asked, 'Why – why can't I come back with you? Why can't I go back to Pomeroy now?'

Numbers answered a little sadly, 'It's in your interest that you stay here.'

'How could *you* know what's in *my* interest—'

Numbers interrupted her with an uncharacteristic touch of recklessness. 'There's nothing left there – nothing but debts.'

Debts and banks and things were of no interest to Idie so she said, 'That doesn't mean I can't *be* there . . .'

Numbers watched her and added, more cautiously now, 'The land's been sold off, field by field. Pomeroy stands almost alone now in her park, with nothing to sustain her. There's nothing left, Miss Grace. You're lucky to have this. That house was built because of this one, because of the wealth that was created here.' He warmed to a topic on which he felt at ease. 'An immense fortune was made here; sugar was worth more than gold in its day, sugar barons were richer than kings. The money that was made here went back, in those days, when the same branch of the family owned both estates, to build and maintain Pomeroy.'

All this took a bit of thinking about so Idie was silent awhile before saying, stoutly, 'Benedict'll live at Pomeroy one day and he'll make it all better.'

Numbers bowed his head, laid his palms flat on the woven surface of the table and inspected his hands. His slender fingers flexed and began to drum the table as if he'd suddenly decided at this difficult juncture to practise his scales.

The tears started in Idie's eyes and she burst out, 'Pomeroy is my *home*.'

Numbers lowered his eyes and twisted his miserable-looking hat around.

'Your mother, Miss Grace, wanted you to have this house –'

'My mother would never have wanted me to be here alone –'

'Miss Grace . . .' Numbers bowed his head as if in infinite sorrow.

She saw the red eczema on his neck, his wrongly buttoned coat, and she thought to herself, *Let him go, he's not much help anyway*, so she said, 'All right, GO – go and just leave me here.' She leaped up and snatched the hat from him and added, 'Go, but I shan't give you your hat.'

'In that case, Miss Grace, you force me to leave without it. You'll not be troubled with the day-to-day running of the house, nor of the estate. You'll want for nothing. All is ably managed.'

In a last bid to stop him, she snatched his glasses.

'Nor your glasses.'

With some dignity Numbers rose and walked slowly, hatless and squinting into the sun. On the forecourt he turned. Blinking furiously, his words a little choked, he said, 'I wish you all the best, Miss Grace.'

*

Idie was left feeling small and angry, with the kind of crossness that comes hand in hand with guilt. Treble made a stagey sort of appearance at the foot of the stairs, attired in a gown that was part negligee, part marquee. Her lips were painted but not strictly in the right places, and that put Idie in mind of Myles, who was just as bad at colouring in as Treble seemed to be. Idie remembered Numbers's hat and glasses and she pulled them under her and tried to sit on them and said sullenly, 'He's gone. *Dear Algernon*'s gone.'

Treble looked about, confused. As the truth of Idie's words dawned on her, her eyes grew wet and her gown grew tremulous as if something seismic were rumbling deep inside her.

Idie took out her book and wrote:

My mother wanted me to have this house.

20

Two new dresses had appeared in Idie's cupboard. Both were soft and loose, but neither had any red in them, which was disappointing on account of the hummingbirds. Today Idie decided that because Celia liked pretty things – dresses and flowers, for instance – there must be some goodness in her.

Alone in her room with Homer and Millicent, Idie watched rain fall in solid sheets from the sky and listened to the rattle and clatter of the leaves.

Life at Pomeroy had accustomed her to the absence of adults. Grancat lived alone there with the children. When his wife had died he'd never thought to find himself another and set about bringing the children up entirely according to his own lights, with only the minimum of interference from schools and tutors. He believed in a system he called Benign Neglect, holding it to be the most advantageous mode of upbringing for all concerned. Thus Idie, Myles and Benedict were left for long hours to do as they pleased. They'd return at tea to tell of their escapades, and Stew would look very pained and tired by them all and Grancat would chortle, 'Good God, Stew, d'you hear that, firing arrows from the east turret. Marvellous. *Marvellous.*'

Gosh, how Idie missed them all. Most of all she missed Grancat. After a while she picked up a pen and paper and wrote:

Bathsheba

13th July 1912

Dear Myles,

Does Grancat ask after me?

Will you come and visit? Your rain is only a half of my rain. Here it rains as if the seas were lifting up and pouring on to the land. And when it is sunny the light rains through the leaves, and when it is rainy the raindrops have sunshine in them.

I have a mongoose called Millie. A mongoose is not at all like a rat. Its tail is long and bushy and its snout is a squirrel sort of snout.

When you have all the punch you want, you don't come out of your bedroom very much, and when you do, you fall down the stairs. Treble fell down the stairs yesterday. First she said her rib was broken, then she decided that instead it was her heart that was broken. If your heart is broken you have to drink lots of punch.

Anyway, it is my aunt Celia whom I told you about who is giving Treble all the punch she wants. Carlisle the butler told her to do that because he is too grand to pour drinks for a governess himself, and Celia does whatever Carlisle tells her to, so Treble will probably fall down the stairs again soon.

Anyway, last night when Mayella was doing the laundry, she discovered that it was only Treble's corset that was broken, not her heart at all. Today Treble says she wants to get on a ship and go home, but I don't think she ever will because she says the roads are ill-paved and the horses are ill-reared and it's a long way along ill-paved roads on an ill-reared horse to get to Georgetown. In any case, because she hasn't got a corset any more she is EXPANDING and has taken to her bed and will never get out again unless a steamer sails over the lawn and lowers its stairs to her window.

The arrangement of my household is not at all satisfactory and the butler is not at all as nice as Silent. I have a friend called Austin, and Austin says that Carlisle eats snakes and lizards and monkeys so he might also eat mongooses.

Love Idie

PS I have done a lot of LISTENING but I haven't found any clues yet to put in the Idie Book except that I know that my mother WAS a nice person even if you said she wasn't.

PPS Nobody has come to visit me except Austin. I do quite like him even if he's almost as annoying as you.

PPPS Sometimes I am a little bit scared.

21

At breakfast Idie found an envelope next to her
napkin.

10th August 1912

Dear Miss Grace,

The butler has been so kind) as to arrange a
berth on a ship home.

    The circumstances being what they are, I offer no
apology for my departure but I will) say that a most
inaccurate description of the terms of my employment
was given to me. Yesterday I discovered) from the
butler facts which render this post untenable. Such
terrible things have occurred) under this very roof
as to make it a most unsuitable place for a
person of my disposition. Poor Miss Grace, you)
are born under <u>an evil) star.</u>

Treble at this point had put down her pen and

wandered off, for when she began again the ink was of a different blue and her words started to meander recklessly across the page.

I shall be sure to make a full report of what I've heard when I give my account to His Lordship at Pomeroy and to my friend Algernon.

Individual letters now sprouted peculiar curlicues and, in three instances, an outcrop of flowers.

I will no longer squander myself in the service of others. From this moment on, I
shall
follow
my
heart.
Yours, Clementine Treble

Idie envisaged Treble parachuting down over turreted Pomeroy on the skirt of one of her gaudy gowns. Idie should perhaps warn Numbers that Treble was about to collapse over him like a resolute flying marquee.

'Has Treble left?' Idie asked Mayella.

'Oh yes. She went quick-quick. Carlisle told her there was no rum left on all the island and that made the governess cry like a child. Then Carlisle say there

128

was plenty of rum on the ship and the ship was in the harbour.' Words flowed from Mayella incessant and fluent as water from a spring. 'The governess she had no shame, she'd run after the man and it was God's truth that the governess was thinking only of the man but it was, in the end, the butler that was making all the trouble; it was the butler who gave the governess the rum; it was the butler who told the governess that the white lawyer man was in love with her. Then the governess's tears were all suddenly gone –' at this point Mayella twirled, holding her arms out either side – 'and the governess flew up from her bed like a bird and was gone and this –' Mayella crossed her arms firmly – 'this was what Miss Celia and Carlisle want.'

'What Aunt Celia *wanted?*'

'Oh yes.'

Idie revised the June-bug theory she'd had for Celia. In fact, and despite the dresses and the flowers, Celia had reptile eyes and was *soft-footed and silent and slippery.* To Mayella she remarked, 'Oh well. Perhaps now that the butler has stopped spending all day supplying my governess with rum, he will be able to take charge of his duties.'

'Oh no,' said Mayella. 'He won't come into the house now the mongoose and the horse and the pigeon are here. He feels safe only in the kitchen.'

Aha, said Idie to herself. *Game, set and match, Carlisle Quarterly.*

22

Dear Idie,

Have you been carried away by pirates? Died of dengue fever? Melted? Has your island been blown away by the wind? Is it vile and horrid?

Grancat says to tell you that Lancelot misses you and that Stables wants to know if there is grass and hay for Baronet. I bet there's nothing but sand and sugar there.

From
MYLES
PS I am not very good at writing letters.
PPS Grancat has stopped sliding down the banisters. He says he only travelled that way to breakfast because it made you smile. He says to tell you that he doesn't hold with letters and things but that he knows your chin is up.

PPPS Benedict is gone back to school and there is not much for me to do.
PPPPS Have you found out anything to put in the I DIE BOOk?

Idie smiled at the boyish brevity of Myles's letter and pictured him sitting alone in the nursery of the turreted grey stone house, trying to think of things to write. She smiled again, through tears, for Grancat, who no longer slid down the banisters to breakfast because she wasn't there.

23

Austin came again at last. At the sound of his voice, Millicent shot out of the basket, across the floor and slithered up on to his lap.

Mayella looked at him with mock suspicion. 'Don't you be leaving no more mongooses here now, Master Austin.'

Austin raised his empty hands and said, 'Mayella, rest assured there's no creature stowed about my person.' He turned to Millie and whispered, 'I hear good reports about you, Millicent. I hear that the people who were supposed to be afraid of you *are* afraid of you.'

Carlisle came out from the kitchen with a tray of lemonade, and Idie was surprised at this and a little pleased, thinking that perhaps her butler had at last decided to actually behave like a butler. Seeing Homer, Carlisle stopped in the doorway. Homer's crown began to quiver and tremble and Carlisle stepped back a foot or two.

Austin rose and took the tray from Carlisle,

and Idie heard Carlisle say, 'The mistress has no visitors except yourself.'

Idie flinched in shame. Austin was silent, watching Carlisle retreat. Then he said to Idie, 'You're tired, you've got rings around your eyes. Have the duppies been bothering you?'

Idie hissed, 'There're no such things.'

Austin watched her carefully for a second or two, then said in his wry, unreadable way, 'Oh, but there are. Mother says you must give them your most deep consideration because they are the little fears and worries that are inside people's heads come to life.'

Idie thought this was very interesting, but she thought about the footsteps in the corridor and knew they were Carlisle's and not just fears inside her head, so she said, 'There used to be noises in the night . . . I think Carlisle Quarterly used to sleep in the house at night, and he is *not* a duppy, nor a little fear inside my head. Besides, it's not normal, is it? Silent never slept on the same floor as us.'

'Oh,' he said, 'I don't know what's normal in a butler. You see, butlers are in rather short supply in my house. But I think you need a monkey to keep the butler at bay. Monkeys are rather good at handling this kind of situation. Yes, you definitely need a monkey, or two: a sweet Spider one for you and some nasty little Cebus for everyone else . . .'

Idie wondered if every boy in the Indies could

summon troops of monkeys at will. She looked at Baronet and saw that he'd taken himself off to the fustic trees to flirt with Austin's mare. Idie was a little put out because she thought Daisy a rather second-rate local kind of creature for a horse like Baronet.

'Would your governess object to a monkey or two about the place?' Austin whispered.

Idie was terribly keen on the idea of monkeys coming to Bathsheba so she said in a hurry, 'Oh, Treble doesn't notice things like monkeys and, in any case, because there's no rum left in the house and because there's plenty on the boat, she's left to follow her heart. Following her heart means chasing Numbers, my trustee, all the way back to Bristol.'

Austin regarded Idie thoughtfully for a minute or two.

'So you're here alone.'

Idie nodded.

She smiled, but had to force her smile to stay in place, and when she could no longer keep it there she dropped her head and bit her lower lip because it began to tremble whenever she thought quite how alone she really was. Despite the unusual sense of normality that life at Pomeroy had given her, Idie knew that being left alone on a remote plantation on the other side of the world in the company of Mayella, whose fears came to life as duppies, and Celia, who was made of water, Phibbah, who was a sphinx, and a butler who thought he was the master was not at all in the usual run of things for a child.

'Golly,' said Austin. Then he jumped up and laughed and said, 'What fun you'll have. We'll fill the house; station a guard in every room. We'll put turtles in the bathtubs, hummingbirds in the hall, monkeys in the rafters . . . You'll whistle them out in the mornings . . .' He took a pencil stub from his pocket and read as he wrote:

'Monkeys, Cebus, plenty
Monkey, small Spider, one
Jack monkey, one
Toucans, two
Sun fowl, female, one'
'Turtles, plenty, small

Let's see, what else . . . ? They'll be the elders of the house, your personal retinue, your household cavalry, they'll sit in judgement . . .'

'They will *not* sit in judgement over me,' said Idie immediately.

'Not over you, silly, over everyone else of course.'

Idie smiled then and said, 'I'll paint the house the colour of the sky and the moon, the windows will always be open and the winds will blow from front to back, and the stars will hang inside . . .'

'And you will dress in rainbows . . .'

'YOU WILL DRESS IN RAINBOWS,' echoed Homer, adding as an afterthought, 'YOUR EXCELLENCY.'

PART III

November 1912

Bathsheba

22nd November 1912

Dear Myles,

I am not scared any more because I have
all sorts of animals. You see, Austin's
father wishes he was a biologist, and
specimens and animals from all the
jungles of the world arrive at his house.
Austin's mother gets annoyed about that
and tells Austin to bring them here.

These are the animals I have:

1. A mongoose called Millie that you
know about. She makes hissing noises
when NOT NICE people come near.

2. A sulphur-crested parakeet called
Homer. He thinks he's better than anyone
else because only he can talk. He's a

true and faithful friend, but neither his conversation nor his character have developed at all, and I can't say anything serious to him as he is so prone to repeating secrets in front of people.

3.   A family of Cebu monkeys that live in a spare bedroom. They are really not very friendly.

4.   A Jack monkey that lives in another spare room. He has to live there because the Cebus don't like him. You see, Jack is bitter in his heart and thinks the world is against him, but he's as happy in the guest bedroom as he could be anywhere because of the canopy over the bed. He perches there and swings down suddenly to terrify anyone who comes into the room. So you see, monkeys and mongooses can keep NOT NICE people away.

5.   A sun fowl, who lives in the dining room and is a perfectly silly sort of thing with knobbly knees and wings that click and make a noise like a grandfather clock.

6.   A greenback turtle. Tommy is only the size of a beetle but one day he'll

be so big there won't be enough room for him in the bathtub. I have to feed him crabs and jellyfish and keep his windows closed, otherwise the gulls will get him.

7. BARONET, who is still the best.

Do you know, perfectly sensible people here believe all sorts of things and speak in riddles? For example, 1. No one goes to a place called Black Water Creek because they say the devil walks about there at night. 2. Everyone believes in duppies. They are the fears and worries that are inside your head and they come alive and live in silk cotton trees and like to play in candle flames and cupboards, so opening cupboards and lighting candles can be a risky business.

The GOOD news is that the butler hasn't come upstairs since all the animals came.

Treble's gone. She left because she took too much punch and that made her weepy about Numbers. I'll never drink punch in case that happens to me, but please tell Grancat not to send another governess out because it isn't necessary at all.

Tell Stables there's a kind of grass called Guinea grass, and Baronet thinks it's rather good.

Did you know that hummingbirds live in nests the size of walnut shells. I can see one from my window. It is made of spider's silk.

Love Idie
PS The only thing I don't yet have is a Spider monkey and I do very much want one.
PPS Something happened in this house that makes people scared of it and it is why they whisper and gossip. I didn't tell you that before, did I?

25

A small Spider monkey did one day come to live at Bathsheba. When Idie came down to breakfast Austin was introducing Baronet to a strange little thing that was all grey and black and definitely the dowdiest, plainest creature Idie had ever seen. Because Baronet was tall and fine, he snorted and whinnied and made it clear that he distrusted monkeys of all stripes and would have no truck with such a creature. Gypsy was hurt and bent her head and rubbed her eyes and threw herself to the ground and wailed.

'Her name is Gypsy,' Austin told Idie. 'She thinks she's human, you see – that's why she wails – but she can't get any tears out because monkeys can't cry.

The wailing monkey unpeeled a hand from her face and looked out of the corner of her eye at Idie.

'She'll make herself princess of all of this place and you will be her queen,' Austin whispered.

Her grievances suddenly forgotten, Gypsy scampered up and slipped her hand into Idie's, and Idie, because she'd never held a monkey by the hand before, was worried that it was so cold and had no thumb to it. Then Gypsy stood upright as though she weren't a monkey at all and looped her tail round Idie's waist and looked up at her, grinning. Idie took a step and Gypsy took a step, and another, and then the two of them were walking side by side and hand in hand in and out of the fustic trees.

That first breakfast Gypsy sat at the table to one side of Idie, Millie to the other, both with bibs about their necks. Homer was above consorting with monkeys and mongooses and he took umbrage and refused his food, disdaining to eat while there were such creatures at his table, but Idie had to admit that a monkey was better company than either a mongoose or a parakeet.

Mayella came out with soursop juice and a bowl of bananas and rolled her eyes.

'You only pretend not to like them, Mayella,' said Austin, adding in a conspiratorial whisper, 'Besides, you know they do a lot of good.'

Idie turned her attention from Gypsy to Millie and fed her some pawpaw, and Gypsy grew jealous and sprang down and snatched Celia's posy from its vase. Terrifically proud of herself, Gypsy carried the posy high in a curl of her tail, to Idie.

'She thinks such a gift deserves at least one banana,' Austin whispered, 'but you must not *on any account* give in to her.'

26

Austin paused at a fork and took the dark and tangled path to the right. With a sudden arrowy chill in her, Idie whispered, 'Not Black Water Creek . . . ?'

'No. I wouldn't take you there,' he answered quietly.

Idie glanced sideways at him, wondering if he knew why it was that no one went there.

'Sampson says the devil walks about there at night. Is that true?'

'Sampson says that, does he?' Austin chuckled. 'I like Sampson.' His face grew serious. 'No, we won't go there.'

They rode through mangrove forest, the horse-hoofs muffled on the white sand path that led beside a stream. Green balisiers brushed their arms and butterflies kissed their cheeks. There were clouds and clouds of butterflies, crimson and sulphur and tangerine, and it was like being inside a kaleidoscope. Idie captured a yellow and brown one from Baronet's neck because he was jumpy about butterflies.

'Carlisle doesn't come into the house at all any more. Or only into the kitchen, to see Celia, because she has a sort of little sitting room behind the kitchen. That's ever since you bought the Cebus, because if you try to go near them they swing down and squawk and jabber. And on top of that he's afraid of the sun fowl because she clacks her tail at him.'

'Mission accomplished,' said Austin, smiling.

They reached a small and secret bay where the mangroves kept their feet in the green water and the coconuts reached their heads into the sky. Tiny waves broke fussily over the sand. Boats and canoes were pulled up on the shore and men were at work mending sails and wicker baskets in the shade of a manchineel tree.

Baronet was very pleased at the sea and the shade and the general absence of butterflies on beaches and he set about eating the young palm leaves that arched over the sand like lace parasols. Austin rolled up his trousers and waded to the shady fringe of the water under the manchineel tree. He pushed up his sleeves and began to fish with his hands among the rocks.

While Austin fished and Baronet feasted on palm leaves, Idie lay on the sand, listening to the sigh of the waves. The wind was warm and dry and she was glad they'd come.

When she woke and looked about she found Austin had laid a circle of pink conch shells all around her.

He reached out and placed something on her belly. She felt the creepy skittle of crab legs skirling over her skin and leaped up screaming and ran into the water.

Austin swam after her. They surfaced in the middle of the bay, laughing, and a darting splatter and glitter of flying fish broke the water all around, silvery and strange and vanishing as a dream.

Idie hadn't had times like this even at Pomeroy, and the shine of the moment was shadowed with the fear that things might not always be so. She watched Austin and wondered if he knew everything about her, all the things that other people seemed to know, the things that made them whisper. After a while she said, 'I'm surprised you want to be friends with me.'

'Well, that's a good point, because you are a spiky and prickly kind of creature.'

Idie's face was sad and serious and she whispered, 'Do you know anything about my family, I mean any sort of secret things . . . ?'

'No.' He laughed. 'Why, what sort of things? Shall I find them out?'

'Hasn't your mother told you anything?'

'No.' He laughed a little ruefully. 'Mother works on what she calls a need-to-know basis, which means more or less that she doesn't tell me anything because children must find out life for themselves.'

Idie whispered, 'Please don't find out any things about me, because they may not be nice things. I know that because people stare at me and whisper.'

The tears were standing in her eyes so she ducked and swam furiously through the water, and when she surfaced Austin was there beside her and he said, 'We don't mind about the things that other people mind about.'

27

Feeling braver, Idie began to go about the island a bit, and often Mayella would accompany her. Gladstone took them in the cart one day to the market. The lane ran alongside a clear, shallow river bordered with tamarinds, all the way to Carriacou where the houses were all in sweet-shop colours and a stream sang through the middle of the village and children played naked and women carried things about on their heads. Baskets of fruit hung from the tamarind trees and stalls stood here and there in patches of shade.

Gladstone went to purchase spades from the hardware shop. Mayella and Idie went about among the trees choosing fruit and filling their baskets. Seeing the women that carried their baskets on their heads, Gypsy placed her own basket on her own plain little head and cooed with delight. Idie placed her basket on her head too and took Gypsy's hand. Gypsy wrapped her tail around the girl's waist and they walked from stall to stall together. Mayella laughed and Homer looked stroppy at having to share the uppermost parts of Idie with a basket of fruit. They found themselves in front of a stall with bolts of cloth laid out. Idie's hand went straight to a plain red cotton. Gladstone joined them and Idie held out the red cloth and said, 'I should like this one.'

Mayella regarded it doubtfully. 'That plenty money, that one.' She felt the weight of it and said, 'Look, it's stiff and straight as a plank of wood.'

'The mistress want that one, the mistress can have that one, Mayella,' said Gladstone. Smiling, he handed over the money and they walked back through the market, Gypsy's tail around Idie's waist, Idie clutching the bolt of cloth and trying to balance a basket on her head and a parakeet on her shoulder and smiling to think how she would soon go about with a flock of hummingbirds about her too.

Two women stood in the doorway of the little haberdashery on the main street. Idie recognized them from the ship and hesitated. They saw the girl with a basket on her head, a parakeet on her arm and a monkey at her side and they raised their parasols and pursed their lips and stared.

'*Look at her.*'

'*She's gone quite savage, they say . . .*'

Mayella took Idie's hand, but Idie, happy about the red cloth, didn't care what they said.

'*Nobody goes up there, you know. Nobody visits her.*'

'*Look, she goes about with locals.*'

'What will become of her?'

'The staff go up there, of course, but only because they're paid to.'

'Everything was taken out, you know. They had to do that or the staff wouldn't return.'

They peered at Idie and one whispered to the other, 'You'd never tell, would you, from the look of her?'

What you'd never tell, Idie didn't know, but she did know that you had to have your chin very high to carry a basket on your head so she couldn't show them she didn't care by tilting it any higher than it already was, but Gladstone stepped towards the women and raised his hat.

'Good morning to you, Mrs Elder, Miss Elder.' Still smiling he said, 'I'm sorry to say I can't spare any labour for your fields next week. Please tell Mr Elder that – not for this harvest, nor for the next.'

Homer eyed the women and he must've been a quick learner because he squawked, 'WHAT WILL BECOME OF HER?'

He is a pillar, thought Idie. *Homer is a pillar and so is Gladstone.*

28

Dear Aunt Celia,

Please would you make me a dress
ALL in red. Can it be
1. comfortable
2. have big pockets
3. NOT have any sleeves

Thank you,

Idie
PS It MUST be only red because you
have to wear red to be friends with
a hummingbird.

Phibbah sat at the kitchen table. That day she wore a towering turban of lemon and turquoise. There was a chopping board in front of her, and a breadfruit, but she was just chewing her pipe. It was a wonder really that anything got made in this kitchen, Idie thought.

She smiled uncertainly at Phibbah. She'd never asked how Phibbah's muteness had come about, but supposed it had been some accident at birth. Phibbah rose from the table, took a jar from a shelf and held out some cashew nuts in the palm of her hand to Homer, and that made Idie feel that Phibbah was *on their side*. She went into Celia's little room and placed the red cloth there with the note on top of it.

29

Idie stood in a corner of the veranda very much hoping that she didn't look as though she were wearing a plank of wood. She examined herself and the new red dress from all angles, but it was tricky to see all of herself in just a hand mirror. She scowled at her reflection.

'Aha. Red. Red is just the thing.'

Idie jumped at the voice and snatched the mirror behind her, mortified.

Austin was wearing his red shirt. He watched her, amused, as she tried to sit on the mirror, and said, 'You look all right.'

'No, I don't.' Idie was burning with shame to have been caught like that staring at herself.

'Well, I think you're all right.'

'Well, I *don't*.'

Austin paused, watching Idie closely. After a while he said quietly, 'My mother says your mother was a wonderful sort of creature too.'

Idie looked at him astonished. Slowly she took in

what Austin had said and grew hot and shaky. She jumped up and stood before him, trembling and scared at what he might know. The whispers and the scraps of gossip she'd heard began to crowd her head. Everywhere whispers had passed like ripples before her and now they all collected in her ears and grew deafening so she clapped her hands over them.

'Mother says she was sort of like a poem,' said Austin.

'Like a poem?' she whispered doubtfully. 'Like a. . . poem?' she asked in a wavering voice. 'When did she say that?'

'Yesterday.'

'Did she say anything else?'

'Oh well, you know,' Austin answered airily. 'Lots of not very helpful things, along the lines of her being the kind of person that made gardens so beautiful they looked like paintings, and filling rooms so full of flowers that they looked like gardens, and loving to swim at night along the stream of the moon and in and out of stars.' He waited, watching Idie.

'Yes, but she didn't want *me*, did she?' Idie whispered fiercely.

'That's not true, Idie,' Austin said, stern and a little shocked.

'It *is*. That's why she sent me away.'

'No, it's not.'

'Myles and Benedict say she couldn't have wanted

157

me because she sent me away.'

'That's not true.'

Idie bit her lip and turned away.

'Mother says sometimes it's best not to know *everything*,' said Austin gently.

'That's what they ALL say.' Idie burst out. 'All grown-ups say you don't need to know everything, but it's not normal for a child not to know things about her mother, is it?'

Idie waited and Austin whispered, 'She said to tell you, if you ever asked, that your mother loved you very much.'

Idie was quiet for a long while. Then she smiled and said, 'One day I should like to swim through stars and down the path of the moon too.'

'We will.' Austin dipped his finger into Phibbah's honey and jumped lightly up on to the balustrade. 'It is the wrong kind of moment for finding a moon to swim along, but it is the right sort of moment for hummingbirds.'

Idie climbed up too and they both rose slowly to their feet and held out their hands and waited.

30

Later, she wrote in her book:

> *Mother was a poem. I'm not sure, but I think it is probably a good thing to be a poem.*
>
> *She loved to swim along the stream of the moon and in and out of stars.*
>
> *She made houses look like gardens and gardens look like paintings.*
>
> *She DID love me.*
>
> *That is all I need to know because you don't need to know everything.*

After a bit of thought she wrote:

> *I love this place as my mother loved it and she is in every bit of it, in the stars and in the trees and in the sea.*

Then she closed the book and put it away, for there was nothing more she needed to know.

*

From that moment a little flame was inside Idie. Warmth and certainty embroidered themselves about her feet and gave her space to grow. Like a sapling uprooted by a storm, she began to send tentative roots into the dark, damp earth of her new home.

31

One evening not long after, Austin came to take Idie to the beach. The frog-song rose from the trees and the stars hurried out, and the sea was smooth as a mirror. Idie and Austin swam out among the flying fish and the fallen stars and Idie thought about her own mother, who liked to swim in the moon river. After a while she turned and lay on her back in the silver stream and looked up into the stars.

Austin said, 'Father is worried about your soul. And Mother is worried about your mind.'

'I don't need anyone to worry about my soul *or* my mind,' replied Idie.

'Nevertheless, she says your mind may wither away if it is not exercised, but I am under instruction, first of all, to take your soul in hand.'

'How will you go about that?' asked Idie.

'By taking you to church, where you will have to endure one of Father's sermons.'

Idie considered the notion of church. The Pomeroy Graces had not been liable to much church-going.

Grancat said that if you ever had need to pray, there was no call whatsoever to do so in a church. It would be a different thing altogether if the darn clergyman would only let the dogs in, he said, his quarrel with churches and clergymen boiling down, in the end, only to the fact of Lancelot being less welcome than Grancat thought properly Christian.

'We'll go on Easter Day, because Father gives a much shorter sermon then.'

Idie thought about that and decided that there was another significant upside to church on Easter Sunday and that was the hymns, which were on average significantly more fun than the unreliable sorts of hymns one might get at other times. She thought too that she'd like to meet Austin's father because he kept crocodiles on his walls and beetles in his drawers. She wasn't so sure that she'd like to meet Austin's mother at all, because a bit of her was jealous that he had a mother, but she said, 'I should like to do that.'

She ducked and swam further out along the silver stream and the flying fish splittered and plashed above her for as far as you could see.

32

'How-day this Easter Day?' asked Mayella, setting down the tray. Idie looked at Mayella with interest because today she'd shed her uniform and emerged from it sweet and bright as a butterfly in a dress that had all the colours of the rainbow in it at once.

'Are you going to church too?' asked Idie.

'Yes, but me and Gladstone and all the Mayleys, we Baptists. Phibbah and Sampson and Reuben and all the Sealys, they Evangelist.'

'I see,' said Idie, who had not realized that church-going could have so many variations to it.

Austin came for Idie with the trap and they drove to Carriacou. Everyone there was making their way, hatted and gloved, to the sleepy little churches that nestled amidst the tamarinds and palms. Idie saw a white-and-green tin shed that she hadn't noticed on other visits. It was covered with all sorts of notices and admonitions to be or do things or not to be or do other things and had a sign tacked over the door, in hand-painted letters, saying 'Baptist Chapel'. Mayella was there, standing amidst all her seven sisters and five brothers. Her head was bowed, her prayer book clasped to her chest. A little apart from her stood Sampson, in the Sunday suit that stood about him as if it didn't know what to do with itself and he watched Mayella shyly.

'Sampson's in love with Mayella,' Idie whispered to Austin. 'And Mayella's wearing every colour at the same time today specially for him. And being in love is infectious, because Sampson got it from Treble, who is in love with Numbers, and I will have to stop Baronet from falling in love with Daisy—'

Austin laughed. 'Oh, you can't do that. Everyone falls in love with Daisy.'

St Lucy's was perched high on a bluff in a cloud of scarlet flame trees. Plaited palm fronds hung from every window and a host of turkeys wandered between the white gravestones. Austin told a bonneted lady in the porch, 'Miss Grace, of Bathsheba.'

Idie saw the airy, whitewashed nave, the open windows, the glittering sea beyond and she felt the wind flutter from transept to transept like the breath of God.

'Long time since a mistress come from Bathsheba,' the lady told Idie, examining her with interest. She handed them hymnals and led them to a pew at the front. A lady in a large sort of gardening hat was sitting there, very upright, like a post that could lead you to an important kind of place. Idie thought it would be awkward being in a front-row pew with the rector's wife if you didn't know when to stand up or sit down and were certain to get it wrong. Austin's mother nodded in a brisk, businesslike sort of way as they joined her.

'Mother, this is Idie Grace,' whispered Austin.

Idie looked in astonishment from Austin who was so dark to his mother who was so pale.

'Edith Hayne,' the lady said in a foghorn sort of voice as though she weren't in church at all. She stuck out her hand to Idie. 'It'll be quite all right, you needn't worry. I've hidden the sermon from him so he can't find it, and I've chosen all the hymns.'

I need an EXPLANATION, Idie told herself as she shook Edith's hand. She thought of the rain-shiny eyes and sunshiny hair that ran from generation to generation of Pomeroy Graces, obliterating all interloping genes. She looked again from Austin to Edith and Edith to Austin. Austin grinned quietly. His father processed down the aisle and Idie gawped. His brows were white and bushy and they spread upward and outwards across his forehead like wings and he didn't look at all like Austin either. Austin smiled quietly again and sang the opening hymn rather loudly and afterwards gave all the right responses and Idie was left puzzled and confused.

Austin's father climbed the stairs to a very tall pulpit

and stood there, so high above the congregation that he was probably already halfway to heaven, but his sermon rambled and was surely worse than the one Edith had hidden, because it had long pauses in it during which he scratched his head and appeared to wait for some new idea to float down to it from the skies.

All this went on for not very long, because after about ten minutes Edith coughed loudly and lifted her hat three times very high above her head, and Austin's father stopped suddenly and said, 'Yes, yes, quite so,' and launched straight into the Creed.

When everybody knelt, Idie tried hard to pray but her head was too full of puzzles and she found herself wondering what it was that everyone had found to pray about and then wondering why Austin's parents were such a different sort of colour to Austin, so she kept staring from them to Austin and back again until he nudged her and whispered, 'Mother's so forgetful she never remembered to have a child at all, and then when she remembered that she'd forgotten she went about looking for one and found me somewhere or other.'

'So she *isn't* your mother then?' hissed Idie.

'Of course she is, though I belonged to someone other parents first, but they didn't need me, so she's been my mother ever since.'

'Quiet, children. Empty your minds, just pour

everything out, like water from a can,' Edith said rather loudly.

The service ended and Edith rose impatiently to her feet and shooed them from the pew as if they were a clutch of hens and marched down the aisle saying in her foghorn voice, 'Why is it, I wonder, that one always feels so hungry after church?'

33

One afternoon Austin took Idie to the waterfall. He led her along a narrow sand path between tall trees. Shafts of speckled light streamed down as if from high windows, illuminating every leaf with stained-glass brilliance, and it was like being in the nave of a great county cathedral. Suddenly they found themselves in a clearing, a vertical wall of white limestone ahead. Water gushed from high above, fracturing mid-air into a glittering spray. Green and blue lights played through the leaves. Mosses and ferns and arums and other plants whose names Austin didn't know grew right to the water's edge in a tangle of sap greens and yellow greens and green greens. They swam in the cool, soft water, then Idie lay on the white rocks.

When Austin rejoined her, he grinned to see Gypsy stretched out beside Idie and said, 'Everyone's talking about you.'

'Do they say that rainbows run through my windows, that there're stars on my ceilings and moonshine in my lanterns?'

Austin was silent awhile, and then he grinned again and said, 'You are a strange creature living in the strangest of circumstances.'

Idie thought that was a funny sort of thing to say. 'I don't know what you mean.'

'Let me count the ways. First, you live alone in a faraway place with no one at all in charge of you. Second, you are mistress of a large estate. Third, you were sent from one side of the world to the other and back again. Fourth, and most interesting, you measure the world and all things in it according to a yardstick that is entirely your own.'

'Grancat said you must always live life according to your own lights,' said Idie, a little defensive.

After a while Austin said, 'You love him very much, don't you?'

Idie bowed and nodded her head, mute because the thought of just how much she missed him could come rushing up into her gullet at any time.

'I'd like to meet Grancat one day, because a grown man who slides down the banisters to breakfast is an *unusual* kind of adult, even by the standards of the adults in my own family.'

Idie nodded, but looked away because her tears were brimming.

'Did you ever think it was unkind of him to send you all across the world on your own, all over again?'

'Grancat is *not* unkind. Ever.' Idie turned to him

and said stoutly, 'Numbers told me once that Grancat did what, according to his own lights, he felt he had to do. Numbers said too that Grancat lives according to the rules of *land* and *heredity* and *lineage* and that there is no wrong in that.'

'So many big words,' Austin answered.

34

Pomeroy
North Devon

July 1913

Dear Idie,

Treble says your establishment is most
irregular, that you are wayward and beyond
remedy and go about with your mongoose in
your pocket [I was behind the curtains in
Grancat's study when I heard that], but I
couldn't discover any more about you because
Grancat interrupted her and called for Silent
and told him, 'Silent, get this darned woman
out of my house before she drinks me out
of gin.'

 Numbers was there too, and he said
Grancat should send out another governess,
but Grancat said no, certainly not, because

hopefully you're beyond remedy already.

'Nothing irregular about a mongoose,' he told Numbers. He says that again often, sort of out of the blue, when you wouldn't expect it all, and it's as if he's always thinking about you.

You're awfully lucky to have mongooses sitting up to breakfast, because you can't get one at all in England.

Love Myles

Dear Myles, thought Idie with a pang, picturing him behind the velvet curtains, the Idie Book on his knee, hiding and listening.

35

'Close your eyes.'

Idie heard the clink of a glass as Austin helped himself to some lemonade.

'Keep them closed. I have someone very special for you. She's got long donkey ears and long giraffe legs and her coat is cinnamon and the insides of her ears are white.'

A small, quivering body was on Idie's lap.

'Keep your eyes closed.'

Idie ran her fingers along a curved tremulous spine, a long tremulous limb, a long velvet ear.

'Open,' commanded Austin. 'I present you with Delilah.'

Delilah was all limbs and no body, her legs the length of Idie's arms, her ears the span of Idie's hands, her back rounded like a whippet, her nose tiny and black, her face white, her eyes shiny and anxious and filled with longing.

'Delilah'll ride with you on a horse and sleep on your pillow and devote herself to you till your dying day.'

Idie stroked the tiny nose and Delilah licked her face, but then Gypsy swung down from the calabash and landed beside Idie's chair, trembling and licking Delilah's face and quivering for joy and wrapping her grey tail around Delilah's waist.

'They hunt Guazipita deer in Jamaica and Guyana and all the places where they live. Father brought her back here, but Mother has *drawn the line* at a deer in the house.'

'Oh my Lord.'

Idie and Austin turned to Mayella.

'What now? Oh my Lord, what's that?'

'Mayella, have you a banana?' asked Austin.

Mayella set down a pitcher of lemonade and a plate of coconut cakes. She turned and her voice drifted across the lawn behind her pretty personage like a twisting ribbon. 'What I going to tell Phibbah? What she going to say when there no more bananas?'

It was Celia who returned with the banana, and Delilah leaped from Idie's lap and bounded towards her.

'Peel it and hold it out for her,' whispered Austin.

Celia did as she was told, all the while her eyes on Delilah. Idie watched, interested, thinking that this might represent a *new development* in what she knew of her Aunt Celia's character. *Perhaps Celia can be CONVERTED*, she thought. Delilah lifted her little black nose to the banana and bit at it and bit again. A hesitant smile came to Celia's lips and a soft dreaminess into her eyes. Delilah stepped forward and licked Celia's hand and gazed up at her and whimpered. Delilah licked her face and Celia clasped the little creature to her and hugged her as though she were a child, and from then on Delilah devoted herself to Celia and followed her about the place wherever she went.

36

Bathsheba

August 1913

Dear Myles,

A little deer has come to live at Bathsheba. She was supposed to devote herself to me till her dying day but she has fallen in love with Celia instead and that is good because it is bringing out the SOFT side of Celia and driving a wedge between her and Carlisle because he doesn't like any sort of animals.

AND I have two toucans. Do you know that toucans are the silliest things you ever saw? You couldn't even make a toucan up because their claws go backwards and their bills are the colour of postboxes. They don't really do anything except sit on a drinks trolley and eat bananas all day, but they DO make you smile every time you see them because of being so absurdical-comical. They're very spoilt and won't eat any of the things they're supposed to, like flies or bugs, because their tree was cut down when they were in the nest and Austin's father saved them. Their faces are violent blue with green frills around and they have white ruffs on their necks and their bills are as long as my arm and can gulp a whole banana in one go. They are called the Crockets – he's Cricket and she's Croquet. Homer and Baronet are sulking and in a slough of despond at having to share the house with such vulgar-looking creatures.

Love Idie

PS My foreman, Gladstone, is going to take us fishing. If he is not at work or in church he's always fishing, and he has promised to take us too.

Feeling rather pleased, Idie folded the letter and placed it in an envelope. Myles would be jealous about the toucans and would definitely come to visit her.

37

Idie stepped up into *The Word of the Lord*, which was Gladstone's little blue-and-yellow boat. Gypsy clambered in after and Gladstone grinned, and there in the shadow of the manchineel tree, which liked to keep its feet in the green-and-turquoise water, Gladstone's smile broke over his face like sunlight. 'I see you're still making trouble for the housekeeping, Miss Idie.' He chuckled, looking at Gypsy.

Austin pushed *The Word of the Lord* off and jumped in, and Idie watched Gladstone's old, handsome face as he tugged at the engine cord and felt blessed that she had such a man working at Bathsheba. *He is a pillar*, she thought to herself. *He and Sampson are both pillars.*

They went far out over the shimmering, undulating threads of petrol, indigo and turquoise to a cluster of islands, tiny spots of land, small as crumbs left for birds, and the wind was soft and the air silky and minuscule silver fish flew about the boat, breaking the water like a gospel.

Austin leaned over the edge and ran his fingers through the water and then ran them over Gladstone's hand-painted lettering, *The Word of the Lord*, and Gladstone threw a line for tunny fish overboard.

Idie, watching Austin, asked, 'Don't you think about your *real* mother?'

'She is my REAL mother. Mother and Father are my parents and I've never needed any others. Hey-ho.'

Dolphins burst in concert from the blue, rising as one and falling as one. There were porpoises too and sea hawks and grampuses the size of Devon cows and turtles that slept on the waves, and Gypsy huddled at the bottom of *The Word of the Lord* fearful of the great size of the sea that was all around her and of all the water that seemed to be in it.

When they turned for home Hummingbird lay before them, floating carelessly on the silver waves, melting as a dream, a happy, careless thing that God once had let slip from his pocket and never remembered to pick up and put somewhere more sensible.

Those were the years; the years that Idie later came to think of as the Bright and Shining Years; the years that Austin came every day to Bathsheba. Those were the years that the island and the house wound themselves around her heartstrings; the years that the warmth of the place ran down into her soul; the years of creeks and waterfalls, of lemonade and picnics, of dappled light and blossomy shade, of molten marigold sundowns and rushing violet nightfalls; the years Idie felt at peace because she had no more questions to ask; the years in which grown-ups played almost no part in things at all.

Idie had never wanted to go to the races. When Austin came for her, she said, 'Why don't we go to the beach instead, or the waterfall?'

'It's for your education. Mother says it's *entirely necessary* that you go a bit about the world.'

'I see,' said Idie doubtfully, amused that horse racing was considered educational in Austin's house. Even Grancat had never made such a claim.

They passed the garrison and she saw the parasols and fans and she tightened a little inside because of all the people that were there. Austin drew up and said, 'Don't worry, it'll be fun. Look, we'll head for the paddock first, then place our bets . . .'

The members' enclosure was a raised and covered stand overlooking the racetrack. It was crowded with pastel-coloured ladies and dark-suited men. On the other side of the track the pastel-coloured women sat about on the grass, like posies, their bright skirts puffed out around them on all sides.

'Father's up there – look – let's go and join him,'

said Austin, gesturing. Idie looked up at all the white and pastel ladies there and hesitated.

'Come on,' said Austin, taking her hand and leading her on up the stairs and weaving through legs and between tables and chairs. They found Austin's father engaged in intense conversation with two other men. The pipe that was clamped in the corner of his mouth looked as though it had once grown there and decided to stay forever after, except for the fact of it having to be taken out for sermons. Austin and Idie waited for the men to finish talking, but they went on for a long while about Serbia and Yugoslavia and an archduke who'd been assassinated.

'There'll be a war, you know,' whispered Austin.

'Why?'

'Because of the archduke who was shot.'

'I see,' said Idie, who of course didn't see at all why the one thing should necessarily lead to the other.

'Father . . .' said Austin finally, and the circle opened to them.

'Idie Grace,' said Idie, stepping forward and holding out her hand to the rector. Grancat had taught her it was courteous to give one's *full* name always so as to be as helpful as possible, a spirit of helpfulness being the only justification for manners.

'Quite, quite, of course you are. I'm delighted to meet you, Idie Grace, quite delighted. Miss Grace, this is Venables, and this is Elder.' Idie remembered the Elder ladies outside the bank in Carriacou and she flinched. Venables and Elder raised their brows faintly and gave a scant nod to Idie, before meeting each other's eyes and withdrawing a little.

Austin's father took Idie's small hand in his large one and, clasping it, bent down to her. Idie, standing in a cloud of tobacco smoke, kept very still, wondering if he'd mistaken her for a curious species from a remote jungle country. She stared into the tangled white hair that was level with her eyes, thinking that it didn't get much tending to and one might perhaps find a new sort of bird nesting in it. Then she noticed his pockets, bulging with magnifying glasses of all shapes and sizes.

'Very good. Very good.' The pipe reverberated as he spoke. 'Magnificent, yes, yes. Your mother, of course, was a beauty too.'

'Tell me about her,' she wanted to say, but Venables whispered to Elder, 'Good bit of land she's got up there.'

He and Elder withdrew a step or two and the air between them all grew sharp and glassy, but Austin's father seemed not to have noticed because he was still inspecting Idie, while at the same time giving Austin a tip. 'The third race, number nine, son. That's the one to put your money on.'

'Terrible shame about the mother,' said Elder, and Idie wondered if Venables and Elder thought she were deaf.

'Father, your tips are never any good.'

'Number nine in the third, number five in the fourth.'

'*That strange chap, the butler there, said it happened in the creek below the house . . .*'

'*Well, he'd know, all right, wouldn't he?*'

'*Said it was a mercy really, her being . . .*' Venables dropped his voice and whispered, but it seemed to Idie that the whole room could hear.

'*It runs in the blood, you know, that sort of thing.*'

She shrank back, her hands over her ears, shaking, and Austin's father shot up and boomed, like a gust of wind across the glassy space, 'Polecats, the pair of you. Elder, d'you know, you can find another rector to marry that dreary daughter of yours.'

39

Idie put two and two together and wrote:

Bathsheba

12th July 1914

Dear Myles,

Something happened here once and there is a secret that I don't know, but it is the reason why people are scared of the house and things had to be taken out of it.

No one will tell me what it is, but I think it happened at Black Water Creek and that is why no one will go there. Also there is something in my blood that makes people stare at me and whisper.

That is for the Idie Book.

Love Idie

PS Tell Grancat I went racing. I didn't like it very much. [Don't tell him I didn't like it.] DO tell him that Baronet is thinking about siring a new bloodline with a mare called Daisy. [I don't think he knows that he can't because of being gelded.]

PPS Austin says there will be a war because of an Archduke who was shot.

40

'Mother's changed her mind about you. She says children can be *entirely ruined* by going to school and coming across grown-ups.'

'Oh good. I am so glad,' said Idie, 'because I have no intention of going to school or going anywhere about the place very much in fact. It is much safer staying here.'

'However, she says you are her new *project*. I have to warn you it is dangerous being a project of Mother's, but the good news for you is that this one won't involve her at all except for the giving of instructions from a distance. You see, I am to be her intermediary. So, now that your soul has been taken in hand, and your education ruled out, we are to tackle your estate. Come with me.'

They led the horses across a patch of rough ground overgrown with Guinea grass.

'When you abandon the cane, the Guinea grows up, you see, and smothers it.' Austin took a piece of it and put it in his mouth and chewed it. 'Gladstone should get the cane growing here again.'

'Was it all cane here once?'

'Yes, once, almost up to the walls of the garden.'

They rode together between the nutmeg and on along a sand track thickly carpeted in leathery rustling leaves, through the cacao plantation. The cacao bushes were spreading and lush, their large, glossy leaves making glittering waves on the ground, like light on the surface of water. They watched a line of men at work, poking pods to the ground with sticks.

'You have responsibilities, Idie, to Bathsheba and to the people on it,' said Austin. 'You must know the hours they work, the amount they're paid.'

'Yes,' said Idie, 'I must.'

'Father says sugar'll be very profitable, you know, because of the war.'

Austin and Idie were silent as they rode home, and Idie wondered if Austin was still thinking about the war too, because thoughts of it kept sneaking back into her head.

After a while Austin asked, 'How old are Myles and Benedict?'

'They're too young,' replied Idie promptly. 'Benedict has one more year of school. Myles is just a boy, and in any case, he'd be no good in a war; he has freckles and falls out of trees and only ever eats pancakes.'

'He was just a boy when you last saw him, Idie, but

boys grow up. Things change whether you want them to or not.'

'It will be over before they're old enough,' said Idie. 'Grancat doesn't believe in war. He says the world should be run by women because they have more common sense. Myles and Benedict wouldn't ever fight and neither would you, would you?'

Austin answered, 'Father doesn't believe in wars either.' After a while he added, 'I have to creep into the Dungeon to read the newspapers now, because that's where they get put.'

'The Dungeon?'

'Mother and Father don't read letters or newspapers. There's a special room we call the Dungeon for letters and bills and things, and they all just get popped in there. They're in a huge pile, and Mother just shuts the door on it to stop it flooding out, and Father says it's amazing how many problems just go away if you don't read about them.'

Idie rather liked the sound of Austin's home, because not only did it have crocodiles on the walls and beetles in the drawers but now it also had a sort of Dungeon where bad things could be locked away, but she said doubtfully, 'I don't think wars go away just because you don't read about them in newspapers.' Then she added, 'Wars go away if men don't go to fight them. *That's* how they go away. And that's why no one should go to war.'

41

Pomeroy

September 1914

Dear Idie,

Benedict has joined the Scots Guards.
That is a family regiment and he is very
proud of that. He does look quite grand in
his uniform, but he shows off too much and
wears it much more than he needs to, i.e.
to DANCES and things.

He says he's going to show the Germans
a thing or two as soon as he can. Grancat
says it's all stuff and nonsense because the
war will be over before Benedict can even
get anywhere close, but still I am a tiny
bit jealous.

Love Myles

Idie couldn't see how Benedict had got grown-up enough already to wear uniform and go to dances and things, let alone to be thinking of showing the Germans a thing or two. How silly of Myles to be jealous because Benedict had a uniform; how silly all boys were about uniforms and things, and how good it was that Austin was different to most of them. Furious, Idie threw the letter aside. It was just as well it would all end soon, long before Benedict would get to France.

42

Austin didn't come again till Sunday. Every day that week Idie had hoped he'd come, and every day she'd waited for him.

'I've a picnic ready,' she told him. 'Let's go to the beach.'

'Oh, I don't know,' he answered.

'Come on,' she insisted.

They walked together along the path that led to Carriacou. Austin paused in the shade of a Tamarind, where the stream met the sea. 'They've formed a West Indies Regiment, you know, Idie.'

'That's silly!' she retorted. 'Why ever would the men from here want to fight? Why would they want to fight for something so distant and far away?'

They walked for a while in silence till Austin said, 'It won't end soon, you know, the war. It might go on a very long while.'

Idie digested this, thinking that if it went on for a long while more, then Benedict *would* get to France before it was all over.

'There's a German battleship in the waters just off here; it's been seen.'

'Is there?' she answered absently, because she wasn't much interested in things like German battleships unless perhaps they happened to sail into her bedroom, but *in the waters off here* sounded actually rather close at hand, and she'd never imagined the war would be here on her doorstep.

Austin paused by the fish stall to admire the strangeness of the creatures that were pulled from the sea, and Idie read the notices pinned to the wooden post of the canopy.

A RESERVE REGIMENT WILL BE FORMED IN EVERY PARISH
for
LOCAL DEFENCE

Another read:

WAR RELIEF FUND.
Women Form Local Organizations to Send Woollen Clothing.

Idie sighed, hating the reminders of the war that were everywhere, and thinking of Numbers, who'd written that he'd not be coming until the war was over because the ships weren't getting through, and of Mayella who considered that war in Europe had absolved her of all responsibility for household dust and disorder.

'Mayella has given up on cleaning altogether. Now she does nothing but knit. She's scared the soldiers will die of cold when they arrive in England.'

Austin laughed. 'Mother spends all day knitting too. She's even formed a Woollen Organization, but I know she'll get bored of the knitting soon and, besides, she's not awfully good at it. She says the price of everything's going to go up and there'll be food shortages.'

They moved onward, thoughtfully, and Idie asked, 'Even if you were old enough, you wouldn't fight, would you?'

Austin never answered because Carlisle was there, leaning against the door to the rum shack, a rolled newspaper in his hand. As they approached, he touched a hand to his hat, a slow, ironic gesture, and raised his brows at Austin's creel and wicker basket.

'Good afternoon, Carlisle,' said Austin, very polite. He gestured to the notice for volunteers. 'Will you be going? I hear many men've volunteered already and gone to Georgetown.'

'It's a white man's war,' Carlisle answered. He unrolled the paper and held up the front page.

WE ARE SECOND TO NONE IN OUR LOYALTY TO THE BRITISH CROWN

AND WILL RISE TO THE OCCASION,
KNOWING THAT THE PEOPLE OF
THIS ISLAND ARE BEHIND US IN ANY
SACRIFICES WE MAKE.

'But what will the British Army pay the men from here? And will they pay our transport? Will they treat us the same? Oh no.'

Later, sitting on the white sand between clouds of sea grape, Idie said, 'No one can get out here now from England, can they? We're cut off.'

Austin nodded.

43

Two days had passed when Mayella came running up to Idie's room,

'Hurry, Miss Idie. The German ship coming in soon. Master Austin is here with the trap. Sampson and me, and Celia, and Phibbah, we all going. What dress are you wearing this day?'

To the great delight of the sun fowl, breakfast, on account of everyone being in a hurry, was set in the dining room. This was her kingdom, the domain of white linen and silver, and she went up and down the table, picking her way on her knock-knee ostrich legs, opening and closing her tail and clicking in a disapproving manner as she passed the monkey, though she had no objection to mongooses or parakeets at all.

When they drew close to Nelson Bay they heard drums and brass bands. Austin pulled aside so they could watch the Georgetown Rifles march past. Celia looked at them and her eyes grew soft and dreamy. Mayella looked and her black eyes filled at the sight of so many uniforms and ribbons and badges and fine men. She whispered to Sampson that he'd look handsome in uniform, and Idie rolled her eyes at Austin. Sampson was quiet and watched the Rifles longingly.

They joined the crowd at the quayside and the men lifted their hats to sing the national anthem, and the breeze ruffled the skirts of the ladies and lifted the hair of the men and fluttered the blue and the white and the red bunting and the canon fired and HMS *Essex* steamed into the mouth of the bay. The *Dresden* was towed in behind her, tail between her legs, and the crowd roared.

Someone made a speech and said that from this great British anchorage the Spaniards had been once kept at bay, from this same anchorage Lord Nelson himself had kept the French at bay, and now from this same anchorage a great German battleship had been captured. The Georgetown Infantry Volunteers marched the prisoners off the ship to the beat of the brass band, and the thunders roared from the crowd and Austin cheered and Idie turned, discomforted that he should feel such joy at it.

'Oh my Lord,' whispered Mayella, her eyes filling once again as she clutched Phibbah's sleeve. 'What's he doing there? Not him, not my own father . . .'

Idie turned. *Nelson*, Mayella's father, Gladstone's son, *Nelson, at the recruiting stand*. Mayella was running towards a makeshift table proudly draped in the British flag, a sign pinned to the canopy saying 'RECRUITING STAND'.

Nelson, the man who'd gone to Pomeroy to fetch her back. Nelson, who'd been turned away at the door by Silent. She looked, horrified, at the long line of men that queued there, so eager to rush to the defence of a country they barely knew. Nelson turned and kissed Mayella's forehead, put an arm around her shoulder and stepped forward to the table even as she pulled him back.

'Why?' Idie asked Austin. 'Why do so many want to go?'

'They'll all go, Idie. There's so little work here. The price of everything is rising, wages are falling. What choice have they got?

That night Mayella said to Idie, 'My father says this war is his chance, this war will be an opportunity for us, good for the people here. But what if he never comes back? What kind of a chance is that? Thank the Lord, Sampson not going – you know how much money they need – fifteen dollars every man from here must pay. And you know what they say – the English don't give guns to the black men, only to the white man, and the black man he does only the digging and the carrying. Oh my Lord, my father is going to go all the same, but what sort of opportunity is just carrying and digging?'

44

As the months of the war trickled by, discontent and unrest grew. There were strikes and rising prices and food shortages and the world had been at war for over a year when Gladstone came for Idie and said, 'You're fifteen now, missus, there or thereabouts. It's time you saw all the things you have.'

That year Austin came less often and Idie began to spend her mornings riding about the estate with Gladstone. At his side she came to understand the timing of the crops, the risks, the rewards, the prices, the conditions, the hours her men worked and the payroll. Slowly she tried to understand the web of interlocking lives of those that worked there, of the Quarterlys and Sealys and Mayleys. Clement Mayley kept Numbers informed by letter as to things regarding the estate. Gladstone, Idie noted, held everything in his head; it was his grandson Clement who committed the accounts to paper and wrote the reports for Numbers.

'We lose two men this week, mistress, both of them

signed up,' Gladstone told Idie one day. 'And there're strikes everywhere, all across the island. It's possible we'll have them here.'

'Strikes here?' asked Idie.

'The wages are low. That makes them discontented.'

'Can't we raise them?' she asked.

'Yes, mistress. I am glad you've asked. We will do that.'

Idie rose to leave Gladstone's office, but at the door she turned and said, 'Why do they want to fight? Why do they leave and go so far away to fight for Britain?'

'George is our king. We're fighting for him, just as the British are,' he answered simply.

'It'll be over before they get there.'

Gladstone said, 'Some think that if they fight it will help us –' Idie saw his fingers touch the dark skin of his arm – 'that it will help advance us in government and things.'

That simple touch of his fingers to the skin of his arm told Idie of all the differences and divisions that scarred the little island, and she was silent awhile and thoughtful till she remembered what Austin had said and asked, 'Gladstone, can we increase the amount of sugar we grow? It'll go up in price if the war goes on.'

A broad white smile broke over his face as he looked at the young girl who sat at the large desk with a parakeet on her shoulder and a monkey at her side and he said, 'Yes, mistress, I have for a long time wanted to do that too.'

Gladstone spoke slowly always, his words considered and kept to a minimum. *Men of few words are the best men*. Grancat had taught Idie that, telling her it came from Shakespeare. Idie still thought it surprising, a) that Shakespeare should say such a thing, given that he was so prone to outpourings of words himself, and b) that Grancat knew any Shakespeare at all.

When Austin did come to visit, Idie was aware of the increasing distance between them. He no longer wore red shirts to summon hummingbirds nor did he go about with creatures in his pockets. It was as though he'd taken a leap towards adulthood and left her behind. If they went to the beach he did not swim, nor hunt among the rocks for crayfish or whistle for lizards. Something in him had changed, but when or how it had changed Idie didn't know. As for herself, the war, the strikes, the rising prices, food shortages and discontent were pressing their dark, sharp teeth into the dreamy consciousness of her girlhood, but she was still a girl, still a girl who didn't want to be an adult.

45

Bathsheba
St Lucy

7th March 1915

Dear Myles,

Do you know I am fifteen now? That
makes you sixteen. The war will be
over before you can sign up, but if you
do sign up I'll write and tell them your
feet are flat because I know they are.
Please send me more news of Benedict.
I do wish he wasn't going to Gallipoli
and I do wish you would write to me
more often and longer letters. I know
girls are much better at writing than
boys, but please do try.

Did you know there's voluntary
enrolment here? King George said he

wanted troops from the West Indies so each island must send some men. Lots of them want to go, but they have to pay their own passage and the only things they are allowed to do are the carrying and digging. That doesn't seem right, but in some ways I am glad because it means Sampson can't afford to go. Gladstone says we can't lose any more men or there'll be no one left.

The sugar is fetching a good price because of the war, but we cannot get lots of things now because so few ships get through. For example, we can't get fabric for clothes or new pots and pans or anything.

Love Idie

46

More troops left from the Indies soon after this, and all the people of the island gathered to see them go. Mayella wept and the brass band played 'Soldiers of the King'. The trained men of the British West Indies Regiment stood on the dock and the feathers of the topis of the colonial police fluttered and a breeze stirred the leaves of the palms and the hearts of all that watched as the brigadier said, 'Some of you may be killed, many wounded, but may those who fall, fall gloriously, your faces to the foe, the light of victory on your bayonets.'

The dark horses and the white uniforms and the beating flags and everything looked grand and splendid. The brigadier bellowed and someone bugled and the sun rose behind the white building of Government House and five hundred fine young men embarked to serve their God and country. Fleecy clouds veiled the sun and cast a shimmering light over all the pomp and panoply, and Idie looked on as if it were all happening in a dream. She'd thought the war would be over by now, not that men would be boarding ships as though the whole thing had only just begun.

'All the men are going and leaving us here,' sobbed Mayella. 'Is nine penny a day to cut the cane and the British Army it pays eighteen penny a day, so, what you see, all the young men they're going to go.'

Idie wondered whether she could raise the wages at Bathsheba still higher.

'Father he says the war will be good for us, that after they going to give us place in government and give us all the things the white men have, but what do we want all that for if all the young men be dead?' Mayella wondered aloud amidst fresh tears. Idie took her hand and together they watched the men embark, Idie wondering what they'd make of England when they arrived, and what the white soldiers would make of them.

Phibbah unclamped her pipe from her mouth and jabbed a scrawny arm towards a troop of scouts parading past the garrison.

'Master Austin,' whispered Mayella, open-mouthed, turning to Idie. Then added with a wicked smile, 'He very handsome, missus.'

Idie tensed. *Austin? Did he* mean to go one day too?

The scouts drew closer. Idie pursed her lips as they passed. Austin was at the head of the column, taller and older than his troops, and he winked as he passed

Idie and swung his arms smartly. Idie noted the long socks he wore, the green gaiters, khaki shorts and khaki jacket with two stars above the breast pocket. She scowled again. He had a stripe on his sleeve and badges all the way up his arm, on his hat the badge of a patrol leader, and all those badges and stripes were upsetting when he'd never told her anything. That stripe meant something, perhaps a year in service. A *year*, and he'd said nothing.

'Maybe Master Austin will go to war also. All the scouts they become soldiers one day,' commented Mayella.

'He will not. We don't believe in war. He *promised*. Anyway, he's too young.'

'All the young boys they grow up,' commented Mayella. 'He's maybe sixteen now.' That was the moment, when Idie was fifteen and saw Austin march by as head of the scouts, that the world around her sharpened and came into view, the moment when trust, the shield of her childhood, shrank back and when all the shifting shadows in her head began to gather.

47

Idie went alone to St Lucy. She wasn't prone to going to church but she needed somewhere to be alone and think. She was often lonely now, and when she was alone she'd think of the times she'd spent with Austin. She stored those times she'd spent with him like precious marbles in a chest, and as she sat there alone in St Lucy she ran her fingers through those marbles, remembering the long, lovely, shining days.

She rose and left the church and wandered out among the turkeys and the gravestones. She looked out across the sea. Somewhere far away over that sea was Benedict, who wanted to show the Germans a thing or two, and Myles, who wanted to wear uniform.

She rested her hand on a gravestone. The granite was cool and smooth and newly polished and her eyes fell, idly, on the engraving that was sharp and all picked out in black. A jar of ginger lilies stood there, gaudy and jarring with the restraint of the stone. Idie stepped back and saw, with a clutch at the throat, the inscription:

In Loving Memory of Arnold Grace.
Born 1830, died 1875.

Arnold. *My grandfather.* She touched her fingers to the stone and kept them there awhile. Of course the Graces would be buried here, being Anglican. This church was where they'd've been christened, blessed, married and buried. She lifted her head. Her mother and father would be here too and yet she'd never thought to look. She searched about for other Graces, but as she turned she found Carlisle before her.

'Mistress Grace,' he said. He nodded to her and, still watching her, he crossed himself and knelt. He placed a prayer book on the ground and stood the vase of ginger lilies more upright. Idie watched, confused and frightened that he should be there straightening the ginger lilies and kneeling before her own grandfather. Carlisle crossed himself again and rose, and Idie straightened herself, stood up tall and took a deep breath.

'Where are my father and my mother buried?'

'No, mistress,' he answered. 'There was no church burial for them.'

Idie didn't know then why they might not have been buried in a church, but she heard the scorn in his voice and she willed herself to look him straight in the eye and her voice to betray no weakness, and she countered as casually as she could, 'Thank you, Quarterly.'

'Good afternoon, mistress,' he said, and turned and left.

Idie stared at the ginger lilies, suddenly hot and frightened. Then she saw on the ground before the lilies the prayer book Carlisle had forgotten. Trembling, she bent to pick it up and held it, not liking to touch it much, for it was Carlisle's. It was of ivory leather, a little freckled with mildew. She opened it and saw, written in blue ink, in hesitant, careful letters:

Honey Quarterly

Beneath it a photograph was pasted. Through the grey speckles of its surface, a woman gazed frankly into the lens, her eyes dark and large and lovely, her strong dark arms cradling a bundle in a snowy shawl. The lace collar of her dress formed a bow beneath her collar bone, the ties of it falling loosely to the baby, whose tiny hand reached up to them.

Idie heard a short, bitter laugh and looked up.

'That is the only picture I have of her,' said Carlisle, holding out his hand for it, his eyes shining and strange.

Idie gave it to him and watched him leave. *Why did he kneel at her grandfather's grave? Was it he who put the fresh flowers there?* A sudden, strange, spinning feeling came into her skull.

48

At Bathsheba Idie found Gladstone and Sampson in the stables.

'Gladstone, tell me about Carlisle.'

The men turned to one another.

'Who are his family?' Idie asked.

Gladstone paused. She saw the apprehension in his eyes, heard the hesitation in his voice, the careful words. 'As you know, his father is Enoch Quarterly.' Gladstone paused again. Idie waited and he went on. 'His mother was Honey Quarterly.'

'Where is Honey now?' asked Idie.

'She died in childbirth. He's been angry, always, since then.'

So this was the reason for the bitterness in Carlisle. His mother had died giving birth to him, and ever since he'd felt guilty, and angry too perhaps, with that vicious kind of anger that comes from guilt.

'I see,' said Idie to Gladstone. 'Thank you.'

She turned and walked towards the house, then stopped, something new suddenly coming clear to her. If Carlisle was the baby in Honey's arms, then Honey had died giving birth not to Carlisle but to some other child. Honey had had another child, but Carlisle had no brother or sister that Idie knew of.

The spinning feeling came into her skull once more. She lifted a hand to her forehead as if to quiet the shadowy, flapping thoughts that were in it. The skin of her forehead was burning to the touch. She went upstairs to the loggia where it was cool and fresh and she'd be alone. She gazed out over the nodding mopheads of the palms. The sea was stirred and fretful in the wind, but she felt hot and limp and the breeze had no power to cool her. The separate things she knew were like the pieces of a puzzle. Only they were swelling and changing shape and growing confused with one another:

The butler who knelt at her grandfather's grave.

The baby his mother had died giving birth to.

Idie's own parents' wish that the butler should have life tenure at Bathsheba.

The creek where no one went.

None of the clues joined together or made any sense at all, and they were all dark and shifting.

49

Dear Myles,

You have made even less improvement in letter writing than Homer has in conversation so you will have to come to visit me instead when the shipping can get through because I know you will like it.

Delilah has broken the spell that Carlisle had over Celia, because Celia is growing softer. She makes dresses for me, and the two things that make her happy are sewing and Delilah. She feeds Delilah bananas and knits scarves for her. Delilah loves bananas, which you wouldn't really expect in a deer.

Anyway, I am going to tell you some things that I know for the Idie Book and also some things that I don't know:

1. Carlisle, the butler, can live here forever because that is what my father wished.
2. Carlisle's mother is Honey. Honey had another child and when she had that other child she died.
3. I don't know who that other child is.
4. Carlisle kneels at my grandfather's grave and puts flowers there but I don't know why he would do that.

OTHER THINGS I DON'T KNOW:

That's more or less EVERYTHING else, e.g. why no one will tell me ALL the things that are NORMAL for children to know about themselves.

Love Idie
PS & MOST IMPORTANT:
PLEASE visit soon. Austin doesn't come round very often any more, and even if you have monkeys and parakeets and turtles it can be lonely and sometimes my head gets hot and swims with all the things inside it and sometimes I am scared.

50

Thoughts of Carlisle troubled Idie throughout the night, and when she rose next morning she determined she would go back to Gladstone.

At the foot of the veranda she paused, a hand on the balustrade, weak with the heat and dizzied by the scent of the ivory flowers that grew there.

Mayella stepped out of the kitchen and Idie said, 'Please ask Enoch to cut these flowers down today.'

'Carlisle told his father to leave them there.'

'It is *my* garden,' Idie hissed.

'But Enoch is afraid of his son. Carlisle he angry, very angry jus' now, he like a burning thing, more angry than he ever were, and Enoch he scared.'

Idie crossed the lawn and the dead hand of the sun was white and fierce on her bare head, the blue of the sky too vibrant, the green of the trees too green and gross. She sank against the cool stone wall of the stable and said, 'Sampson, please can we saddle the horses and go to Gladstone?'

'Storm is coming,' Sampson said, hesitating.

'Fetch the tack,' Idie commanded testily, and Sampson bowed his head and turned for it.

A weight at the back of Idie's head throbbed and the space behind her temple pulsed. As they reached the cacao plantation, Sampson pointed, grinning, to the red and orange pods that hung on little stalks directly from the boughs. Beneath them, supervised by Gladstone and Clement, stood a line of workers, poking sticks upward to jolt them down.

'Cacao does not hurt the hands like sugar cane,' said Sampson. 'Is good.'

Idie shivered. Her arms were shaking and sort of uncontrollable and she was glad Baronet was behaving himself. Clement held out a hand as she dismounted.

'Mistress?' asked Gladstone, smiling gently and lifting his hat.

Leaving Clement and Sampson with the horses, Idie and Gladstone walked together between the trees, the dead leaves crackling beneath their feet. Idie said, 'Honey was Carlisle's mother; Enoch was his father.'

'Is so, mistress.'

'Then why does he kneel at my grandfather's grave? What is he to do with my grandfather?'

Gladstone lifted his hat and rubbed his forehead with the back of his fist.

'Is Carlisle giving you trouble, mistress?'

Everything oscillated and swam; the reds and oranges and greens had become pulsing circles of colour that came and went before Idie's eyes. She held out a hand to the branch of a tree to steady herself.

'I – I – I don't like him. He doesn't want me here.' Idie swayed and recovered herself.

'You're not yourself, mistress,' said Gladstone. 'It's fever perhaps?'

'Why is Carlisle here?'

Gladstone rubbed his forehead again, then with a long, low exhalation said, 'He can live here long as he likes, keep his house till the day he dies. It was what your mother wished. She wished that because your father wished it.'

Idie held a hand to her forehead and bowed her head and whispered, 'I know, but why did they wish that?'

The leaves stirred and whispered to one another.

'That's not for me to say, mistress,' said Gladstone eventually.

The pain in Idie's head throbbed as if to burst her skull; the light burned her eyes and she covered them with her hands, giddy and swaying.

Gladstone stepped forward. 'You're not well – Sampson, help.'

Idie's legs gave way and she fell.

51

Idie spent two days resting in the cool and dark of her room. On the third day she felt strong enough to go down with Mayella to the kitchen, for Celia wanted to fit a dress. They helped Idie up on to chair and she stood there, still a little weak, her hand in Mayella's to steady her. Celia's head was bent over the hem, a flock of pins in her mouth. The air of the kitchen was heavy and still. Idie turned a quarter-circle so Celia could begin work on the other side. The air thickened and seemed to swell with the heat, and Idie's head began to swim.

Everything was silent, but for the *drip-drip-drip* of the old brass tap and the clicking of the kitchen clock.

'She grown some more . . . She's got a nice waist, nice hip,' said Mayella, who was, Idie noticed, not in fact looking at all at waists or hips but instead staring dismayed in the direction of a paltry flying fish by the sink. 'How we going make lunch with one fly-fish and one breadfruit? That all you buy, Phibbah?'

Phibbah, inscrutable, chewed her unlit pipe. Her

long, sharp knife lay beside a breadfruit on the marble chopping board. Carried on a swathe of heat from the stables, voices wafted in through the window, riffling the still of the room.

Celia removed the pins from her mouth and placed them on the table. She shifted to the window and stood there, wary and attentive. Not a blade of grass moved. The birds fell silent as if the hammer blow of the noon sun had stupefied every living creature. Idie, standing on the chair, waited. She heard Gladstone's voice, first almost inaudible, then louder.

'Where's the will, Carlisle?'

A shadow passed across Celia's face as though a ghost had walked there. Her eyes narrowed and flickered. Phibbah's knife remained poised, suspended over the breadfruit.

'Give me that will, Carlisle. I want to know what's in it.'

'You'll never see it, Gladstone Mayley,' Carlisle answered, jeering.

'Carlisle's got no respect. No one talks to my granfer like that; he an old man,' said Mayella. Celia pulled the leaf of the casement window to. She held the needle to the light, but Idie saw the tremor in her fingers, the quivering thread. Mayella turned and slipped from the room. A fly droned above the table, its buzzing filling the room till it settled on the breadfruit, and for a few seconds there was silence, everything paused and held in time, Phibbah's knife hovering above the breadfruit, Celia's needle and thread in the light of the window, everything utterly still but for the ticking of the clock and the dripping of the tap. Somewhere something heavy crashed and fell, the sound of timber crashing and splintering, of metal clattering on stone. There was a piercing shriek, then a sustained, shrill scream. A figure staggered from the yard, shirt unbuttoned, jacket open – Carlisle – dazed and blinking in the white sun. A look of wild release overtook him and he was running towards the gates and laughing with a strange violence and hysteria.

Sampson ran out from the yard and stood, open-mouthed, arms helpless and loose on either side, as if too astounded for a second to move or call out. Then, 'Help! Miss Celia! Phibbah! Call the mistress. Is Gladstone.'

Idie found Clement and Mayella in the forge, Mayella's hands and blouse red with fresh blood. In her arms was Gladstone, beside him on the ground a flat-headed hammer. Mayella stroked his bloodied hair, circled his staring eyes with a tender forefinger, kissed his smooth, broad forehead.

A little apart from the Mayleys stood Enoch Quarterly, his eyes loose with fear. Celia stood to the other side, cowering against the wall. All were dumb with horror.

Phibbah knelt. She pulled Mayella's head towards her and held it there against her chest, and with her other arm reached down and closed Gladstone's eyes.

'What happened, Clement?' whispered Idie when she was able to speak.

Sampson answered for Clement. 'They shout an' argue all about the will. Carlisle he push Gladstone 'gainst the wall an' shake him an' shake him like he shake de whole world with his anger, an he fall an' the hammer it fall too from the shelf an' –'

Celia moaned. She was transported by the sight of Gladstone, like one pulled from a long sleep into a violent and terrible world, her white cheeks flushed with rose as if she were a wax doll to whom blood had suddenly been given and it was rushing now in her veins where it never had before.

Idie bowed her head, faint with horror, fear and grief. 'Where's Quarterly?' she whispered.

'He gone,' said Sampson.

'I will call the police,' she said.

Sampson glanced at Enoch, paused, then went to him and said, 'It were an accident, Enoch; it were what your son wanted, but it were an accident.' He turned to Idie. 'Mistress, is best maybe I call only the priest.'

Enoch nodded at Sampson, gratitude in his eyes, and Idie saw that she was tangled in the web of loyalties and enmities, in the lines of family and blood and love that criss-crossed Bathsheba.

The dressing of Gladstone was done by Phibbah. Mayella, her seven sisters and the Baptist church took control of the house. People came and went long into the night, praying in the library where Gladstone now lay, weeping in the hall, gathering on the lawn. Gypsy huddled in the rafters, rubbed her eyes and tugged her ears. Baronet, disgruntled at all the people that were coming in and out of his hall, removed himself to the stables.

Through that long and ghastly night Idie sat in the library with Mayella and Phibbah and with all Mayella's seven sisters and five brothers, but Mayella was stiff and cold with Idie, and Idie wondered if it were better she weren't there. She longed for Austin to come, and thought she might send word to him, but the heat and the giddiness was in her head again and there was no one to send for him, for all were absorbed in their grief. Mourners left and more mourners came and Mayella asked over and over, 'Carlisle, where's he? Where's he?'

Near dawn she said, suddenly, 'Gladstone asked Carlisle three times what was in the will that Carlisle make him sign. Carlisle say it no business of his, and Gladstone told Carlisle, "I signed that paper and is my right to know what in it. One day I going to tell the mistress that I don't know what was on the will I signed." That when Carlisle push Gladstone to the ground and shake him and . . .' Idie was still wondering what was in the will that Gladstone had signed when Mayella turned and said to her with sudden violence, her dark eyes burning, 'It's on your account my granfer died. He loved this place, this house, this land.'

52

The funeral took place the next afternoon in the green-white tin shed Baptist chapel. Gladstone's boat lay below the altar. Old Enoch was rambling and incoherent. Clement, Reuben and Sampson were among those that carried the coffin on their shoulders and placed it in the boat.

Neither Carlisle nor Celia were there. Mayella and Clement stood together beside Nelson and all their brothers and sisters. The congregation overflowed the chapel and the yard and so stricken was the outpouring of grief for Gladstone it seemed to Idie that the roof might burst and Gladstone go sailing straight to heaven in his boat and that at heaven's gate the drums would beat and the trumpets blow and the silver sunfish splatter the seas, and she hung her head.

It's on your account my granfer died. He loved this place, the house, the land.

Afterwards, she stepped out of the chapel and stood alone in the shade.

Sampson drew Mayella aside and took her hand

and Idie heard him whisper, 'Next time I here is for I marry you.'

Idie saw how, for all her grief, Mayella's beauty lit up when Sampson spoke to her, as if the sun had placed its palm on her for the first time.

Idie crept away and returned to Bathsheba alone.

Everything was still and silent. She felt hidden watching eyes. A cold, trickling fear threaded her veins. Who was there? And where was Homer? And Gypsy?

She broke into a run, screaming, 'Homer! Gypsy! Millie!' She raced up the stairs to the veranda, tripping and stumbling and screaming, 'Homer, Homer!'

There was no Gypsy in the rafters, no Crockets on the trolley. Idie whirled around, calling into the trees and skies. She flung open the door and ran into the hall. Brushing the hair from her eyes, she paused and stood in the centre of the hall, listening, all her senses taut. The door to the dining room was ajar, the door to the study ajar. Idie went to the study.

Celia was there, looking a little odd and stiff, sitting sideways to the desk, her legs crossed. A cut crystal vase of scarlet ginger lilies stood on the desk before her. That had not been there that morning when all the flowers had been white for Gladstone. Celia looked at Idie, her eyes hard and vacant, and Idie wondered at the sudden reversal that had come over her; yesterday she'd been as one drawn into life for the first time, now she was again withdrawn and empty.

Idie took a deep breath and said inwardly, *She is my aunt. I must look after her as my mother would have wished. Be calm, be gentle, Idie Grace.*

'Are you quite all right, Aunt Celia?' she asked.

Celia smoothed the collar of her dress and toyed with a trinket on her wrist and said in a shallow, brittle voice, 'I am fine, very fine. Just taking some afternoon tea and doing correspondence.'

Idie saw the blank paper in front of her, the closed inkwell and said, very slowly, 'I see.' She half turned, then paused, picking her words carefully. 'I'm sorry you didn't come to the funeral, Celia.'

'Gladstone was a foolish man.'

'Carlisle told you that, did he?' asked Idie.

'Gladstone couldn't read or write. Carlisle is educated—'

'I see. This all has to do with Carlisle, doesn't it . . . ? Aunt Celia, you must stay away from him.'

Delilah's little scarf, the one Celia had knitted for her, lay across the lacquered surface of the desk. Celia picked it up and threaded it to and fro between her fingers, pulling it out one side, threading it back through the other. 'I read and write.'

'So I see.'

Again Celia pulled the scarf through her fingers.

'Where's Delilah?' asked Idie.

Celia opened her mouth to speak, then closed it. Her eyes went to the door. She threaded the scarf through her fingers once more.

'*Where* is Delilah?'

'It's not proper to have her follow me, now I am a lady.'

'Oh my word. Carlisle says it's not proper, does he?' Idie stepped closer and whispered, 'Where's Delilah? Where's Homer? And Millicent? Where are they all?'

A look of cunning came into Celia's eyes.

'WHERE ARE THEY?'

Celia whispered, 'Hidden.'

'*Hidden?*'

'In Phibbah's rooms.'

Idie discarded the June-bug theory once and for all. Celia had cunning in her and duplicity. She'd hidden Delilah and the animals from Carlisle, yet she was still his puppet. Idie stepped away from Celia and said, 'Well now, being a lady, Aunt Celia, I am sure you will keep Delilah safe because you know how she loves you.'

'She loves me,' repeated Celia in a soft, faraway voice.

'And because you are a lady, you will keep Delilah and all of them safe till I return, and you will tell me where Carlisle happens to be.'

Celia's eyes darted towards the dining room, then back to Idie.

'Thank you,' whispered Idie, turning. Celia snatched at Idie's sleeve as if to warn her of something, but Idie pulled free and marched across the hall.

Carlisle sat at the head of the table, a crystal decanter of dark liquor beside him. He put down his glass, wiped his lips with the back of his hand and looked at her.

'Where's Delilah?' Idie asked, very quiet, very controlled.

He laughed. 'Gone. It's not yours. None of it is yours. That's why they're gone. All of them. Because I'll be master here soon, Mistress Idie, this house'll be mine. Mine. It's my inheritance; it's what your mother wanted.'

Idie answered, calm and steely, 'No, it's not, Carlisle Quarterly; it's not what she wanted.'

He took some rum and laughed. 'It is. I have the paper to prove it.'

Idie fought for control of her anger, and finally, through her teeth, said, 'You are butler here, Carlisle Quarterly, no more than that. You may wish that Bathsheba were yours, but it is not.'

'Your own mother gave this house to me in her will. You didn't know that, did you, Miss Grace? Her will makes everything over to me. When I give that will to the bank, then –' he drank again and rose unsteadily – 'all of this will be mine, Miss Grace.'

Idie shook her head from side to side, telling

herself, *No, no, she never did that . . . my mother would never have done that.*

'I'm going to tell you one more thing you don't know . . .' He laughed again and waited, watching Idie. There were beads of sweat on his brow. 'We've the same blood, you and I.'

Idie gasped.

Carlisle laughed. 'Honey, my own mother, was your grandmother, the mother of your father . . .'

Idie put her hands over her ears and backed against the wall, but he laughed and she felt his breath on her face.

'That's right,' he growled, adding with a curling tone, '*mistress.*'

Idie smelt the drink on him.

'I was taught in the same schoolroom as your father, treated like a brother to him.' He placed a hand on the wall on either side of Idie, pinning her there. 'You see, I am the half-brother of your own father.'

His foul rummy breath lapped her face. Idie pressed herself against the wall.

'Your father killed my mother the day he came into this world. He was no good from the day he was born. He killed her –'

The anger was coiled in Carlisle like a spring.

'And your mother, Miss Grace, was insane. Insane, crying at the trees and the sun and the birds, begging for the dark . . .'

Insane?

Carlisle leaned closer and hissed, 'They didn't tell you that, did they? She was afraid of the light, afraid of birds and trees and flowers, afraid . . .'

Idie tried to step back, but he caught her and she bent her head and covered her eyes and her nails clawed the skin of her face.

'*Insane*, Miss Grace. A lunatic.'

Blinding illumination shot through Idie, shaking her to her roots, howling through the foundations on which she'd built her happiness.

'Her own child wasn't safe. Nothing was safe with her, not even her own child. That's why you were sent away. They didn't tell you that either, did they? Didn't tell you that she killed herself?' He stepped back to see Idie's face.

'Insanity runs in the blood, Miss Grace. You have it too.' He laughed. 'The fear of the light. . .'

He laughed again, and in that second she broke free and fled.

PART IV

October 1915

53

The fever that had before only simmered in Idie's veins returned, full blown and furious. She was febrile and burning, sweating and shivering, her skull straining as if it couldn't contain the heat in her head.

They had to take me away from her to keep me safe. It runs in the blood. There will be no escape from it, no escape from myself.

There'd been a doctor some time ago – how long – a doctor had been there and his words found a space in Idie's crowded head: 'It's nothing more than a simple fever. Give her fluid and bed rest. Plenty of fluid, plenty of rest. Keep her cool. Keep the windows open.'

So the windows had been opened and the scent of the trumpet flowers flooded the room. Homer was unsettled and noisome, his feathers glowing whitely in the night. Shadows vibrated across the room, the palms made close muffled sounds, the vines rattled against the shutters and Idie tossed and turned, groping for the peace that comes with sleep. Palm leaves scraped the sky, their giant fingers grotesque and distorted. Heat moved in leisurely swathes across the room bringing voices on its back: *Madness runs in the blood, you know.*

I am mad. It is in my blood. I will fear the light. There will be voices in my head. Already the moon that is in the sky is not right; she isn't as she should be. She's yellow and fallen on her back and the stars are hung incorrectly, disorderly and too bright. They're bright with tears and sliding through the black and nothing can stop them falling.

The candle flickered. The flame grew long and thin and the pale face in it grew narrow as a snake tongue, then twisted and strangled itself. Idie shivered and turned away. Idie's nightdress was damp and clinging, her mouth dry and bitter. She shut her eyes. She'd have no candles for there were faces in all the flames. It was the madness in her that made her see the faces, made her fear the light.

Things stirred outside. There were startled bird shrieks, shrill and metallic.

The frog song poured in through the window, only it wasn't song, it was a million million whispers, a million million deafening whispers from the birds to the frogs and the frogs to the birds.

She is mad, she is mad. These things run in the blood, you know, they said to one another, and their whispers joined the laughter of the moon, and the scent of the trumpet flowers and they swelled together as if to fill

234

the room and erupt the walls of it, and in Idie's head all the puzzle pieces that had lain about disordered rose all at once, twirling like confetti and turning their dark undersides to her.

The vines were creeping, inch by inch, into the room. Even if she closed her eyes tight she knew they were still there, twining themselves around the head of the bed, clinging to her hair, tangling their tendrils around her and thrusting their jeering trumpet mouths in her face.

Burning and shivering by turns, Idie clung shaking to her pillow and to Millicent, who squirmed and protested at the ferocity of her grip.

54

The heat grew in Idie's body and the thick fog of fever swelled in her brain. The vines flapped and rattled. Black clouds banked up. The wind rose sharply and seemed to blow from all sides of the compass at once. The doors and windows creaked and the air grew sulphurous. The palmate devil hands of the breadfruit tree clawed the watery sky. A damp chill rose in wreaths from below the window and curled upward, carrying with it the sinister scent of the trumpet flowers.

A procession of goblins slid in and out of Idie's tremulous consciousness: grinning gravestones and rummy men, a face clear as water and slippery as glass, the simple sister of the mad mother, a pair of sewing scissors in her hand.

With no warning the sky roared and split. Thunder burst and cracked as if to blow the world apart. Rain fell in solid sheets and the fever in Idie raged.

Morning came finally, grey and late and sluggish, and pushed the rain aside. Mayella came in with the tea tray.

'Where is Carlisle?' asked Idie.

'He gone. No one seen him.' Mayella turned her attention to the floor and tutted at it. 'Roaches . . . come in when it rains. Plenty rain in the night, plenty roaches in the mornin'.'

'Roaches?'

'Big fat roaches. All over de place.' She gave a gesture that encompassed the entire room and bed and furnishings as though the roaches might be in the cupboard and in all places, but Idie was built now of solid darkness and no longer cared about such things. The roaches could creep and crawl through all the cracks and crevices of her house. *They didn't matter. Nothing mattered any more. Nothing meant anything now.*

Mayella tutted now at the window. 'That jumby tree is maybe stopping your sleep. Too many duppies in him. I going to tell Enoch to plant overlook peas in all the corners.'

'Overlook peas?' asked Idie weakly.

'Oh yes, the overlook pea stops the evil eye.'

Grancat was right: if you lived in wet and boggy places you knew as fact that there were fairies, and if you lived in hot and sticky places, you knew as fact there was an evil eye and that therefore you must have overlook peas.

'Where is Celia?' asked Idie.

'No one seen her, and no one seen Carlisle.'

'Did anyone report him?'

'No. He is your father's family, Miss Idie, and he is Enoch's son. That why.'

Idie turned away.

'The Crockets?' she asked. 'And Delilah?'

'They was all in Phibbah's rooms. Celia she put them there. The pigeon is here with you. The mongoose is here with you. The monkey is thinking she ill with fever and she thinking she must have a big soft bed with four posts to it of her own. The toucans are on the trolley now. The horse is in the hall. Sampson is looking after them all like they his own children.'

Idie reached a hand out to Millicent and knew it was good to have a parakeet and a mongoose in your room, but perhaps, to be on the safe side, one needed an overlook pea as well.

In the late afternoon Mayella came again. She lit a candle, then went to the window. 'I close the window. That stop the duppies coming in.'

Idie, with a little fear, thought of the night that was coming again and heard herself ask, 'Are there duppies in your house?'

Mayella beamed. 'Oh no, certainly no, thank the Lord, my house has no duppies. The dragon's blood bush, that stop them.'

The dragon's blood bush was a new item to Idie, but it was the duppies in her own head that she must fight to keep away.

'Why do the duppies come?'

'They come only when a coffin is not closed, if you're not buried proper in a church.'

An unclosed coffin . . . That was Mother's coffin. Mother was not buried in a church because she killed herself. She killed herself because she was mad and haunted and I am haunted too.

'Don't leave me . . .' Idie whispered.

'It's all right, mistress – me and Phibbah stay in the house with you tonight.'

55

Pomeroy
North Devon

November 1915

Dear Idie,

Everything is rationed, but we still have our
hens and don't have to eat powdered eggs
like everyone else. Do you remember the
house cow, Clover? She's getting old and
doesn't make creamy milk any more. Stables
has signed up with a machine-gun regiment
and Silent says he'd go too if only he were
younger and Stew grumbles all the time that
it's hard to find anyone to help in the
house. As soon as I'm seventeen, which is
not very long, I'm going to sign up, because
there is nothing wrong with my feet at all.

Love Myles
PS The clues you sent for the Idie Book don't add up to anything but I think you shouldn't find any more clues because they might not be good.

'My mother was mad, Myles,' whispered Idie. 'She killed herself. It runs in the blood, madness. I haven't told you that, Myles, because that is a thing I can barely say to myself, let alone commit to paper.'

56

In the dark nights that followed the storm, there were no stars, no moon. Mayella and Phibbah took turns at Idie's side. For a fortnight her body burned like a furnace. The doctor came again, once, perhaps twice. Gypsy brought Idie wet flannels from time to time, and from time to time Homer said, 'Water for the mistress.'

On the fifteenth morning, when Mayella came, Idie asked, 'Why did they send Nelson to Pomeroy for me?'

'Gladstone work here a long, long time and he love this place. He saw Carlisle grow greedy and he saw Carlisle mean to make trouble. First your father died and then your mother, and when she die, that when my granfer send my father to fetch you back.'

'Tell me what he knew about my mother. Tell me everything, Mayella, everything.' But when Idie turned to her she found Mayella had slipped from the room.

Idie crept down the stairs to the dining room. Clutching her notebook she stood before the portrait of her grandfather Arnold and looked up into his sad eyes, and saw then that he was looking towards the gatehouse where Honey had then lived with Enoch. *Honey*. Idie pulled up the sleeve of her nightdress and stared as if mesmerized at the bare skin of her arm. She lifted her other hand and touched it to her skin gently. She stared down and then stretched out both her arms and looked at them wonderingly, turning her palms first uppermost then downward.

'I never knew –'

She dropped her arms suddenly and turned to her father and saw for the first time that Cecil's skin was so much darker than her own, and how his eyes were black and troubled. *Did you know what was happening to my mother, that it ran the blood, that it would happen to me?* She howled and tore at the book in her hands, page after page ripped till all the pieces of it were shredded and she was blind with tears. She collapsed sobbing to the floor, the shredded papers all about her.

Somewhere there were alarmed calls. Shouts rang through all the empty spaces of the house.

'The missus! Where the missus?'

The voices came again, nearer, and now there was another voice among them.

'Get me a blanket, cold water.'

The same voice came again, whispering, 'Why did no one tell me? Why did you not call for me?'

Idie clasped her hands over her eyes because of all the lamps and lanterns. 'Fasten the shutters,' she instructed. 'Put out the lights. Put out the voices in my head.' She tore at her hair, and banged her fists against her forehead. 'It – it was always here – here – here – always in me – in my blood, in my veins . . . waiting.'

A blanket was placed around her shoulders.

'How long's she been like this?' Austin whispered to Mayella, and Idie looked his way with wild, unseeing eyes.

'They sent me away from Pomeroy. I wanted rainshine eyes and sunshine hair, I wanted to stay there, to be like them . . .'

Austin put an arm around her shoulders and whispered, 'It's rather good you're not.'

'She – sent me away when I was small . . .' Idie's fingers clawed at the blanket. 'She put me on a boat . . . she was mad and cruel. There was no church burial – haunted, my house is haunted because of her, and she gave it to Carlisle – they sent for me again – and brought me here but it is not mine – and one day I will leave, and where will I go then? . . . Carlisle and my mother's watery sister will live here – the trumpet flowers told me that when they crept into my bed and put their taste in my mouth, their smell in my veins.'

'Get the doctor back, Mayella,' said Austin. 'Send Reuben for him, quick.'

Idie clawed at the blanket and clutched it up to her chin. 'Poison,' she whispered. 'They're trying to poison me. I am scared of the light, scared of the moon when she grins and laughs – and scared that the stars will fall –'

'It's all right,' Austin whispered. 'It will be all right.'

57

After a week or more the rain stopped suddenly, as if turned off by a tap. The mildewing books on the shelf by Idie's bed gave off a damp earthy smell that mingled with the wet of the vines. The fierce, long fever was ebbing, the heat running out of her veins, leaving only fears and shadows inside her.

The door opened and a current of air came through, brisk as a dash of icy water. A cool hand was placed on her forehead, her hand turned over and the pulse of her wrist counted.

'The fever's dropped. She's overwrought, no more than that, nothing more sinister. She'll return slowly to herself in due course.' The doctor put his things back in his bag.

Then Austin spoke and Idie was surprised that he was there. 'Stay with her, Mayella, don't leave her side.'

The door shut and Mayella bathed Idie's forehead. Idie asked weakly, 'Baronet?'

'Sampson groom the horse in the house, feed the

horse in the house, make the horse fine and shining.'

'Bring Enoch to me, Mayella.'

Enoch came and stood in the doorway, a little anxious. Idie looked for a minute at the man whose wife was her own grandmother. His hat had grown still more dilapidated, tufts of it sticking up now at all angles and fraying as though a bouquet of flowers had sprouted there. Idie smiled, thinking it was good to have someone about the place out of whose head flowers grew. She pushed the sheets aside and rose and went to him.

'Enoch –' she asked gently – 'Enoch, Honey was your wife?'

Enoch smiled broadly and removed the fragile hat and said, still beaming, 'Yes, mistress, Honey my wife.' He beamed again. 'She were a beautiful woman.'

'She was my grandmother.'

He smiled again and chuckled. 'She love me but also she love de master, your grandfather, Master Arnold, an' Master Arnold he love her, because all the world loved Honey. Yes, mistress, is so, for she were pretty like the sun, an' pretty like the night.'

Idie smiled and took his hand and held it in both her own.

58

The next day Mayella bathed Idie from head to toe and led her to the wardrobe. Austin had sent note that he was coming to see how Millicent was, and Idie thought how like a boy it was to say he was coming not to see her who'd been so ill, but to find out how a mongoose had been faring all this while on a soft and downy pillow.

'The doctor tried to move them out of the room, the mongoose and the pigeon. And that little mongoose she only small as a mango –' Mayella bared her own pretty teeth and snarled – 'but she got sharp teeth and she go like so and then the pigeon he fix the eye like so on the doctor, and the feathers on the pigeon's head, they tremble like all the wrath of heaven is in him and like the Day of Judgement is come and then the white doctor he step quick-quick to the door. Oh yes, they like two angels, the mongoose and the pigeon.'

'PARAKEET,' said Idie.

Mayella then said she'd get the egg for the mongoose,

banana bread for the pigeon and lemonade for Massa Austin because Phibbah in the kitchen was too busy waiting for the Second Coming to put the cake on the plate. Mayella buttoned Idie's dress and placed Homer on Idie's shoulder, Millicent in Idie's straw basket.

'Baronet,' breathed Idie, leaning over the balustrade. She went to him and rested her head against his cheek, and then she felt a little cold nose nuzzling about her knee and looked down to see Delilah there, her eyes deep and full of sorrow.

'Aunt Celia?' asked Idie, noticing then that there were no cut flowers on the hall table.

'Miss Celia she not here. No one seen her,' commented Mayella, 'and that Delilah she cryin' all mornin' and walking in circles roun' Miss Celia's chair.'

For a moment Idie was withdrawn and lost in thought. *Celia is my mother's sister. Whatever she may have done or want to do, it is my duty to look after her.*

'Come, missus,' said Mayella. 'Master Austin is waiting on the terrace.'

At the door she said, 'Master Austin, the missus still not herself. You stay ten minutes only.'

'Mayella,' answered Austin, 'your mistress is prickly as a porcupine and is sure to drive me away long before ten minutes is up.'

Idie walked slowly out and stood before him, her

head high, her heart numb, her arms wrapped tightly around herself.

He was once my friend, she thought. *But now he knows what is coming, what I will be. Now he knows what is in my blood . . .*

'Why did you come?' she asked.

'Of course I came. Why would I not come, Idie?'

She whispered, 'I am a bad lot.'

'Oh, I know that,' he answered airily, smiling at her.

But Idie was overwrought and burst out, 'You knew all along, didn't you? Knew everything and never said – all those times we spent together and you never said –'

'Knew what? What did I know?'

She clutched his arms and shook him, saying, 'You never said. Never told me anything.'

She swayed and fell to the ground then, and Austin called for Mayella and for the doctor.

While he held her, he whispered, 'Told you what, Idie? Who've you been listening to? I told you all you needed to know.'

59

The next afternoon, Idie began to teach both Mayella and Phibbah to read and write. There was a space in her now, a crater in her centre like a grave, but she would do some good while she was here, while she could. They were upstairs in the loggia where the breeze was brisk and cool.

'D, E, F,' said Idie.

Phibbah's concentration was fierce, her bony hand gripping her pencil like a vulture's claw clutching a tiny mouse, her letters swift and precise.

Idie found it hard to keep Mayella's mind on the matter in hand, for she was distracted and absent. She watched the girl's brow crease, her hand hesitate halfway through a C. Gypsy sat beside Mayella, with her cheek and own paper, making a mark on her paper if ever Mayella did on hers.

Mayella slammed the pencil on the table and looked up, eyes brimming. 'How do I think about this, mistress, when my head is so full of worry? When Sampson is going to go in two months from today?'

'Sampson?' breathed Idie, stricken. 'Not Sampson?'

There were footsteps in the corridor and Idie turned. Sampson and Enoch walked together towards the loggia. Behind them was Sampson's brother, Reuben. Sampson was self-conscious in khaki uniform which stood about him like a cardboard casing meant for someone else entirely.

Phibbah rose squawking from the table and she ran at him and tore at the buttons of his tunic, and reaching as she did only up to his collar, she beat him about his chest.

'Grandma, I am going; there's nothing you can do,' he said gently, taking her hands from him and turning to Idie. He smiled, shyly, proudly, as he spoke. 'Mistress.'

'Not you, Sampson . . .' whispered Idie.

Sampson turned the black peaked cap around in his hands, fingering the badge, the Tudor crown and ship of Columbus in full sail proper, its laurel-and-palm wreath.

'Is in maybe six month from now that I will go,' he said.

Mayella looked at him, the tears shining in her eyes.

'Mistress, I am going to miss this place, the horse and all,' said Sampson, and Idie was put in mind of Stables and she reflected that it was a sign of good character to work with horses. Perhaps the horses made the man good, not the man the horses.

'I bring Reuben here.' Reuben stepped out from behind Sampson, too shy to raise his face to Idie. 'He's a good boy, my brother. He will stay till I come back, take good care of everything.'

'I know,' said Idie, smiling at Reuben, 'but I'll miss you, Sampson.'

Sampson shuffled a bit and said, 'I bring Enoch also. He wants to talk.' Enoch stepped forward and raised the ancient hat from his head.

There was silence for a while, Enoch looking at the floor and turning the tufted hat about in his hands.

In the silence Sampson said, 'Enoch got something to say, mistress.'

Enoch looked at the floor still, and after a second or two Sampson said, 'Maybe I say it for him.'

Idie drew herself up, cold pins of fear pricking her skin. 'Yes, Sampson, go ahead.'

Sampson looked at the old man and Enoch nodded at him. 'Mistress, Carlisle, he's going to make trouble. He's got the will and Enoch think he's going to take that will to the bank.'

'It is no matter,' said Idie quietly.

'But we don't know what is on that will, mistress. Gladstone he witnessed it, and he sign it but he never knew what was in the thing that he signed. He signed it only because the mistress your mother told him to, but she were not in her right mind.'

'She was not in her right mind?' asked Idie quietly.

There was silence and Idie asked, 'Why didn't Gladstone tell me about the will?' She looked from Mayella to Sampson to Enoch. 'Why did no one ever say anything to me?' She bowed her head. No one had said anything about it of course, for Enoch was much loved and Carlisle his only son. Idie was a small thing caught up in the ties of family and marriage and blood that threaded the people here one to another.

After a while Enoch said, 'He was ashamed, mistress, same as I. Ashamed he cannot read.'

Gladstone couldn't read or write. Idie winced. She'd been so blind and had never thought. That was why Clement did the accounts and paperwork. All that Gladstone had achieved over the years he'd achieved without knowing how to read or write.

She stood and looked at each of them again. 'Why didn't anyone tell me about the will?'

'I was also afraid. I live here all my life; I never want go nowhere else and Carlisle is my son,' said Enoch, his old head still bowed.

Idie lowered her voice and said gently, 'I would never make you leave, I promise.' Then she asked, 'Where is Quarterly?'

'No one knows,' answered Enoch. 'He's been seen roun' here and he goin' make trouble. He hiding maybe, but that will – is certain now he gon' take it to the bank, for now that Gladstone is gone there is no one to say that Gladstone could not read and could not be a witness to that will. There were no one else there but Phibbah, and Carlisle knows Phibbah never gonna speak in all her days.'

Phibbah chewed her pipe and stared into the middle distance. Sampson, Enoch and Mayella watched Idie, but she said, wearily, 'It is no matter, let Carlisle Quarterly take all that he wants.'

Enoch and Sampson then stepped back and Sampson said, 'Is all, mistress. We sorry for your troubles. I glad you teach them writing. Mayella she say she gon' write to me when I be gone.'

'God bless you, Sampson, and keep you safe,' said Idie. She sank on to a chair and dropped her head.

Phibbah rose, and as she passed Idie she laid her hand on Idie's shoulder, light and cool as the claw of a bird.

When news came later that day of the British disaster at Ypres, Idie took a sheet of writing paper from her desk.

Myles,

Your feet ARE very flat and I know that because I used to tie your laces. Lots of things change when you get older, but one's feet do not get less flat with the passing years.

Idie

Austin came and they sat together beneath the calabash tree but he was uneasy and distracted. *It is as if I am an invalid or dying relative that he must do his duty by,* Idie thought. *His mind is elsewhere; he does not want to be with me.* She turned from Austin and watched old Enoch go about the garden, then smiled and said, 'It is as if I have a grandfather about the place. Enoch's wife was my grandmother. Did you ever know that?'

Austin nodded. 'Mother told me that when you were ill.'

Idie stretched out her arm in the sun and turned it up and then down and said, 'Mayella says my father was not one thing nor the other. I should have seen that from his portrait but I never did.'

'You don't look for such things, Idie, because they're not important to you. Mother says your mother never cared about those things either. She says no one else would have married your father in those days but her. It would have been hard for him, you know.' He looked down at the skin of his own arm and said,

'These things run deeply here.'

As he rose to leave, Austin asked, 'Has Carlisle been here at all?'

'No one's seen him, not since Gladstone died. Nor Aunt Celia.'

Something slipped from Austin's pocket, making a small metallic clatter across the floor. Idie snatched it up. She opened her palm flat. The badge of the Boy Scouts was there.

'I see now what takes up your time,' she said, very quiet.

All the things she'd thought meant so much to them both were turned to dust by that badge, and she looked up at him and saw his face, the way it was more set, the bony adult shape of it showing. She flung the badge at him.

'Go on, go back to them, go back to your scouts.'

'Idie—'

'Go, go to war if that is what you want.'

Austin bent his head and paused, then rose and left and she was again alone, thinking of the times they'd roamed the creeks and gullies, the times when the ground had been firm beneath her feet and the sky blue above her head, when the rain had had sunshine in it because she'd known she'd had a mother who was strong and kind and capable; now the mother of her imaginings had been taken from her and another put in her place, Idie was scared and frightened of what was to come. She sat alone, all the sunshininess in her gone, and she ran her fingers through those times that were round and shining as marbles and knew that they would never come again.

When Carlisle returned he would present the will and Bathsheba would go to him, but Idie no longer cared. She'd do what was right until Carlisle returned; she'd dedicate herself to the running of the place, plant cane and cacao, raise the wages, teach those who couldn't to read and write and then one day Carlisle and Celia would come, and she would go.

Austin had come but he'd not stayed for long, and in her loneliness Idie picked up a pen and wrote again to Myles.

Bathsheba

February 1916

Dear Myles,

I did get a fever like you said, but I didn't die.

I have got an overlook pea and a dragon's blood bush because now I know that terrible things can happen in life, but the worst thing would be if you went to war.

For so long I hoped you would visit me, and now even if you wanted to you can't because of the war. When it is all over, I will still be somewhere here, with a mongoose and a monkey at my table, waiting for you, should you ever come.

Love Idie

62

After what may have been a week or more, Celia reappeared at Bathsheba. Idie was at her window when she saw Celia drifting about the garden, a basket on her arm and scissors in her hand. Delilah skipped and skittered about at her heels, finding joy again in everything, but Celia's movements were slow, and the broad and flopping sort of hat she wore added to the picture of melancholy she presented.

She's here because this is the only place she knows.

Gladstone had said that, oh so long ago, when Idie'd been small and strong.

Idie watched Celia gather a bunch of lilies and was overwhelmed with sadness for her. Because my mother was afraid of the light, Celia wanted to close the shutters. Because my mother loved the house to be full of flowers, her sister goes about the garden still with her scissors.

Delilah trotted after Celia, and Idie saw Celia's soft, sad smile as she caressed Delilah's uplifted face.

The thoughts in her head are like water – any man

can give them the colour he wants, said Idie to herself, remembering Mayella's words.

She dressed and went down to the garden. Celia was bent over the lilies.

'I'm glad you're back, Aunt Celia,' said Idie.

Celia seemed hesitant to rise.

'Celia –' began Idie.

Celia lifted her head and looked into Idie's eyes.

'Celia . . . ?' whispered Idie, startled, for Celia had a black-and-purple bruise on the fine white skin of her temple and one eye was swollen and half shut.

'Carlisle?' asked Idie.

Celia gave no answer and it was as if she'd never heard the name, for as she gazed at Idie, her eyes clouded and grew strange and remote. Very slowly, she stretched out a hand, the fingers of it hovering before Idie's face, moved, trembling, to Idie's hair, and Idie asked, 'Am I very like her? Am I very like your sister?'

Celia nodded and her eyes glimmered with tears.

London

March 1916

Dear Idie,

A long time has gone by since I last wrote, and so much has changed. I have enlisted [despite the persistent flatness of my feet] and am bound for France. There was an order to evacuate Gallipoli. They had a terrible time of it there and Benedict was not himself when he came home on leave. He's posted now to Alexandria so we'll be far apart.

Love Myles

PS I'm glad you didn't die of your fever and glad you have a dragon's blood bush and some overlook peas, and if your island hasn't fallen into the sea I will visit when the war's over.

Idie was very alone in the time that followed the fever. As she grew stronger she went sometimes with Phibbah or Mayella to the market in Carriacou. She heard the white women whispering that she went about only with the local people, that she had no visitors, that she kept the company only of animals, but she'd not been brought up by Grancat for nothing and knew better than to care what people said. Mostly she was at Bathsheba, knitting or teaching Mayella and Phibbah their letters and thinking of Myles who was in France, of Sampson who would soon leave Bathsheba.

Mayella scowled at Idie's knitting. 'You think the soldiers will wear that? The cold going to come in through that hole . . . and that one . . . and this one . . .'

Idie looked at the perfectly formed sleeve that hung from Mayella's needles. She saw too the gaudy orange of it and doubted that any grown man would wear such a thing even if it did have no holes in it. Sighing, she put her own knitting down and gazed up into the improbable leaf-circles of the calabash. A wave of melancholy swept through her. She remembered how she'd once thought that they were so round and so green that Myles might have drawn them.

The leaves stirred and whispered as if to tell of faraway events, and the jasmine shrugged her blossom to the grass. The outer world had crept in on moonshiny Bathsheba, the shadows of distant happenings fell now in jagged shapes across the lawn.

Gypsy grasped Idie's knitting and coiled it around her own little neck, thinking she looked mighty fine.

'That for the soldiers. Why does that monkey think she needs a sleeve for round her neck?' demanded Mayella. Gypsy looked up at the sky and into the calabash tree and at the guilty ground doves in it, who had surely put that knitting about her neck and not she.

Four years had passed since Idie had first seen that calabash tree. Myles was now seventeen and had enlisted. Benedict, now an officer with pips on his sleeves, was in the desert fighting the straightforward Turk. She herself was sixteen, and all the sunshininess was gone from her and in its place lay the shadow of the insanity that would one day swoop down on her like a dark bird of prey and take away her reason.

'The newspaper, mistress, come,' said Mayella. Together they rose and walked to the kitchen. Idie would sit with Phibbah and Mayella and read aloud to them from the papers. Sometimes Celia would be there and she would sew and Mayella would knit and Phibbah would stare as if backwards through all the sorrow and all the grief of all the ages.

The Greeks' continued refusal to withdraw troops from Salonika . . .

Phibbah's mouth puckered and the lines down her cheeks hardened and deepened like ravines.

The withdrawal of Allied forces from Macedonia . . .

'Where's that?' Mayella's eyes widened.

Western Persia occupied by Russian forces . . .

The West Indies Regiment serving on the Eastern Front . . .

'Where's that? Oh Lord, where's that? Is my father there?' Mayella cried.

Phibbah chewed her pipe.

Celia picked up her sewing and, watching her, Idie said, 'Aunt Celia, I will buy you a machine, a sewing machine. Would you like that?'

Celia looked up and smiled then at Idie, but Mayella snorted and rose and thrust some sheets of paper into Idie's hand. 'There more important things you must do,' she commanded. 'First you write to the lawyer man. You better now, mistress. Is time you stop feeling sorry and find some fight in you.'

Idie stared at the sheet in her hand, at the pen Mayella placed before her. 'You write, Miss Idie, or what's gon' happen to us all? Only you can stop what Carlisle plan to do.'

'It is no matter what he plans or doesn't plan to do,' said Idie

'It's not for you, Miss Grace; it's for us all as work here,' retorted Mayella.

Idie took the pen. She glanced briefly at Celia, but Celia's head was still bent deeply over her stitching, so Idie then began to write.

Bathsheba

20th May 1916

Dear Mr Webb,

You may have been notified by Mr Pugsley of Barclays that a will has been lodged at the bank by Carlisle Quarterly.

Satisfied, Mayella left the room.

I am told this will is my mother's and that it entails the estate to Mr Quarterly. I do not know where he is, but it is certain he intends to claim it.

Idie looked out through the window to where the sun rained through the leaves of the candle trees on to the white stone forecourt and thought, *What does it* matter? I will not be able to look after these people. Perhaps Carlisle will do a better job. Still, she finished the letter then took a second sheet and wrote to Myles.

Bathsheba

10th May 1916

Dear Myles,

I am learning to knit. If you go to France you are in <u>great danger</u> of getting one of my jerseys. You'll know it's mine if it has big holes in it. I am afraid for you and for Benedict but I am glad he has at least left Gallipoli.

We've raised the wages and done all we can, but still the people from here leave to serve YOUR king and fight YOUR wars. I pay them all I can, but still they go. Even Sampson has signed up and will soon leave.

My foreman died. It may have been an accident or it may not, but Carlisle has gone into hiding. My foreman's name was Gladstone. I was very fond of him and he was a pillar of the place.

Aunt Celia has come back. She disappeared for a day or two and no one knows where she went but now she is back with Delilah and I am glad she's here. I am so glad too that one day you will visit me. I shall count the MINUTES from here till then for I am so alone and Austin rarely comes to see me now.

Love Idie

65

Pomeroy

1st July 1916

Dear Miss Grace,

I am sorry you should have had this worry about Carlisle Quarterly. That and the death of old Gladstone must have been quite a blow.

He took good care of things, ran a tight ship. So a loyal man is difficult to replace, but Pugsley tells me young Clement is capable and has his father's spirit, and I am glad there is another Mayley to hold the reins.

With regard to Carlisle Quarterly, I have made enquiries and have discovered that there is a search warrant out for him. He will be found sooner or later. Pugsley tells me that it was Miss Celia who went to

the police. It appears Carlisle had promised
to marry her and share the place with her.
After Gladstone's death he turned against
her and beat her and she went then to the
police.

The war wears on and still I am unable to
return to Bathsheba. We pray and hope that
it will soon end.

Yours,
Algernon Webb

Poor Celia who thought Carlisle would marry her and
had been dreaming of that all these years. Idie looked
out into the garden and saw old Enoch there, clipping
the hibiscus. *Enoch.*

She rose and went out to him.

'Enoch, there's a warrant out for Carlisle's arrest –'

Enoch's old eyes misted with fear. He looked at
Idie and said, 'Is God's will maybe . . .'

'No, he is your only son and he is my half-uncle
and you *must* warn him, Enoch, about the warrant.
Tell him to get away from here, perhaps go to another
island where they will not find him.'

66

Idie saw the word *Egypt* in the dusty paper at her feet and bent to pick it up.

**Our Boys are Doing Splendidly in
Egypt, Mesopotamia and France
ANOTHER CONTINGENT OF THE
BRITISH WEST INDIES REGIMENT
WILL BE SAILING SOON
ROLL UP, MEN, MAKE IT THE BEST**

GOD SAVE THE KING

More men, dear God. Must they have more men? Myles had been in France a month or so, but there'd been no letter from him.

'What's that?' asked Mayella, scowling at the words on the poster.

Idie screwed it up and put it in a bin.

'Why you do that?'

Idie turned away and ploughed on through the

crowded market towards the post office. There was a letter waiting. She saw the handwriting on the envelope and she clutched Mayella.

'Myles! Myles has written.'

She turned away from the counter, tearing at it, and Mayella stepped forward in her place and said, 'The mistress needs two stamps for England. She's not thinking straight now she got a letter full of words.'

Idie slipped outside and sat on the bench beneath the tamarind beside the woman who sold fresh coconut water, while Mayella went from stall to stall filling her straw basket.

67

Ypres

August 1916

Dear Idie,

Grancat said once that war puts everything in
perspective, and now I have so much time on
my hands to think, I know that he was right.
I've been thinking so much of you and of how we
treated you, and I am ashamed that I could once
have written in the Idie book, 'IDIE IS NOT
ONE OF US'; that so petty a difference could
once have meant so much. I've been thinking too
of how you were sent so very far away, so young
and so very much on your own. I asked Grancat
before I left for France why it was that he let
you go. He said it was for your good, or that was
what he thought then. He was silent awhile and
then said, 'Some things are easier when you're

young. You see it takes experience and the passing of the years before we're able to tell what will be a turning point in life and what won't. I only hope Idie didn't understand what a turning point leaving Pomeroy would be. They say children don't have the wisdom to tell what's in the ordinary sort of run of things and what's outside of them. I hope that was the case when Idie left, Myles, I hope that was the case, because it's all I have in my defence, God help me.'

That evening by the fire when I thought he was dozing he suddenly turned and said, 'Never look back, Myles, never look back.' But he'd been looking back. I know that because he must've been thinking about you all along.

There was head and heart – somewhere – in what he did to you, though I'm sure you couldn't see it then. I think Grancat thought sending you away was giving you your best chance in life, people and society being what they are. Did he ever tell you that? I shouldn't think he did. He's always been economical with words. Only the dogs, in his opinion, require any great amount of converse.

Have things turned out all right? I do hope they have and that you forgive us all for what we did to you. I will write again soon.

All love, Myles

PS As soon as the war's over I'll come and visit. All attempts to educate me will be over and I'll have a penny or two of my own.

PPS Benedict's been transferred to the British West Indies Regiment in Egypt. He's a bit put out about that as he thinks its rather infra dig to fight alongside the colonials. It's a funny thing though, isn't it, to think that there might be some of your lot alongside him. How unexpected life is.

Mayella handed Idie an envelope. Idie saw the precise, careful hand she'd last seen so many years ago when she was just a child. Grancat's hand. *Oh God.*

Pomeroy

30th August 1916

Dear Idie

Myles is dead. He died at Ypres. He'd been there only two weeks. Two weeks, good God. He was writing to you when the sniper got him. I enclose what was found in his tunic.

You'll be sixteen or so now, though of course I'll always see you as you were the day you left: a brave, dark-eyed child, holding a fine English horse.

You know I don't hold with words or letters much. Forgive me.

Yours aye,
Grancat

Idie's trembling fingers slowly unwrapped the tissue paper from around a photograph. On the reverse was written:

Ypres
For Idie
Are your suns always gold and your leaves always
green? I will visit your equatorial idyll and dine
with mongooses . . .

Then the sniper had found his mark.

Idie turned the photograph over.

Myles, in the uniform of the Scots Guards, the thistle and the wreath he'd so wanted on his cap. The sunshiny hair, the rain-shiny eyes, the freckles still on his clear face, Myles, the attic room they'd shared, the long summer evenings, the dark winter nights, his hand clutching the brown velvet of the curtains, Myles who put wishes on stars, Myles who kept a list of all the things he knew about Idie, Myles of the pirates and picaroons, Myles of the blackberry stains and undone laces, Myles whose tears were so round because his heart was so much bigger than everyone else's.

Myles, dead.

Idie lifted her head and saw the leaves so unlikely-round and green that Myles might have drawn them. She clasped the paper in her hands and howled, with the brief short howl of an animal whose throat is cut.

69

Bathsheba

September 1916

Dear Austin,

Once I told you I was surprised that you wanted to be my friend because no one else would be. I didn't know then quite how surprised I should have been because then I knew nothing. Now I know so much that nothing can ever hurt me again, and if you never do anything else for me, promise me one thing only:
    THAT YOU'LL NEVER GO TO WAR.

From Idie

On the envelope she wrote:

For Austin Hayne
DO NOT PUT IN THE DUNGEON

70

Austin sat a little awkwardly on the balustrade.
Through the window Idie watched him carefully. He
didn't swing his legs nor whistle. He'd not come for a
long while, this boy who'd once been her friend.

'Not *him* too . . .' she breathed. 'Not him, please,
not him . . .'

She saw folded and sticking out from his trouser
pocket a piece of paper and wondered if it was the
note she'd written.

'Missus! Where you? Master Austin has come.'

Idie shrank back against the curtains as Mayella
came into the hall.

'Miss Idie. You come with me. Master Austin
here.'

Mayella took Idie by the hand and led her out.

'Idie,' said Austin gently.

Mayella led Idie to a chair but Idie didn't sit. As
Mayella left, Austin went to her and tried to take her
hand.

'Listen Idie—'

'Why should I listen now when once you could have told me something, something about someone that was so important to me, and you never did?'

Austin was silent. He bowed his head and said eventually, 'Look, Idie, I never spoke because – well – what could I have said? There was nothing I could say that wouldn't only have made things harder for you, nothing that could help you.'

'Go, Austin. Go away.'

'No. Don't send me away, because I've something I must tell you, something you must hear only from me.'

Idie stepped back towards the door. 'No.' She clapped her hands over her ears.

'Idie, hear me out. Idie, I've enlisted—'

'No!' she yelped as if scalded, snatching her hands now over her eyes. 'No, no, Austin, not you too. Not now – now – Myles – Myles died, *Myles*, Austin, did you know that?'

Through all the empty space that was inside her, pain howled and gusted. She bent her head and her hands scraped the skin of her face.

He came close to her and placed a hand on her shoulder,

'I leave tomorrow, on the same ship as Sampson.'

Idie shook herself free and walked into the hall. Her back turned, she said in a level, dead sort of voice, 'Go. If that is what you want, go.'

Austin followed her into the hall and said from the foot of the stairs, 'Look forward, Idie; no good ever came of looking back. Live your own life, and live it the way you want it.'

71

'Come, mistress.'

Mayella's dress today was of white broderie, her hair freshly braided and ribboned. She led Idie to the wardrobe. 'You're coming with us. Reuben and Clement are going to take us all, me and Phibbah and Miss Celia and –' she hesitated – 'Enoch he come too. It's not good for you to stay so much in the house. Sampson and Master Austin both are sailing today.'

There was a new dress in the wardrobe, and when Idie went downstairs in it Celia was there and she smiled shyly at Idie. Idie went to her and hugged her, and when she drew back she saw that Celia's eyes were filled with tears.

An immense crowd was gathered in the harbour. The BWIR marched along the waterfront and people stretched their arms out to them. Idie watched them pass, saw their shining eyes and smooth young faces and shrank back, numb with horror at what might lie ahead for them.

Celia started and Idie turned and saw.

'Quarterly,' she breathed, 'enlisted.'

Idie saw the trembling in Celia's hands and the tears in old Enoch's eyes and she went and stood between them and took each by the hand and stayed with them.

The bands played and the flags flapped and Sampson passed by, tall and smiling, head turned as he searched the sea of faces for Mayella. Mayella saw him and waved, her eyes shining with pride. Idie watched Sampson pass by and started with fear for the boy who was so good and gentle. Panic stricken, she searched the ranks of men for Austin, but it was Mayella who saw him first.

'Is Massa Austin there; he very handsome, mistress.'

Idie started with shock to see him in full uniform. She saw then that he was strong and tall and fine, and when he marched past he turned his face a fraction to her, and Idie saw then that the boy she had known was gone and in his place stood a man who would never again go about with mongooses in his pockets.

The sun sank and streamed across the water, the ship sailed out and the band played and people waved and there were tears in the eyes of all that were there.

Taking Gypsy's cold dry hand in her own, Idie turned for home.

72

There was a letter on the hall table.

Bissett

22nd September 1916

Dear Idie,

I took a risk and came back to say goodbye.

Mother says do go to her if ever you need anything. She's not at all a usual kind of person and you'll be all right with her. She's working at Boscobelle. It's a special sort of hospital. Some of the first men have already returned - the lot who went to Africa in 1915. The ones whose nerves have been fractured by the shelling and the noise are housed and cared for at Boscobelle.

Father sails with me. I see now, only too late, that you didn't know that, did you?

He is chaplain to my regiment. You see, I could never have let him go and not gone myself. How could I not have gone, when he is going? How could I not when he is sixty and I am seventeen? My first duty is to him, and besides, I couldn't make anything better for you by staying.

You are a spiky, porcupiny kind of person and I know you won't write, but I, at least, will miss you, and you, at least, might. Wish me luck.

Love Austin

73

Idie folded the letter carefully and that night she took Tommy from the bathtub and walked down to the beach and watched him follow the stream of the moon, flip-flopping on his paddles down the sand to the sea.

She remembered the tiny beetle-sized turtle that Austin had brought to Bathsheba and put in her bathtub. She remembered Myles who was dead, Benedict in the desert, Sampson and Austin bound for Egypt. She thought of the boy who'd once filled Bathsheba with monkeys and toucans and knew that he had changed, that the girl she'd been was also changing. Shadows had gathered and massed in her, and her spirit at seventeen was the ghost of what it had been at twelve. She was as if stripped bare, the last strands of childhood finally falling from her.

A wave ruffled over the sand and carried Tommy away on a flurry of moonlit surf. Watching him go, silent tears slid down Idie's cheeks for the sadness of all the things that change.

PART V

March 1917

74

1917 was the year of the alphabet and of knitting. There were newspapers that came all too often and letters that came only too infrequently. Neither the police nor the postal service were operating; the people of the island were restless and discontented.

In the mornings Idie rode about the fields with Clement, learning the nooks and crannies of the place. In the afternoons she stayed with the women in the kitchen, Celia at her new sewing machine, Mayella knitting, Phibbah writing in her exercise book. Gypsy rope-danced in the bougainvillea, Baronet wandered about the hall and Homer looked down on all the inferior species in the garden from the balustrade, and it could seem that nothing at Bathsheba had changed. But when the palms were shaken by a breeze it was as if they'd some news to tell, as if their torpor had been ruffled by the roar of distant guns.

Idie raised her eyes to the kitchen window and scowled. Homer had acquired a new skill. He'd begun to whistle and he favoured Austin's rowdiest sort of tune and the sound of it jarred on Idie's nerves.

'G, H, I, J,' said Idie, her mind still on Homer's annoying new habit.

Gypsy made jabs at her page with her pencil and Mayella said, 'Oh Lord, even that monkey is faster than me.'

'K, L, M, N.'

Reuben came to the door and waited, hesitant to enter the women's domain.

'Miss Mayella . . .'

Mayella saw the envelope in his hand, the words 'ON ACTIVE SERVICE' and the ring of the Army Post Office, leapt to her feet and snatched it from him. Idie saw Austin's handwriting and started at it.

Mayella tore at the envelope, lips trembling, pulled out the letter and looked at all the words on it.

'Oh my Lord!' Mayella's face quivered, like the surface of a stream. Deep-eyed and picturesque indignation formed on her face. She looked from Idie to Phibbah and back again.

'What Sampson do that for? What he want write so many words for?'

Phibbah rose, waving her arms about, and shooed Reuben from the room with squawking cockerel sounds.

Reuben grinned. 'All right, Grandma, I goin' now.'

Idie picked up the letter and read to Mayella.

Jordan

April 1917

Dear Miss Mayella,

I am in Machine Gun Crew number 162. We all West Indians and men from Guyana from the Bahamas also and we are working with the Australians. We are always digging or marching. We march across Sinai desert and see no enemy all the way. At Gaza many men were killed by the Turks and many men sick of the malaria. It's mighty hot, hotter than home. Your father here too, but not in the 162 crew. He's a lance corporal now. I have bit of trouble from a white officer but is nothing to worry for.

Miss Mayella, you keeping well? And the mistress? She well? And young Reuben? Does Reuben look after the mistress's horse good?

Write to me soon, and I will ask someone here read your letter to me. Master Austin write this letter. I tell him what to write and he write it all down. Maybe the mistress read it to you.

Is a fine place there, Miss Mayella, back

home. Now I seen all the other bits of the world, I know you, Miss Mayella Mayley, be in the best bit of it all.

Sampson Sealy

Phibbah looked with concern and affection on Mayella – whose lips were trembling and whose eyes were deep with moonshine – who loved Phibbah's own grandson so.

'Oh my Lord, my own father a corporal – and what does that mean?' demanded Mayella. 'And Sampson –' she took the letter from Idie and squinted at it in disgust – 'Is so, I going to learn to write quick and tell him there is no reason to be putting them words on paper. If he only stay here, there no need to write them when he's by my side to speak them.'

She snatched up her pencil crossly and formed a determined, triumphant sort of A.

75

'Sampson gets money from the army, all the men from here get land by the Rio Grande, we'll buy a house maybe one day together, me and Sampson. The government is giving the soldiers land for cattle when they come back, land and money,' said Mayella one afternoon.

Idie looked up, stricken, but Mayella bent her head and pouted in mock annoyance at the letters she was to copy.

As Idie tried to accommodate the idea of Mayella one day leaving, the door opened abruptly and Austin's mother Edith walked in, brisk and small and bright-eyed. She yanked off her hat, revealing white hair cut in such jagged layers that it might have been done with garden shears. With an air of incontrovertible authority and the volume of a gong, she said, 'I have it on good account that you are not faint of heart. Idie Grace, are you faint of heart?'

Idie had not yet formulated an answer when Edith said, 'No, I don't think you are. Well, get your hat.'

She stared at Idie and mused as though thinking aloud, 'Marvellous. *Most poetic*. One couldn't make her up, could one? I must use her.' Edith turned to the door. 'No time to waste, we're doing the afternoon shift.'

Idie stared at her. *Most poetic? She told Austin my mother was a poem*, Idie thought. *So she thinks we are alike. She thinks I will one day end the way my mother did.* Idie shrank inwardly from Edith, who had known her mother. *I do not want to talk about these things. I do not want to know more than I know already.*

'Of course, certain things won't do at all.' Edith was looking about the room, and Idie too looked about the little kitchen, at the knitting on the table, at Phibbah and her pipe, at Celia, at Gypsy, wondering which particular element of it all would not do. She concluded it was the fact of the small monkey at the table, pencil in hand and the alphabet written out for her.

'Get your hat, girl, chop-chop,' said Edith, and Idie did as she was bid and selected a straw hat from the array of them behind the kitchen door, placed it on her head and tilted her chin at Edith to tell her that she didn't care that certain things would not do. Gypsy sprang to Idie's side and selected a hat for herself. She tended to favour the yellow one, possibly on account of it being the same colour as bananas.

Edith paid no attention to the monkey in the yellow that clambered into the trap and sat beside her. Daisy trotted away and poor Baronet whinnied that

Daisy should be leaving so soon.

'Number one,' said Edith, 'I shall bring Celia my *Vogue* patterns. She's got a good hand but a poor eye. She needs direction, direction's the thing. Number two, poetry. For the women. No good copying out dull old prose when learning to write. No, no, no, poetry's the thing. Number three, most important, I'm under instruction to take you, Idie Grace, in hand.'

Idie wondered if all Austin's relatives made lists and took people in hand with no warning and at unexpected hours. Idie thought that Edith was as strange and unconventional a person as she'd ever met but perhaps all poets went about giving robust instructions to comparative strangers without drawing breath while at the same time driving traps without the use of any reins at all.

When Idie could get a word in edgeways she asked, rather meekly, 'Where're we going?'

'Boscobelle Hospital, afternoon shift. This week I'll be collecting you every day at two and dropping you off at eight.'

While Edith took a notebook from her bag and busied herself with what seemed to be another list, Daisy, without any instruction at all, followed the white road that curved through high, shimmering cane. A man was hobbling towards them, hatless and meandering, in the violent sun.

With barely a glance up from her notebook Edith

said, 'Oh, do stop there, Daisy, just by that fellow.'
And Daisy did as she was bid. His home-made crutch
was bound with rope and he was singing and praying,
drifts of sense, of nonsense and of prayer, all colliding
with one another like songbirds into window panes.

'Your name?' asked Edith.

'He who calls on the name of the Lord shall be
saved . . .'

'Here, you are in need of a hat.' She placed her
own rather unusual confection firmly on his bare
head. 'Now tell me your name.'

'He who calls on the name of the Lord shall be
saved . . .'

'Oh dear, poor fellow. We'll send someone up for
him. Oh dear, how will this little island cope?'

Idie didn't answer as Edith seemed to be conversing
only with Daisy, who heaved a sad sigh by way of
answer and trotted on. Edith took up her list again.
As they crossed the spiny ridge of the island the wild
glitter and flash of the east coast came into view. On
the outskirts of Boscobelle a group of men stood
beside placards advertising the Caribbean League.
Edith pulled up and peered closely at them.

THE BLACK MAN WILL GOVERN
HIMSELF IN THE WEST INDIES. IF
NECESSARY FORCE & BLOODSHED
WILL BE USED TO ATTAIN THAT OBJECT

Once Edith had managed to read the words she said loudly, 'Force and bloodshed. Can't blame them, I'm afraid. Of course they want higher wages.' She turned to Idie. 'Another strike coming – I hope you've enough of everything?'

A young man on crutches put aside his placard and raised his hat.

'Good day, Mrs Hayne.'

'Ah, Errol,' Edith said to him, then turned to Idie and said loudly, 'Errol's feet were amputated, clean off, the pair of them.'

Idie was deeply shocked. She stared resolutely at Errol's head, but Errol simply nodded and said, 'Is so.'

'He was one of the first lot to come home. The ship was diverted to Nova Scotia and they got frostbite – no blankets on the ship – a hundred of them lost all sorts of bits of themselves. There's nothing for these men, they're destitute, no pension, nothing.'

'Is so,' said Errol again, with no trace of self-pity.

Idie, flooded with sudden anger, said through her teeth, 'That would never happen if women ruled the world. Women don't wage wars and they never forget about blankets.'

Edith turned sharply to Idie and looked at her all over, top to toe. 'Quite so, quite so. You are most advanced, *most* advanced.'

Edith had communicated somehow to Daisy that

they were to move off again, and Daisy did as she should. They drew up outside a huge stone building surrounded by a handsome garden.

Edith marched Idie across the lawn into an empty high-ceilinged hall, saying, 'Work alongside me till you know the ropes.'

A soft wind blew from one end of the place to the other. From behind closed doors and from upstairs came screams, song, prayer, moans and whimpers, all confused in a continuous incoherent stream.

Idie paused.

A refuge for the insane.

Is this where I will end my days? And am I to work here until then?

'Come along. No time to waste,' said Edith, and Idie braced herself and followed and together they moved from room to room, leading patients out into the garden, walking with them among the trees or settling them in chairs. Some were noisy, some violent or scared, wounded or maimed, but the mind of each and every one had unravelled.

Edith cajoled a man into a rattan chaise she'd placed in the speckled shade of a mango tree.

'Abraham was among the first to go out. He volunteered in 1915. The government made no provision for the wounded, none at all. There's nothing for Abraham now, he's destitute.' Edith was as flat and matter of fact as though Abraham were not there. Abraham himself was entirely silent, as though he'd been once so astonished that he'd fallen permanently into shock and would never talk again.

Idie, standing by, placed Abraham's prayer book in his hand and spread a blanket over his legs. Abraham's fingers scratched at the pages of it, and Idie turned away from Abraham, whose eyes would never see again, whose fingers could never find the page they sought.

'Not a bad place at all for a troubled mind, is it?' said Edith, looking towards a skirt of flowers around the foot of a tree fern. 'A garden's the thing, and a view of the sea. Green and blue.'

'But Abraham can't see the green and blue,' said Idie, turning away and looking out through the flame trees towards the flashing turquoise sea. She thought of Benedict and of Sampson, and wondered if Edith thought of her husband and her son.

'Oh yes, Abraham, you can, can't you? And you can hear them in your ears, feel them in your veins; they are quieting as a psalm, the green and the blue, are they not, Abraham?' Edith plucked a flower and handed it to him. 'Blue bougainvillea, Abraham. It is as a balsam to you, is it not?'

A man wandered alone about the lawn, an odd rhythmic twitch to his shoulder, as if he were forever adjusting the position of a rifle on his back. He fell suddenly to the ground and cowered in the centre of the lawn, his arms about his head, whimpering.

'Oh dear. There's Virgil,' commented Edith. 'Poor Virgil, the screaming shells, he'll carry them forever in his ears – it was the noise, you see, that cracked his sense. He's only oddments of memory left and they come and they go like birds.'

Gypsy, delighted by Virgil's antics, plucked a posy of flowers and took it to him curled aloft in her tail. She soon became a pet of all the men. Their song and nonsense enchanted her and there was no end of men to give flowers or fruit to; no end of attention and affection in return. And Idie thought, *Gypsy, at least, will love me still, when my time comes, when my own mind unravels.*

76

'The drawing room,' Edith said one morning as they drove through the gates of Bathsheba.

Idie looked up and wondered at this most recent of Edith's many mysterious pronouncements. For all Idie knew, all poetesses were moved to cryptic utterances at unexpected moments, and this time Idie decided to ignore Edith, but Edith insisted.

'Do you never go in there?' Without waiting for an answer she went on, 'No, no, I didn't think you did, and that's as well because when you do you'll find you've no curtains in there. Yesterday it was the library curtains and today it's the drawing-room curtains. Celia will strip your house naked.'

Idie looked at the yellow-and-white sprig print of her dress and giggled, 'Well, I've no need for curtains and things.'

'It was clever, you know, to get Celia sewing, very clever. Everyone's a better person for a sense of purpose and, yes, that reminds me, *Vogue* patterns.

Vogue patterns for grown-ups, because, after all, you might one day grow up.'

'I've no ambition to grow up,' said Idie. 'I've done quite enough of it already and I find the benefits of it debatable.'

Edith looked at the young woman dressed in drawing-room curtains, at the monkey beside her, and raised an eyebrow and said, 'Quite right. No point to growing up at all. Nevertheless you might one day find it's just happened to you without any volition of your own.'

Idie darkened to think of the unavoidability of any further growing up.

'Most poetic, of course you know, to hold on to your innocence while others rush to throw it off. Nonetheless, the misty layers of that childhood, like the skins of an onion, will fall away whether you like it or not.'

Quite so, thought Idie. *So many have already fallen away that there is nothing left of* me.

'Austin took a leap away from you without you noticing, didn't he? The journey towards adulthood comes in fits and starts, and he somehow leaped ahead of you.'

At that Edith bent her head and busied herself over notes in her book: *1. Vogue Patterns.*

They reached Carriacou and, without any kind of instruction from Edith, Daisy drew up outside the post office.

'Read it to me,' instructed Edith, handing a postcard to Idie.

Idie took it and looked up, hesitating.

'I've not got my reading glasses,' said Edith, looking into the middle distance. 'Besides, I've not the courage. You read it.'

Daisy set off and Idie read aloud:

Southampton

June 1917

Dear Mother,

Filthy cold here but the people lined the streets to meet us and stared and cheered, amazed at the colour of our hair and skin. The English don't appear to have even heard of such a place as the West Indies and had no idea we are part of the Empire.

Our men are very surprised for England is the country whose anthems we sing, whose history we've learned and whose flag we have come to serve under. I will write again when I have more time.

Love Austin

77

Idie heard news of Austin only by reading his letters to Edith. In September 1917 a letter came from Egypt.

Dear Mother,

We're in Jordan, mainly on fatigues, which is a bore, but there's lots of hanging about so I can write a little more now.

The men enjoyed the training here and had a chance of some fighting at Umbrella Hill and they've proved to the world that the men of the West Indies are as soldierly as any other. But now the BWIR are back on fatigues as usual. What's worse is that the War Office doesn't want us armed even though our duties are often in the line of fire. Dammit, it's not a native battalion - the men volunteered, but they're not being treated as a regular fighting unit, they're being treated as a native unit as if they weren't suitable for the front line, and made to dig water pipes and trenches, do road mending and construction.

It would be a fine thing if you, with your fierce sense of justice, were here, Mother, to knock some sense into some of the officers. My men aren't even allowed to play cricket. I would dearly love to give them a game - they watch so eagerly as the white men play. They've been cheerful and uncomplaining, but now there's a bit of discontent because they just want to fight. Yesterday there was some trouble. The men were stacking shells alongside the railway line again. They came under fire - infantry fire - but of course they themselves couldn't fight back - one of them was a fellow called Nelson - do you remember him? He's Mayella's father, from Bathsheba -

Idie looked up at Edith. *Mayella's father -*

a stern, quiet chap who works the docks at Georgetown - he was amongst them. He survived but the men either side of him fell. A young chap called Sampson, who's always looking out for Nelson, went to his officer and remonstrated with him, begging that they be able to defend themselves against enemy fire, but the officer tried to strike him. So you see, the senior officers who are seconded to us from the English regiments don't understand the men from home at all and can be high-handed with them.

Nelson, Sampson, Austin, all in Egypt. Nelson who'd stood at the door of Pomeroy and been turned away by Silent for the colour of his skin, Nelson who'd taken a small baby all the way to England for the sake of an estate that was not his, then returned twelve years later to fetch her back again. Nelson, Nelson, who stopped to talk to horses in the rain, Nelson, father of Mayella and of Clement, of all in all eight fine daughters and five fine sons, had gone from this tiny faraway island to fight for the motherland and not been issued with a gun because of the colour of his skin.

Idie braced herself and read on:

Egypt is a strangely beautiful place. There's something heroic and dashing about the quality of the fighting here - it's hand-to-hand combat and charges with bayonets. You've at least got a chance here, not like Flanders; here it's man against man and the best man wins. I only hope my men will get another chance to fight. I'm glad to have seen the Promised Land, the Pyramids and the Sphinx, but none of it is as lovely as home.

Do send some books - and binoculars if you can spare them. Send them to the camp at Kantara as we'll be there soon and I'll pick them up on leave. Oh - and do please send jam. Army jam is lousy. In fact all the food, if it comes at all, is lousy.

Are you keeping well? Does your poetry improve at all, Mother, for Father's sermons don't, though he's much loved by the men here. Anyway, poetry and sermons both are improved by brevity. Do you hear anything of Idie Grace? Is she well? Do send news of her for I know she'll not write to me.

All love, Austin

'Heroic and dashing. Hand-to-hand combat and charges with bayonets,' snorted Edith in disgust. 'Toerag. No jam for him and certainly no binoculars.'

Idie said fiercely, 'He's right. You must recruit a regiment of women and go to Kantara and tell the English officers how to look after the men from here.'

78

One day in February Idie received a letter from Benedict.

British West Indies Regiment
Cairo

10th October 1917

Dear Idie,

I'm rather put out on account of one of the chaps in my regiment knowing you — fellow called Austin — seems a reasonable enough type — but really, Idie, you can't go about with that sort. What has become of you?

The heat is a strain on the nerves, and your colonials should be better suited to it than we, but they're falling like flies, ninety per cent of them down with malaria.

Chaps here from your neck of the woods,

they're not really up on the rules, any of them. Had to give one or two of them a bit of a talking-to the other day. Must be difficult living among those sorts, though I expect there are some better types there too.

There're regimental games tomorrow – camel racing and all kinds of fun. Still I'll be glad when it's all over and I can get back to jolly old London and dances and clubs, though you can have a bit of a laugh in Cairo, all sorts of bars and things there.

I hear your sugar planters are making a fortune because of the shortage of sugar so I see things have turned out all right for you. Perhaps I'll pay you a visit once all this is over.

Did you know I've had another promotion?

Love Benedict

Idie wondered about regimental games, London dances and Cairo bars. Benedict might come and visit. She looked across the lawn to the long, low white house, the veranda with its trailing vines, the calabash and the moonflower trees and thought how Benedict would love it all. She wondered about the West Indians being so ill with malaria and wondered too that they were not up on the rules and thought then that Benedict would help them and soon love the men from here; he was Grancat's son and would know how to look after his men.

79

Once again Edith handed Idie an envelope from
Austin and Idie read it to her.

Kantara
Egypt

15th November 1917

Mother,

No jam, no binoculars and we're still stuck
just stacking shells. They want to make
us a native regiment so they don't have to
give us the pay increase - everyone else gets
1/6d now. I've written to appeal as there'll
be trouble otherwise. The men are making
the same sacrifice other regiments make
and that has to be recognized, regardless
of race. The temperatures are growing high
among the men though they seemed to

enjoy the Cairo bars and now at last they're allowed to play cricket, which helps. We've won seventeen out of the twenty matches we've played at the Alexandria Cricket Club. Our star player is Sampson, from Bathsheba (the one I wrote about in my last letter), though you'd never believe it from the look of him.

Mother, I cannot imagine you make a kind nurse. Go easy on your poor patients - don't be all vim and bicarbonate. You've not been out here, you can never understand what they've seen.

It's not all beer and skittles in this corner of the world, you know, so do please send the jam and binoculars.

Love Austin

PS If you send the jam, I won't say anything horrid about your poetry again.

80

'I've a letter to read today,' Idie said, her voice shaking, because this was a letter from Austin and it was the first she herself had received from him.

Edith looked at Idie, sort of long and quiet and sideways, and said, 'You don't have to read it to *me*, you know.'

Idie wondered at that but answered brightly, unfolding the letter, 'Oh, I do. You share yours with me.'

Kantara

20th December 1917

Dear Idie

I'm forced to beg you to send me some jam because Mother's taken um and won't send me any of hers.

Edith chuckled.

Do ask Phibbah, that pipe-smoking sphinx in your kitchen, to make some of her guava jam. You can send it to me at Kantara – we'll be stuck here for a while.

Your second cousin once removed, Benedict Grace, and I are in the same regiment. I think you know that – though he doesn't think much of being placed with us lot.

I want you to read the next bit of this letter to Mayella. At last we had another bit of fighting and the men were armed and given a chance to show again what they can do.

In the Jordan Valley we climbed 4,000 feet and walked fifteen miles, with no water and no rations, and then had to go straight up and raid the Turk trenches. Nelson and his men went in as calm as if they were on parade and never faltered even under heavy fire. I was standing with the major. We watched the men advance at point of bayonet into a hail of artillery fire as if they were simply walking through a rain shower, and the major said, 'My God, Hayne, don't they know what shells are?'

We took forty prisoners and captured

fourteen guns, and Chaytor, the general, said afterwards he could wish for no better men than the BWIR. Nelson was awarded the DCM and promoted to corporal.

It is cold in a desert at night and I strongly suspect that the jersey I've been issued was made by you, since it is full of holes. My battalion has one hundred and twenty mules and thirty-six camels attached to it, though not a monkey or mongoose in sight. Idie, is your chin -

She stopped reading aloud and scanned the next few lines. Edith looked straight ahead and for once picked up the reins and fidgeted with them, in such a way that Daisy, with a toss of her head, made clear was entirely unnecessary.

- still high? Is your heart still laced with moonshine? Do you dress in rainbows? I would like to bring you back a camel. You don't yet have a camel.

These are the other animals I can offer you:

1. Scorpion
2. Snake
3. Mosquito

They are all, for various different reasons,

unsuitable; 1. A nuisance as they get under the blankets. 2 & 3. Self-explanatory.

So I will do my best to squeeze a camel into a kitbag though it might be a little awkward.

Love,
Austin

'Don't forget to send the jam,' Idie said aloud, improvising, 'From Austin.'

She was silent for a while and cross, for he had written to her as if she were just a child.

81

Early in 1918 a telegraph boy came to Bathsheba. Idie stared at the envelope in her hands, at the handwriting on it, the unfamiliar hand of some GPO clerk. She saw the words 'URGENT, PERSONAL', and hesitated to open it. Mayella and Phibbah read on Idie's face the dread in her heart. Idie stepped away from them and walked alone into the garden.

Kantara
Egypt

April 1918

Dear Miss Grace,

Be alone when you read this, God bless you, and steel yourself.

Idie turned the paper over. The Reverend Lionel Hayne. *Austin's father.*

Not Austin, *please not Austin too.*
She read on, trembling.

Nelson, poor man, has asked that you break
this news to Mayella before the official notice
comes.

Sampson. Dear God, not Sampson. Stricken, Idie raised
her eyes to the kitchen window. She saw Mayella in
there, a red hibiscus in her hair, dancing a pasodoble
around the table with Gypsy. *Oh, Mayella . . .*

The trouble we knew was brewing has come
but, dear God, that it should come in such a
way.

One of the men from Bathsheba, Sampson
Sealy, is dead, executed by firing squad.

Damn them all - the British officers provoked
this. The West Indies Regiment came to fight,
but for two years were forced only to dig
pipes, stack shells and clean latrines. Two days
ago the men were made to unload white
men's kit from the train and that was when
the trouble started. On some minor account
of ill discipline, Sampson Sealy was given a
field punishment. It was not warranted, for
he was never insubordinate, but a certain
officer has had it in for Sampson from the

start and had Sampson confined and punished. It is claimed then that at some time during that punishment Sampson assaulted a military policeman. I can't believe it of him, nor can anyone who knew him.

The highest price is paid for this offence.

Forgive me, Miss Grace, there is no gentle way to tell what happened. I was called to attend the execution and went at dawn, together with my medical officer. Sampson stood close to the wall, naked from the waist up, as gentle-looking a man as I ever saw, waiting his moment with grace and dignity. the staff were hesitant, the little quartermaster white with fear, the assistant provost marshal fidgeting with his revolver and shuffling. Only Sampson was still and calm. the dawn rose and gathered all her light on him. The firing party huddled, twenty or so feet away, their faces drawn. the QM stuck strips of plaster to Sampson's heart, his fingers trembling while Sampson gazed ahead, his eyes soft and shining.

As the QM fumbled to tie the handkerchief around his eyes, Sampson said, 'Is all right, reverend, I can die with my eyes open.' I whispered that it were better he didn't as this would be seen as an act of defiance. 'All right, sir,' Sampson said, and the handkerchief was tied.

Afterwards a stunned silence fell over us all.

Tell Mayella that a chaplain had been with Sampson all the preceding day, that I was there and gave him the last offices and that he died in readiness to face his God. Tell her too that his last words were for her, asking that I tell her that he had seen all over the world now and knew for certain that the best lady in all of it was sweet Mayella Mayley. He asked also that his brother Rennben take good care of her.

I am sorry to be the bearer of such dreadful tidings.

Yours, Lionel Hayme

Mayella came and set down a bowl of golden pawpaw for Homer. Idie started and looked up, clutching the paper to her chest.

'I bring you banana bread, hot chocolate, mango. We have the bib for the monkey, the bib for the mongoose.'

Idie stared at Mayella aghast.

Mayella saw Idie's distress and said gently, 'The war it gon' end soon and the men they come home . . .'

'Mayella . . .' Idie began.

82

Mayella's grief and silence was the grief and silence of a whole house. She didn't sing nor dance nor speak in riddles and Bathsheba became a sad, dim place.

Gypsy never swung from the rafters, nor did the sun fowl click her tail, nor Homer whistle, nor Baronet whinny. Every creature drooped and bent his head in shame that such things could come to pass. Everything was muted, the sprinkling of moonshine on the lawn faint and dingy, the song of the tree frogs flat, and there was no coconut cake, no lemonade.

Sampson was dead. Myles was dead.

The armistice came and went unmarked at Bathsheba.

Ships began to reach Georgetown, and the shops, after three long years, filled their shelves. Benedict had written that he'd been released, would come soon, was in need of a rest. Men began to return from Europe though Austin, like many of the BWIR, was still stationed at Taranto in Italy, waiting for transport home.

In January 1919, Austin wrote to Edith of a mutiny among his men. The BWIR Taranto in Italy were doing labour fatigues alongside the Egyptian troops. The matter of the recent pay rise for the English troops had come up again. Austin had petitioned on behalf of his men for an equal rise, but in response was given an order that his men start to clean the latrines used by Italian labourers. Tempers burst, the men mutinied and were tried. Forty-nine were found guilty and imprisoned to hard labour, among them Carlisle Quarterly.

One February morning Mayella whispered, 'My father is coming. He's on the next ship.'

'We must all go to welcome him home,' Idie said.

Phibbah braided Mayella's hair and Celia had made her a new dress.

When Nelson's ship came in they stood, Idie, Celia, Phibbah, Clement, Reuben and Mayella together amidst Mayella's sisters and brothers, on the dock at Georgetown. Red, white and blue shone from every post and tree. Mayella's new dress was fresh and pretty as a doily, and Reuben stood close beside her.

The steps were lowered from the ship. The military police formed a flank on either side and the first of the men began to disembark. They fell into line on the dock. Heads peered and strained as they searched for the faces of those they loved. A group of nearby women glanced at Idie and whispered, but Idie didn't care; she'd live her life as she wished, among the people she loved.

'*They say she's not quite right, like the mother you know, the same thing . . .*'

Idie lifted her head and looked away. What did it matter what they said, or what became of her?

The crowds roared and the bands struck up in every corner as the returning men paraded into the square. They came to a halt before the crowd. Idie scanned their faces, thinking idly that Carlisle wouldn't be among them, him being a prisoner in Taranto, but that made no difference to her now. Fear of him had been long displaced by larger griefs.

Sampson should be there among those men, returning to marry Miss Mayella Mayley in the little Baptist chapel.

Nelson stood at the far end of the line in the front row.

Idie touched Mayella's sleeve. 'There – Mayella – your father – do you see him, at the front on the left?'

Nelson's arm was bandaged. He wore a medal on his chest, a badge on his cap and the twin stripes of a corporal on his sleeve. He was thin and scarred and his eyes were deep and sad, but when he saw his clutch of children there together on that dock he smiled and it was as if the sun had risen in his face.

On the podium in the centre of the square, the governor waited for absolute silence.

'Men of this sweet island, you're home again. Look

at this harbour, at these white sands, these hills and trees, and be sure you are not dreaming.

'Many of you standing here today remember the first contingent of men this island sent; many of you will still feel the tears on your faces, still see the ship sailing out as the sinking sun streamed across the water and the band played the last strains of the Soldier's Song.

'Four years have passed since then. The war has been fought and won. More than ten thousand men left this shore, of whom a thousand will never return.'

Mayella dropped her head and murmured a prayer. Reuben took her hand in his.

From each corner of the square a brass band played a chord and the soldiers and the police, the governor and the onlookers and all the people of Hummingbird broke into song and sang with all their hearts till their anthem resounded from the mountains to the reefs and shook the plumes of the palms, and somewhere deep and buried, a still light and living corner of Idie was stirred.

Afterwards Edith sought out Idie and said, 'We still have long work to do, you and I, for armistices do not mend the minds that war unravels.'

And together they made their way to Boscobelle, each alone with her thoughts.

83

Bristol

March 1919

Dear Miss Grace,

I board a ship tomorrow and hope to arrive at Georgetown within ten days.

I bring Benedict with me in the hope that he will have a period of rest and calm at Bathsheba. He contracted malaria in the desert and is in need of some warmth and quiet.

His Lordship asks to be remembered to you.

Yours,
Algernon Webb

Idie put the letter down and looked up.

She had left it at twelve, was now almost nineteen,

but Pomeroy wasn't far away and long ago to her. It was still the measure by which she lived; Grancat, Myles and Benedict still her yardsticks. She'd make Benedict proud of her. She'd show him the land, show him the cane fields and the sugar works, show him how the new cacao crop was faring, how it didn't hurt the hands of the men as cane did.

84

Later, standing again on the kitchen chair, she turned a quarter-circle as Celia pulled out the tacking stitches along her hem.

Benedict was now an officer and decorated. He went to balls and bars and regimental dances and he was coming from the other side of the world to visit her. The Jack monkey must leave the guest bedroom and the sun fowl must be persuaded out of the dining room.

Idie thought too of Mayella and of how light and song was returning by degrees to Bathsheba. Since that day on the quay when Mayella had waited to see Nelson's return, she'd begun to hum and dance and hum again as she went about her ineffectual, pretty sort of dabbing at the household dust. Gypsy's spirits had rallied with Mayella's and she too had taken up a mop once more and cradled it and turned in circles, and Idie smiled, glad to think that others, at least, could still find some lightness in their hearts.

The door opened now and Mayella came in, but

she stomped across the kitchen with her bucket, filling it noisily at the dripping tap.

Then she put her hands on her hips and demanded, 'Why must that Jack monkey move? Who this man coming that is so special he must sleep in the monkey's bedroom?' She stomped out, pail banging, the water slopping on the tiles.

Idie shook her head in bewilderment at Mayella's reversal in temper, but she put Mayella's sourness aside because Benedict was coming that afternoon. She lifted her head and ran her hands down the silky cloth of the new dress. Now the ships were getting through, there was fabric in the shops once more and she no longer had to wear the drapery of Bathsheba's windows. Idie turned another quarter-circle, a little offended that Mayella had said nothing nice about her dress, for Idie was sure it was very pretty.

She bent to Celia and said, 'One day I will set you up a shop in Georgetown, and when I do you will have a line of customers from there to Carriacou.'

Celia smiled shyly and Idie thought that she must ask Clement about premises. She looked out through the window to the new cane fields, thinking too that she'd show Benedict how she'd managed, show him the new offices, the accounts and payroll system. Benedict would bring news of Pomeroy. He'd tell of her of the years Idie thought of as the missing years, and most of all of he'd tell her of Grancat and

Lancelot, of Stables and Pomeroy, and together they'd remember Myles too.

Idie looked at the counter where the coconut cake stood ready, the squash and guineafowl prepared for dinner. She and Benedict would eat perhaps on the lawn under the moonflowers, where the breeze was coolest. Benedict needed rest and peace and, because of that and because of Benedict being so grand, the Jack monkey had been removed from his room.

The kitchen door swung open once more and Mayella set down the pail abruptly, folded her arms and said, 'The lawyer man is here. Only him. The other one is not here.'

The floor beneath Idie fell away. For a second or two she could not move. Then she lifted her head and yanked the thread from her neckline, stepped down and walked to the window. Numbers stood alone on the forecourt, dismissing the driver.

She hesitated there, gripping the windowsill. *Where was Benedict?*

Numbers's face was leaner, more lines had grown between those that were there before and his glasses sat on his face as though they'd blossomed right there before his eyes and then thought they'd stay in just that place forever. Idie bowed her head a second, biting her lip and fighting the hurt that was welling inside her. Benedict hadn't come; it was because he was not well perhaps, or weak after the sea journey.

Celia and Phibbah stood either side of Idie, each looking with concern at the young woman who stood between them.

Idie lifted her head, smoothed her dress and walked with slow dignity through the dining room and out into the hall. Numbers was climbing the stairs to the veranda. Gypsy sat on a rafter, scratching her cheek and tugging her ear, uncertain what to make of him.

'YOUR EXCELLENCY,' Homer said, and Numbers smiled and raised his hat in response.

'Homer.'

And at that Gyspy decided resolutely in favour of Numbers and sprang down beside him and, to his confusion, curled her tail about his waist. Numbers looked in alarm towards the door and there saw Idie, and slowly, with the monkey's tail still about his waist, took stock of the young woman the small girl he'd last seen had become.

'Miss Grace.'

Idie looked at the man who'd transported her this far side of the world and left her here. Anger gathered in her and she said, a little acid, 'Tell me, did Miss Treble settle over you like a sunset? Did she whisk you away in a cloud of lilac chiffon?'

Astonishment silenced Numbers for a moment or two. Then he blinked and said, 'You've lost none of your candour, Miss Grace.'

The Crockets, like spectators at a tennis match,

turned as one, their long beaks from Numbers to Idie when she retorted, 'Mr Webb, you left me here *with* Treble . . .'

Gypsy uncoiled her tail from about his waist and Numbers stepped across the veranda, circumnavigating at a safe distance the Crockets.

The good in Idie, along with the mischief, surfaced like a cork and she smiled.

'All right, I won't be beastly, I promise.'

She drew up a chair for them both and sat. Millie slipped from her basket and settled, like a coiled ribbon, on her lap.

'Miss Grace.' Numbers opened his mouth and closed it. Then he smiled and said, 'Fishes do that.'

Idie grinned. 'I believe a horrid little girl may once have told you something along those lines.'

'I never met a horrid little girl in all my life. I once boarded a large ship in the company of a large horse and a brave little girl who wouldn't wear her hat. She caused me all kinds of trouble and taught me all kinds of things.'

He looked down and twisted his hat in his hands as if astonished he'd said so many words in one go, so Idie asked what she most wanted to know.

'Where's Benedict?'

Numbers opened his mouth to speak but no words came out.

'Fishes,' said Idie.

He nodded and said, 'He's at the governor's house. He's involved with the cenotaph they're building and, well, there's a dance there tonight. But he needs rest – please make him rest; he's weaker than he knows and reckless and, well, it may just be his age, but he's perhaps too fond of parties.'

Idie, still sensitive to such things as other people going to dances and not she, understood at once that there would be a dance that night and Benedict would go but that he'd not take her. She lifted her head and swallowed and said, as if talking of a stranger about whom she had only a mild curiosity, 'Is he well? Was the journey all right?'

Numbers looked straight at her. 'He is. He'll come soon. He said to tell you he'd be along in a day or two.'

'A day or two?' asked Idie quietly.

Numbers nodded, then he said, 'You very much want to see him, don't you?'

All the years of pent-up longing for Pomeroy and all it meant to her burst from her and then she answered, 'How could I not? It's been seven years . . .'

Numbers waited a minute or two, then said, 'He's not well. He won't say so, but he's not. The army never knew, you see. The chest problem, he hid it from them, and the desert, being so dry, was dangerous for him . . . In any case, he's not himself.'

Idie nodded. She knew indeed what war could do

to a man's mind, for she knew the screams of Virgil and of Abraham and all the men at Boscobelle.

Numbers looked out across the lawn and rubbed his temple, then turned back to Idie. 'Gladstone –'

Idie nodded sadly.

'I'm sorry. That must have been a difficult time. Gladstone gone and Sampson too.' Idie bent her head and Numbers waited. After a while he said, 'We're most impressed, Mr Pugsley and I, most impressed, with the bookkeeping, the accounts, the crops, the yields . . .'

'We were lucky,' said Idie simply. 'We had sugar when the world needed it.'

He looked straight at her, silent awhile, then nodded and said, 'His Lordship was right, of course, about you. He always said you'd be equal to whatever you were given in life . . .'

'How is he? Tell me –' she asked in a flat, quiet voice.

'It's hard in England for the large estates, Miss Grace, and there're harder times ahead. Many won't survive; many have gone already. His Lordship, well, the fight went out of him when you left.'

'I DIDN'T LEAVE,' Idie burst out. All the sorrow in her, all the anger and the fear, flared in a sudden blaze. 'All of you LEFT me. Grancat sent me away when I was only twelve, and then you left me, and then Treble left me, and no one ever came to see me till now. And people talked and stared and whispered, but none of you had the courage to tell me anything. ANYTHING.'

Numbers looked her in the face, unflinching, and there was a deep sadness in his eyes as he asked quietly, 'And now, Miss Grace, knowing what you know, do you wish we'd told you?'

Idie bowed her head and struggled with herself awhile. After a moment or two of silence, she whispered simply, 'No.'

When she'd regained her calm, she met his eyes and said quietly, 'Thank you. Thank you for the years that not knowing gave me. It was kinder that I knew nothing.'

The breeze sighed through the trees and the sun dipped further and spilled orange and pink over the land and the sea, and the tea Mayella had brought out for Numbers remained untouched. He rose slowly, as though his bones suddenly ached more than they once had.

'With regard to the matter of Carlisle Quarterly, we'll have to wait until he returns. It is, you know, entirely possible that your mother wrote a will in his favour.'

Idie interrupted, nodding, and said, 'No matter, but do tell Benedict to come soon, that I long to see him.' She turned to the serving table and added with a sad smile, 'See, I've your old hat and glasses still. I kept them there, there where I could see them as a reminder to me not to be so horrid. You see, there were times when I missed you.'

Numbers bent his head. He removed his glasses and rubbed his eyes as if there were suddenly dust in them.

85

For three days Idie's new dress hung from the handle of the cupboard door. On the fourth day she placed it inside the cupboard. Edith came that morning and this time Idie didn't make the excuse that a visitor was coming, but went with her to Boscobelle.

Edith, sprightly and wry, saw Idie was subdued and watched her closely. At the end of the day as they returned to Bathsheba Edith remarked, a little drily, 'You've a visitor.'

Idie saw the sleeping figure on the chaise and mouthed, 'Benedict.'

She leaped from the trap and ran calling to him.

He opened one eye slowly, then the next and looked at her. He wore uniform, was tall and broad, big and bearish now almost as Grancat, fair as he'd always been, only there was stubble now on his chin, perhaps two days' worth.

Idie stood in her white uniform before him and he gazed at her, bleary. Gradually, as he came fully to his senses, a smile formed on his lips and he rose and opened his arms wide. Idie hesitated, looking at him, seeing Grancat there before her almost for they were so similar in shape and size and gesture.

'Little Idie?' said Benedict, and Idie smiled because it was all now as it once had been, she the small and tiresome girl, he the older boy, mildly amused, mildly irked.

'Benedict,' she breathed, but the impulse to run to him was checked by his leisurely survey of the young woman he'd last seen as a girl of twelve. 'When did you come?' she asked. 'And how did you get here? I wish I'd known. I wouldn't have gone out if I'd known you were coming.' As Idie raced on she never heard the gravel churn beneath the trap as Edith left, never noticed Gypsy huddled in a corner, knees to her chest, like a schoolgirl at assembly. 'Did Mayella bring you some tea?'

'Slow down,' said Benedict, arch. 'And yes, in fact, a sweet, dark-eyed person did come out but was quite foul to me.'

'I see you're quite at home nevertheless,' responded Idie, smiling.

'But then a white witch glided past and took pity on me and brought me tea and cake. It was rather good, in fact, that cake, but, oh, by the way, I've asked her to put those birds somewhere else.'

Idie wondered if Benedict had seen the sun fowl in the dining room and felt guiltily grateful that

Millicent was in her basket and the Jack monkey rehoused in the stables. 'A gentleman can't kip in an aviary. Idie, you're grown quite savage; you're every bit as unpresentable as they say.'

Gypsy crept up and curled her tail about Idie's waist. Idie wriggled a little and tried to unwind Gypsy's tail, but Benedict grinned and said, 'You got the better of Treble, didn't you?'

'It wasn't me, in fact; it was the rum,' said Idie.

'Ah yes, Grancat always said she could drink even Pomeroy out of gin,' answered Benedict, and they looked at each other and suddenly all the things they'd shared, all the things of their childhood – the trees and turrets of Pomeroy, Stew and Stables and all the things they'd known and loved – lay shining there between them bright as tears.

Benedict turned and looked about across the lawn and into the trees. 'I never realized then, really, what was happening, how far away you were going. It must've been a bit rough on you – was it?'

'When you're small you don't question things, you just do what grown-ups tell you to.' Then Idie added, with a mischievous smile on her lips, 'More or less you do.' She took his hand and said, 'Come, I'll show you everything . . .'

Benedict stretched. 'It's damnably hot –'

'Would you like to rest?'

'Idie, I do NOT need a nurse,' he interrupted

sharply. Then he eyed her uniform, grinning, and said, 'No, I was just long at lunch, that's all.'

Idie flung herself down again and leaned forward and cupped her hands around her chin. 'Tell me everything. Pomeroy – is it all just the same?'

He sighed and ran a hand through his hair. 'It's all as it was and more so. God knows how we'll manage now.' A sadness blew over his face like a sharp squall and seemed to take him away from her for a second or two. There was a fluttering in his fingers, and Idie wanted to hold his hands to still them. 'It'll all be different now, Idie; the world is changing, those big places, so many staff . . .'

Idie thought about Myles and hoped Benedict might speak of him.

'You know, Idie, it'll be the same everywhere. There'll be difficult times ahead.'

He rose and she watched him, anxious, admiring, proud, seeing Grancat in his gesture as he lifted a sherry decanter from the drinks trolley. Idie took it from him and poured, thinking it was strange Mayella had not come to serve the drinks.

'I'll have a lie-down before changing for dinner,' Benedict said.

Idie wondered whether she too should change for dinner, since he seemed to think dinner dress was necessary.

Benedict indicated to the hall and to a small green

trunk that stood there in the centre. 'We found it in his room, marked for you. You see, I think he knew – even before he left – he'd never come back. I heard that often out there, men saying they knew, just knew that they were going to die.' He paused, about to say more, but then looked down and turned and went inside.

When Idie opened the box she found all the tiny playthings of their childhood: a special smooth and magic stone fished from the river, her crown and his arrows, a story she'd once written him, the fleur-de-lis playing cards. She lifted the battered pack and held it in her hands, remembering the feel of the nursery carpet on bare knees, the games of Pelmanism. The knave of hearts had been lost then, would still be missing now. Tears fogged her eyes and she was submerged by a tidal wave of memories, tumbled, turned over and inside out in the surf of times gone by.

She put both hands in that chest, searching blindly for what she knew was there. Tentatively she fingered the cover of the book, and, wiping her eyes, opened it and in it saw Myles's careful rounded letters. She saw them and remembered too the roundness of his tears and in his tears saw all the depth and goodness of his heart.

1. *Idie is not the same as us.*
2. *But she has the same name [GRACE].*
3. *Grancat is mine and Benedict's father but not Idie's.*

4. Someone just gave Idie to Grancat, like a kind of parcel.
5. Then [later, when Idie was bigger] a letter came telling Grancat she had to go back to where she came from at the start.
6. Grancat says it's because she is a lady of property now. We don't know if that's good or not.
7. Grancat says that Blood is THICKER than Water. We don't know what that means, but the result of it is that Idie has to go to a small and faraway place called Hummingbird Island.
8. It is in the WEST INDIES and they are dangerous and only Treble will go to them because she is greedy for the money. You have to pay someone a good deal to go to them because they are awash with brigands and bandits.
9. Idie won't ever come back because the Indies are so far away.

After these first childish entries came, in tidier, joined-up writing, the facts noted over the years from Idie's letters. Beneath those, more recently, he'd written:

How I missed you then, miss you still, dear Idie Grace. Pomeroy, March 1916.

Idie closed it, bowed her head, lifted the book to her temple and whispered, 'I never told you the other things, Myles, because I couldn't. My mother was insane; that is why I was brought to Pomeroy. Babies are taken away from the insane. I was never able to tell you that, and neither can I say those words to anyone. These things run in the blood and one day I will go the same way as she. Benedict is here, Myles; you never came but he is here, and I promise you that I will look after him till he is well enough to return safely to Pomeroy.'

86

Before the ceremony for the unveiling of the cenotaph, all of the grand sorts of people of the island came up to Benedict and greeted him, and Idie wondered that he should know so many. He told her it was because he was an officer, and would one day be an earl, and she'd never known before that such things should make so great a difference.

'Come, Idie, take your place in the world today,' Benedict said, smiling and half teasing. 'Sit with me.'

Idie hesitated, but he took her arm and led her away from Celia out of the crowds and up on to the dais.

People spoke to her there when they'd never done so before, and she stood at his side among bishops and dignitaries and before ten thousand people.

The governor began to talk:

Our memorial is wrought by island hands from island stone. Let it stand for those who fell.

Idie looked out on the crowd which packed the square and the roof and tree of every building facing the square. She felt the breeze on her bare arms and saw that everything was splendid and shining. She was proud of Benedict and his uniform and his medal, and when she looked at him she saw Grancat in his height and bearing and it was as if she were back at Pomeroy and all the years between now and then wiped out.

The world is girdled with the graves of sons of the Empire. In Flanders and France, Italy and Macedonia, the Dardanelles, Palestine, Egypt, Mesopotamia, East Africa, West Africa, they lie dead. From all the tiny islands and all the golden links that bind the chain of Empire, these men went and these men fell that the Empire might stand.

The Royal Engineers, the Royal Garrison Artillery and all the men of the British West Indies Regiment stood about the stone and with them stood a troop of Boy Scouts, and Idie remembered with a stab of pain another day she'd come to this same square and seen a dear friend there who'd turned away from her and gone to war. Some from Bathsheba were in the crowd, but Mayella had not come, nor Reuben, nor Clement. That Sampson's name would never be engraved on that cenotaph tarnished the shine of the day.

With full military pomp and panoply the cenotaph was unveiled. At its base were marked the names of those '*who came not home*'.

Slowly and amidst absolute silence, the Governor read a list of names and each name rang through the air, but the name of smiling Sampson Sealy was not among them for he had been found guilty of insubordination and incitement to mutiny.

Sampson Sealy, Idie said in her heart. *Sampson Sealy of Bathsheba. He too, that your Empire might stand, came not home.*

Benedict clutched her shoulder and Idie saw that he was strange and sweating and she took his arm. She led him from the platform and he followed meekly.

Next day, when Benedict seemed recovered, they rode together along a path Austin had once shown her, through the mangroves and the palms. When they reached the cane fields, Benedict looked out across them and said, 'They were once owned jointly, you know, Pomeroy and Bathsheba, by our many-times-great-grandfathers. When things were at their height for us Graces.'

Idie said nothing and Benedict said, 'It could be the same again one day.'

No, Benedict, she answered inwardly, thinking of what ran in her blood. But somehow still the sunlight reached then the darkest parts of her and they rode on together and butterflies kissed her skin and made her heart light and it was as if she'd been lifted from an abyss.

Celia placed an envelope beside Idie's coffee cup. Idie glanced at Benedict, then turned aside and read:

Homeward bound

Dear Idie,

Strange and remarkable creature, do you hold court still under a calabash tree? Is there lemonade still and coconut cake at Bathsheba? Do herds of moons hang from your trees and monkeys from your rafters?
Keep them there till I return, and always.

Austin

Idie slipped the letter into a pocket and did not think about Austin because Benedict was here and she must organize the picnic and the horses and her dress for the evening.

Idie pinned some white flowers in her dark hair and turned a little to see her reflection in the glass of the wardrobe. She stroked Millicent a little sadly and placed her in her basket. Benedict was right: you couldn't go up on to platforms and stand beside governors if you had a mongoose in your pocket. She thought briefly of Homer, who had been stationed with the Crockets in the loggia because Benedict complained of his whistling and that he had only one tune.

Idie placed a necklace around her neck. 'It was my mother's,' Benedict had said when he'd given it to her.

Idie had thought of Pomeroy and the distress of the large estates and answered shyly, 'They are the Pomeroy diamonds and they will be for your wife.'

'Quite right.' He smiled and added, 'They should be sold to pay for the roof. But Grancat said they must be yours. He wanted you to have them, Idie, so there they are.'

Now she fastened the diamonds and looked at herself, not quite liking to think how she was wearing a half-acre roof about her neck.

Benedict stood at the foot of the stairs, a Sherry Cobbler in his hand. The string of diamonds about Idie's neck flashed red in the setting sun and he smiled and said, 'You scrub up all right.'

Idie's hand went to the cold hard stones and she paused, then rushed on down the stairs.

'Must you be such a whirlwind?' Benedict asked, laconic and amused. 'Ladies don't run.'

'They do sometimes,' said Idie, a little defensive, then, to herself, *I must remember not to run – no mongooses and no running.*

'Yes, perhaps they do, sometimes, but only if a fine young man is waiting to take them to a dance at the best house in town.'

Idie collected her cape from the chair in the hall. She saw Celia there with Delilah, beside the chair. Celia started then as she sometimes did, as if Idie were a ghost, then held out her hand to Idie's hair and face, and that made Idie smile to think that she was so like her own mother that Celia should start at the sight of her.

'Thank you, Celia, for the dress,' Idie said gently. 'Thank you.'

She stepped towards the door. There, on the balustrade, beside the water that fell in a glittering stream from the gutter, swinging his legs and chewing cane, was Austin.

Idie faltered.

Austin rose, slowly, his eyes on Idie, on her dress and on her face, then on the diamonds about her neck. Idie looked back at Austin, searching in the man who stood before her for the boy who wore red shirts and whistled.

Benedict came out and Austin stood smartly and saluted. 'Sir.'

Benedict nodded casually.

'Are you coming to the dance?' asked Idie, but she knew he wasn't.

'No.' Austin smiled briefly at Benedict. 'That's for rather grand officers, like Captain Grace.' He turned to Idie. 'I'll come another time.'

'Yes, do . . .' said Idie, a little hurt, a little cold. 'Do come back another time.'

Benedict, impatient, set down his drink and said to Idie, 'We'll be late.' He turned and went down the steps.

Austin picked up the bundle tied with string from the balustrade and sprang lightly down.

Idie stepped forward, arm out. 'Oh – don't – where – where're you going?'

'To Mayella. I've something for her.'

'She's not here.'

'No.' He nodded, looking directly at Idie and

speaking quietly. 'No, she wouldn't be here. I'll go to her house – I've things of Sampson's.'

'Come on, Idie, we mustn't be late,' said Benedict.

Austin went to Daisy and mounted. Idie, fastening her cape, heard Baronet whinny piteously that Daisy should be leaving so soon.

Idie and Benedict returned through a night sweet with jasmine and honeysuckle. Idie, who'd been for the first time to a society dinner and danced and been admired, took off her shoes and skipped barefoot across the lawn. She stopped short at the foot of the steps, noticing now the single oil lantern still burning, the figure beside it, head bowed. Numbers lifted his head, and Idie saw in the lantern shadows that flickered across his drawn face the news he brought. The blood draining from her, she took Benedict's arm.

'Benedict,' she whispered. 'Benedict –'

Numbers rose and said, 'I am so sorry, sir – your father – His Lordship –'

Benedict reached for the post of the veranda and clutched it. 'Oh God . . .'

'There was no pain. He died as he would have wished, the *Racing Post* in his hand, Lancelot at his feet.'

Idie stood in the shadows, a little apart. The hall in

which Baronet had eaten scones without a knife and fork because a sensible horse couldn't be doing with such things, Grancat's velvet chair, the banisters, the pairs of glasses stacked on his great head like diadems, the binoculars around his neck, everything came flooding back, precise and vivid as if she'd reached across the oceans and the years and touched those things with her fingers.

Numbers said quietly, 'There was no one like him.' He dipped his head and retreated, adding, 'Take your time. When you're ready we'll meet to discuss the practical side of things.'

Benedict sank into a chair, his head dropped. 'Oh God.'

Idie waited, and when Benedict looked up again she saw the hollowed, haunted sockets of his rainshine eyes, the moonlit sunshine of his hair. He looked away into the garden and said, 'I will never be the man he was.'

She took his hand. 'You will. You are so like him.'

'No, I am of different mettle.' Benedict turned to Idie. 'Grancat was so certain, so sure . . . war takes away your certainties, you see, and God . . . the house.' He covered his eyes. 'I'll be the one that lets it go, after two hundred years, it will be me, the seventh earl, that sells it off.'

His fingers shook a little and his nails scratched the arm of the chair and Idie glanced away, remembering

Grancat sliding gleefully down the banisters for his hard-boiled egg of a morning, and Lancelot waiting at the foot of them, the *Racing Post* rolled up in his mouth for he knew his master always checked the form before breakfast.

91

Next morning Idie found Benedict somehow changed. *He'll go*, Idie thought sadly. *He'll leave so soon, even before he is well he'll leave, and the last strand of Pomeroy will be lost to me.*

'You'll have to go back now . . . ?' she asked, pouring his coffee and watching him. He smiled, but he was pale and his eyes were hard and there were beads of sweat on his forehead.

'I'll go into town. There's the passage to book and things to organize. Hop in with me and I'll drop you off at that place where you work.'

Benedict was studiously casual, but his right eye flickered and his cup rattled in the saucer as he lifted it.

His eyes were on her and he seemed about to say something that would not quite come out. In the trap she watched him again and thought she might distract him with happy things and talked to him of Bathsheba, the people and things in it and of all she'd come to love. But Benedict wasn't listening so Idie grew silent.

When they drew up at Boscobelle he said, 'Idie, I'd like to ask you, well, the fact of it is, to come back with me to Pomeroy. Together, you and I. Would you . . . ?'

'I – I –' She glanced backwards as though Bathsheba and all that was in it might appear there on the road to Boscobelle.

'This place will take care of itself; we'll put someone in charge of it, to run the plantation and so on.'

Idie was silent, confused with surprise and joy and also with anxiety for what she must tell him about herself.

'You don't have to say anything now –'

She smiled and dismounted. Benedict flicked the reins and drove off. Idie watched him go, thinking, *He does not know what I will be, does not know what my mother was.*

92

Edith was attacking a vigorous-looking plant. Idie glanced at its tall stem and cream trumpet flowers and was somehow glad that Edith was digging the thing up. She went to Virgil and took his arm and walked him along the path, her mind on Benedict and Pomeroy.

Wife of Benedict, mistress of Pomeroy. Benedict is not well. I can help him, look after him, but only until such a day as my reason is taken away from me.

She was still in the garden with Virgil when she heard a voice.

'Henbane, Mother, beware. That way lies delirium and madness.'

Idie started at that easy, smiling voice of Austin's. She turned and saw him bend to inspect his mother's work, then take the fork from her and dig a deep and systematic circle.

Delirium and madness.

Why must he talk of such things in front of her? But Austin continued in his airy way. 'Consider the lilies, Mother. The plants are well enough alone.

Dedicate yourself to poetry. Digging is not for you.'

Edith looked at her son and, smiling, snatched the fork back from him and held out some shears.

'No, Mother, no shearing for me today; I'm going to ask if Miss Idie Grace will allow me to walk with her.'

Idie looked at him and thought how he'd been her only friend; the only friend she'd had had left her when she'd been ill and scared and lonely; had gone when she'd begged him not to.

'I've no choice you see, Mother, since you've commandeered her for your own purposes, but to come here if I'm to see her at all.' He stood between his mother and Idie and added, looking directly at Idie, 'She has been TAKEN OVER, by an English captain-cousin several times removed, and by you.'

How like Austin it was to wear hurt and pain so lightly. He was telling her that he knew, and she was thankful for his grace and generosity and able then to look at him then and smile.

Austin took Idie's arm and together they walked in silence for a while, and there was something so tall and strong and upright in him that made Idie feel he knew the heart of her and was standing in judgement over her. She said, a little acid, 'Was Phibbah's jam up to scratch?'

Austin let go of her arm. 'You've lost none of your sweetness, Idie Grace.'

She retorted, 'You left me, Austin.'

Austin's voice was low but burning. 'Did you ever write to me? Did you say goodbye or wish me luck? Did you ever think that I was young and scared and going far away?'

They waited. After a while Idie asked, in a small voice, 'Did you find Mayella?'

'I did.'

He said no more than that, so Idie asked, 'Austin, Sampson didn't do it, did he – what they say he did – he wouldn't –'

Austin was silent and Idie persisted. 'Did the English officers not understand the men from here?'

'They did, some of them did, and grew awfully fond of them; others just never tried.'

'His name isn't on the cenotaph.'

'It is an injustice. I will get his name put on there. I have promised I will do that, to myself and to Mayella.'

'Oh, good,' said Idie. 'Mayella will be so pleased, and Reuben and Phibbah.'

He waited, watching her awhile, then said, 'The doctor and my father, they saw it all. You're right, Sampson never answered back. He was angry, yes, but never insubordinate.'

She nodded and he watched her still, then sighed and they set off again in silence.

She must tell Austin that Benedict had asked for her hand, so she turned to him brightly and asked,

'Did you see anything of Benedict out there?'

Looking straight ahead, Austin nodded.

'Did he make a good officer, Austin? He was always brave and quick and reckless.'

He turned to her. The sun fingered her face and her hair fell loosely from her cap and full about her shoulders and Austin said, very suddenly, 'Don't throw yourself away on him.'

Idie was too taken aback to say anything for a second or two. When she answered it was with an eruption of rage and fury. 'How dare you? How dare you say such a thing?'

'Idie—'

'How dare you?'

'Idie – don't you see –'

'What? WHAT should I see?'

'Sampson – it was Benedict who gave the order.'

A fist twisted in the pit of Idie's stomach.

'Don't be ridiculous,' she whispered, trembling. 'No, no, no – no, he didn't . . . You're lying.'

Sampson who'd gone away to fight for his motherland, Sampson who'd been made to clean latrines, Sampson who'd stood outside the chapel when Gladstone died and said to Mayella, 'Next time I here is for I marry you.' Sampson shot by firing squad at the order of her own cousin.

They stood there, facing each other, Austin and Idie, a flood of hitherto unheeded signs trickling into Idie's head and swimming there and turning her to water; Mayella's absence, her sourness about the removal of the monkeys from the house, Reuben's reticence.

But Benedict was Grancat's son.

Live and let live. Each to their own.

Grancat, for all his prejudice about all the bits of the world that were not Pomeroy, never tolerated injustice of any kind.

Nelson had been at Kantara. She'd find Nelson and ask him.

She untied her pinafore, tore off her cap, left them on the gatepost and ran off down the street.

93

She asked around for him in the docks at Georgetown. A man looked up from his work and gestured and Idie saw Nelson at work among a group of men where the ships were careened on the sand. He was singing and working and was the last of the men to look up. He mopped his brow and pulled on his shirt and he and Idie walked aside together in silence.

'What happened?'

He looked at her and said nothing.

'Tell me, Nelson.'

He understood and answered, 'Mayella's young man, Sampson, he were never violent in his life. He were a brave and gentle boy.'

'Who gave the order?'

Nelson's head was bowed.

'Who gave the order?'

She waited.

'Tell me, Nelson.'

Nelson lifted his head and his voice was measured and certain.

'Captain Grace.'

'Benedict,' Idie breathed. 'Dear God, Benedict . . .'

Bile rose in her throat and she turned and ran, stumbling across the sand.

94

At Bathsheba she found Reuben.

'The captain came back early, mistress. He dressed and went out and said to tell you he come back later when the races finished.'

The races.

In disgust, Idie turned and walked to the stables. She opened the door of Baronet's box and led him across through the gardens to the veranda and into the hall. She went to the kitchen and called for Gypsy and Delilah. She took Homer from the loggia and put him on the balustrade, removed Millie from Celia's sewing basket, wheeled the toucans out of the kitchen and then she went to the garden and waited, pacing to and fro, hour after hour, her stomach turning over to think of Sampson, of so good and gentle a man, put against a wall at dawn and shot, by the order of her own cousin. It was late when Benedict returned, driven in a smart new motorcar from town, but Idie was standing at the top of the steps, waiting. Benedict came to the foot of them, and raised a hand to his neck to loosen his tie.

'Leave this instant.'

Benedict paused, confused.

'Idie –'

He saw the packed trunk beside her, the white sleeve of a dress shirt straggling from it, and his voice tailed away.

'Idie—'

'Leave now, Benedict. Leave and may you carry with you, from this day to the grave, the name of noble Sampson Sealy. And take this too.' She flung the necklace at him. He caught it casually by a clasp and laughed a short, sour laugh. The necklace dangled from his forefinger, trapping the moonlight like a strand of tears

'I sold the biggest stones.'

He swayed a little on his legs and she saw that he'd been drinking.

'No one'll have you, will they? You think I don't know, don't you? But I do. Your grandmother the gardener's wife, your mother a madwoman, her sister a simpleton.'

Idie was all steel and strength then. She lifted her chin and watched him walk alone down the drive with his trunk.

95

Phibbah found Idie still on the veranda in the early morning. She saw the girl's tear-stained cheeks, dishevelled hair. Idie cringed from her and hid her face. Sampson was Phibbah's grandson, he was Reuben's brother, had been beloved of Mayella. How could she face Phibbah? What could she say to Mayella, who'd lost her grandfather on Idie's account and Sampson too. Their blood was on Idie's hands.

Phibbah returned, bringing coffee and a plate of fruit. She unwound Idie's arms and gently lifted her head and tidied her hair. She placed her cool, dry hand on Idie's cheek, keeping it there as Idie's tears ran over it.

Then she took her handwriting book from her pocket and placed it on Idie's lap and waited. Mayella came out from the kitchen just then, and Idie started and half rose in fear, but Mayella gently pushed her back into her chair and bent and planted a kiss on her forehead.

Mayella saw the book on Idie's lap and glanced at

Phibbah. Phibbah opened it and poked a bony finger at the page. Idie attempted to smile and said, 'Not today, no lessons today . . .'

Phibbah jabbed her finger at the page again and Idie summoned another smile because the script was so neat and ran from edge to edge across the page.

I've done some good here at least . . .

Phibbah lifted the book and held it up in front of Idie and jabbed the page again.

'Read it, mistress. All the words in it they are for you,' said Mayella.

Then, finally, Idie understood and lifted the book and read.

96

I, Phibbah, eighty-one years of age, who cannot speak, have found a tongue only with my letters.

I now tell you, Mistress Grace, everything that I have seen, everything that I know. I tell you about your mother.

Idie gasped and looked up, but she was alone.

Your grandfather, Master Arnold, loved Honey Quarterly. Honey, God rest her sweet soul, she was the wife of Enoch and she was the only woman Enoch ever loved but also the only woman your grandfather loved in all his days. When she died, Master Arnold took her other son, the son by Enoch Quarterly, Carlisle, into this house so he be taught alongside his own son, your father, Cecil Grace. That was how Enoch knew Arnold Grace was a good man. That was also how Carlisle came to think he so mighty fine and that how the kindness of your family it grow only as poison in Carlisle because Carlisle think now he's so fine this place must go to him.

Your father he never minded about anything. He was

not one thing nor the other, neither black nor white, but he never cared about anything except your mother. Her name was Lily. He married Miss Lily Rhodes and she come here to Bathsheba with her sister for Miss Celia must be looked after. Your mother was beautiful as an orchid and a hummingbird together and kind as the breeze that come about this house and she loved your father, but she loved you more. Is always so for women. She planted these fustic trees, these moonflower trees, silk cotton tree and all. She always say there is no place on earth so beautiful as here, no child so sweet as you, no man so good as Cecil.

Carlisle see you come, Miss Idie, into this world and he see then there no chance of this house being for him and the anger grow in him.

Your mother she never liked Carlisle, but your father see it his duty to look after him as they half-brothers. Your mother start to get ill with visions. She screaming sometimes, scared sometimes, she scared even of the sun and the light. She forgetting sometime who she is, forgetting even she have a child. She go outside only when it growing dark. That why the shutters were always closed and the house kept dark. She go to swim only when it get dark. Your father start to drink, for knowing he was losing her, and Carlisle he pour the drink always to help your father on his way, and when your father die Lily come to me one morning and you were in her arms and she weeping like a child and she say, 'Tell Nelson to come. My Idie is not safe here. I do not trust that man Carlisle and my daughter must be safe.'

Nelson come and Mistress Lily give him a warm coat and a piece of paper and she say, 'Tell them her name is Idie Grace.'

That what I heard, here where I sitting and writing this, that what she said. Then when you were gone, she like a child, and Carlisle he make her sign the paper that he want and at sundown that day Lily go to swim, same as always, to Black Water Creek, but she never come back because the moon was full and the water high and angry. Later she was found and buried in that creek and no one know to this day if it were her intention to leave this earth that night.

The things Carlisle say to you are not true. She was never wrong in the head. She seeing things, but they were visions from the henbane, the same one that grow once below your window. The henbane, the devil's trumpet they call it here, is in the seeds of the flower. That seed make the mind see things. Carlisle he collect the seed and give it to your mother, and later to yourself also.

Idie remembered the flowers that stalked dreams in the time of her fever, her nights, and she felt the heat rise in her blood.

It was the devil's trumpet turned your mother's mind and killed her.

Miss Grace. I write here from the Oxford Dictionary. It say that henbane give

374

INTOXICATION
DELIRIUM
AMNESIA
PHOBIA
MYDRIASIS

I do not know what these words mean, but they dangerous things and I certain she were all of them because she were not herself. Celia like a mirror – there no badness in her, but she scared and she do only what someone tell her she must do. Carlisle he all pretty-pretty with poor Miss Celia and tell her that this place will be for them, for he and she together. God is my witness, I heard him say so and I see her smile and nod and cry.

I see all this and I hear all this with my own ears and eyes but I have no way of telling till now. You have your father's kindness and your mother's beauty and that why sometimes poor Celia see you and she scared like she seen a duppy, for you so like your mother it sometimes like Lily is here with us once more.

God bless you, Mistress Grace. I know your mother smiling now. She look down and see the woman her baby is become.

Idie didn't know how it was that her head was in the stars but her feet were still on the cool tiles. She looked out through the fustic trees and her heart was singing, because the way was clear and open to her now.

Phibbah had written more, but Idie put down the

375

book and walked alone along the narrow path she'd never taken, a path that led between cannes de riviere and balisiers to Black Water Creek. The air was soft and the water clear and deep. On a sloping bit of land, overlooking the water, stood a pair of crosses, shoulder to shoulder, all overgrown with spathes and a tangled spray of cattleyas.

She sat awhile looking at the winged petals of the cattleya that were a soft deep pink, and at the engraving on the white cross, picked out in gold:

Cecil Grace
Forever in the heart of Lily.

And on the other, plainer:

Lily Grace

A curious peace settled over Idie and she stayed there a long while, still and calm, and a green-and-amethyst hummingbird came and put his long bill into the open part of the cattleya that was deepest pink, and the purr of its wings fanned her cheek and fluttered the sheets of Phibbah's book.

Later Idie turned and watched the silver sea break on the beach. As it came and went it gathered up her fear and hurt and washed them away as writing on sand.

Idie stayed there till the purple night fell from the sky like a stage curtain, till the stars brightened and the moon rose and cast her light, like the touch of a cool hand, on Idie's forehead.

97

It was with a light heart that, some hours later, Idie took up reading again from Phibbah's book.

Gladstone was the only one that know, except myself, that your mother write that will. Gladstone never did wrong in his life except sign that will, but he never knew what was in the will that he signed because he could not read or write. And your mother she was the mistress and Gladstone only the foreman and she telling him to sign and Gladstone he ashamed to say he could not read, and that why he sign the will.

I the only one that saw it all so there was no one to tell what happened because I cannot speak.

When Gladstone die then Carlisle see at last he can present the will for now there is no one to tell that he, Carlisle, forced your mother to sign that will and that he, Carlisle, forced poor Gladstone to make a mark on a thing he could not read. Carlisle see now the house can be his and he have no need of Celia and he tell her, here in this kitchen, that all this house and land would be for him only, not for her. Then when you ill like your mother was, Miss Celia understand then that the bush of henbane is the evil in the house and she go somehow to the police and tell them of the will and she come back and go to the bush of henbane and she trying to pull it with her bare hands. Enoch he find her there by the henbane and he help her, and in the end they kill the thing and that why you were never sick again.

Those two things, the henbane and going to the police, are the only things poor Miss Celia did in all her life that she was not told to do by someone else.

That is all I have to tell.

It is all true, the Lord be my witness.

I, Phibbah, write this for the lawyer men.

This day, 10th May 1919.

Mayella and Reuben came into the kitchen and stood there holding hands, and neither could find their tongue so Idie began to giggle.

Then Reuben took Mayella's hand and said to Phibbah, 'We getting married, Grandma.'

And the old woman rose up waving her arms about and there were shining tears on her riven cheeks and Reuben said, 'Now you stop that, Grandma, or I gon' cry too.'

Idie pulled the white cloth from Celia's sewing table and wrapped Mayella in it head to toe and said, 'The Indies will never see a prettier bride.'

Mayella beamed.

'Till you marry, mistress . . .' she said, adding shyly, 'Master Austin come one day for you maybe.'

'He doesn't care for me,' said Idie, turning away.

Outside the little Baptist chapel, Idie, Homer aloft on her shoulder, waited for Numbers. He told Idie that Lancelot had died of grief, that Grancat lay in the Pomeroy churchyard, buried between the wife he'd loved and the dog he'd loved. He mentioned too, by the by, that Carlisle had been brought home in irons and jailed for his part in the mutiny at Taranto. Idie handed Phibbah's book to Numbers.

Phibbah waited at the door to the chapel, her turban higher, her robe brighter than ever before and she had more bangles about her wrists than Idie had ever seen in one go, though she'd removed the pipe from her mouth for the occasion.

When Mayella came, she was with Nelson, all her seven sisters and five brothers following, and the dress Celia had made for her was as glorious as the foam of a wave.

Mayella paused beside Idie and stroked Homer's beak and said, 'One day you marry, mistress, and on that day all the hummingbirds they be about your head like the company of heaven, and the pigeon on your shoulder and the mongoose and the monkey about your neck, and the horse at your side . . .'

'No one'll have her.'

Idie turned.

'Idie's wayward and spiny and no one'll have her.' Austin smiled and held out his arm to lead Idie into the chapel.

Mayella Mayley married Reuben Sealy that day and the singing swelled the walls and raised the rafters of the tiny Baptist chapel.

100

Idie returned late. The Idie Book was where she'd left it on the veranda table, a pencil beside it, and the moon so low and bright that Idie could read by the light of it. She picked up the book and looked at the new page she'd begun.

THE ONLY THINGS THAT MATTER

1. *My mother did not take her own life.*
2. *She was not mad.*
3. *She loved my father, and my father loved her.*
4. *She loved me too but sent me away to keep me safe.*
5. *Grancat also sent me away to keep me safe, because the world is not kind if you are not the same as everyone else.*
6. *Celia is my mother's sister and I will look after her as my mother would have wished.*
7. *Sampson Sealy's name will one day be on that cenotaph because Austin will make sure that this is so.*

8. My mother loved this place and planted every tree and flower.
9. Let it be written across the sky in fire that I will never leave it.

She took up the pencil, wondering about number 10, because if you made lists it was more satisfactory to finish on a round number.

She looked at the old calabash tree and thought how she was as deeply rooted at Bathsheba as he, that she loved its glittering rainshine, its blossomy shade and its iridescent nights.

She looked up to the spangled sky and felt so light and clear that she might float up and go cartwheeling from star to star, streamers for her tail, comets in her slipstream, go cartwheeling on and on, all the way to morning.

The wind stirred and started a soft, cool hum about the veranda. It danced lightly through the leaves of the fustic trees her mother had planted and it carried on its song the scent of the candle flowers.

Homer whistled, and not even his whistling could break the spell for it rose and melted into the breeze and became part of the song of the breeze that skipped through the leaves.

Idie turned to tap his beak. Only it was not Homer whistling, but Austin, and he was behind her, reading over her shoulder from the Idie Book, and then

Homer started whistling too, and it was good he'd done so much practising for he was perfectly in tune with Austin.

Austin read on and Idie waited, breathing in the scent of candle flowers and honeysuckle till he took the pencil from her and wrote:

> 10. *It is written in fire, Idie wayward Grace, between the stars, across the moon and all along a rainbow, that* I LOVE YOU.

Everything was as it had been, the calabash was in his place, the stars in theirs, the tree frogs in the fustic trees, Gypsy in the rafters, Baronet in the hall; everything was as it had been and as it should be. Only the song of the breeze had dropped and somehow everything was still and suspended for a moment or two till Homer, whose conversation seemed to have developed a little, said, 'IDIE'S WAYWARD AND SPINY AND NO ONE'LL HAVE HER.'

Austin took Idie's hands and said, 'Idie Grace, I give all of me to you if you will have me.'

The wind took up its hymn once more, but now the sound it wound about Idie's heart had something new in it, something clear and shining, and Idie knew that nothing would ever be the same again.

AUTHOR NOTE

Hummingbird is not a real island, only a distillation of memories of different islands. Nor is the Grace family based on any real family, nor Bathsheba on any real house – and neither are place names, though taken from various islands, meant to be read as real places.

However, the flora and fauna described, as well as the historical facts, are particular to the islands of the West Indies and for these I am indebted to, among many, many others, the following books:

The West Indies and the Spanish Main by Anthony Trollope

At Last: A Christmas in the West Indies by Charles Kingsley

Six Months in the West Indies by Henry Nelson Coleridge

A naturalist's sojourn in Jamaica by Philip Henry Gosse and Richard Hill

Two Years in the French West Indies by Lafcadio Hearn

West Indian Summer by James Pope-Hennessy

Sugar in the Blood: A Family's Story of Slavery and
   Empire by Andrea Stuart
The Sugar Barons by Matthew Parker
Jamaica's Part in the Great War by Frank Cundall
Jamaican Volunteers in the First World War by
   Richard Smith

THE BRITISH WEST INDIES REGIMENT

In October 1915 King George V appealed for
recruits from the Empire. A new British West Indies
Regiment would be formed and accepted into the
military fraternity on equal terms with men from
the Motherland. On Sunday 31 October the King's
Appeal was read in all the churches of all the British
West Indies. Men were urged to volunteer, brothers
'to know each other as brother without thinking of
race, nationality, colour, class, or complexion . . . to
join hands and hearts together'.

Men of the West Indies left their islands willingly
and with optimism, pride and enthusiasm. They hoped
to serve their King and hoped also that the war would
bring opportunity for racial equality. In addition
many were driven by fear that German dominion
would bring a return to slavery. The optimism with
which they left was, however, soon to be squashed by
a mighty military apparatus designed to perpetuate
the social structure of empire. The men of the sunny

British West Indies who volunteered to fight for the King they regarded as their own, for the country they regarded as the Motherland, found a chilly reception in England.

There were no firm guidelines regarding their recruitment, the difficulty being whether war officials should or should not accept 'men of colour'. A stream of edicts, inconsistent, ambiguous and contradictory, was issued. The Manual of Military Law of 1914 stated that 'any Negro or person of colour' was an alien and could not hold a rank higher than NCO, but also stated that a serving black man was 'entitled to all the privileges of a natural-born British subject'. In May 1915 the War Office stated that West Indian volunteers would be accepted if their transport costs were met by their own governments and if, on arrival, they enlisted as infantry men only for the duration of the war. In October 1915 the Colonial Office and the War Office agreed terms for men of the BWIR with pay set at standard British Army rate. In February 1918 a telegram was sent to the War Office stating that since blacks could not be recruited to white battalions, they must go to 'native units'. In June 1918 this policy was overturned and black volunteers of the USA, Canada and the UK were recruited directly to regular British units on standard British rations and standard British pay. However, in response to a query from the Colonial Office it was later clarified that this policy did not, in fact, include the men of the Indies: 'It was not, and is not, the intention of the Army Council to accept for units of the British Army natives of unmixed blood from the colonies . . .'

What all this meant in practice was that some black volunteers were accepted and some were not, according to who was recruiting, his personal preference and which particular instruction he had come across. Those who did manage to enlist, once trained and transported out, found that they were to be utilized only for routine manual labour rather than the front-line fighting for which they longed.

Because the BWIR was now to be demarcated as 'native' troops, they were deployed as labour units on fatigues, loading and unloading the kit of white regiments. The BWIR first battalion was utilized for guard duties (the guarding of Turkish prisoners in Palestine), the second deployed on lines of communication in West and East Africa. The first, second and fifth battalions in Egypt did play some much-praised front-line roles, but for the main part, during 1916 and 1917, the majority of the BWIR unloaded shells from supply trains, relayed them from park to dump to ammunition column, built roads, constructed railways, mixed concrete or dug trenches.

Bitterly disappointed, often they found themselves in the firing line yet not allowed to handle a weapon nor fire a shot in anger themselves. They were regularly in exposed and dangerous positions, subject to shellfire and infantry attack, and regularly suffered casualties, yet were without weapons for self-defence.

The refusal to deploy black West Indian volunteers on the front line caused a slump in their morale. Their pent-up desire to feel that they were actually striking the enemy was exacerbated by official blunders, unequal pay, poor medical treatment and racial discrimination. The men of the BWIR were, in general, excluded from the games, cricket matches and other facilities enjoyed by the regular British soldier. The substandard native hospitals designated for West Indian soldiers and 'native' labourers recruited from South Africa, China, Fiji and Egypt were unheated and the food poor, while German prisoners were kept in comparative luxury.

Furthermore, the BWIR, now officially designated a 'native' unit, was excluded from the general pay increase and War Bonus of Army Order 1 of 1918, despite the fact that the BWIR had been specially granted the same pay as other British Army infantry units. Unsurprisingly, many men of the BWIR returned radicalized by ill-treatment and discrimination, and their anger and sense of injustice fuelled the emergent nationalist movements in the islands that were already bent on social, political and economic reform.

ABOUT THE AUTHOR

Sam Angus grew up in Spain. She studied Literature at Trinity College, Cambridge, taught A-level English for a while, designed clothes for a while longer and is now a novelist. She lives between London and Exmoor with an improvident quantity of children, horses and dogs.

SOLDIER DOG

SAM ANGUS

'He'll always be true, faithful and brave,
even to the last beat of his heart.'

It's 1917. In the trenches of France,
miles from home, Stanley is a boy fighting a
man's war. He is a dog handler, whose dog must
be so loyal that he will cross no-man's-land
alone under heavy fire to return to Stanley's side,
carrying a message that could save countless lives.
But this journey is fraught with danger,
and only the bravest will survive.

As the fighting escalates and Stanley
experiences the true horror of war, he comes
to realize that the loyalty of his dog is the
only thing he can rely on . . .